Greyladi

SUMMER'S ...

"The school, empty and expectant, waited within sound of the sea..."

It awaits the Headmistress, Miss Bishop, a detached, successful woman who considers it her duty to be calm and cheerful; Miss Meadows, the Classics mistress, kind, fragile and attempting to become nothing beyond a gentle old maid; Miss Cottingham, house-mistress, addicted to detective novels; Miss Warrender, games mistress, whose face "shone honestly from an admixture of natural good humour and liberal application of soap"; Upper Fifth friends Sophie and Jasmine, "with hair the colour of yellow leaves and the smile of a fallen angel"; Matron, with her straight high cap above a pair of piercing black eyes; Honor Christow, unhappy assistant matron, who "in spite of her twenty-three years and the rather brassy heartiness she cultivated for the benefit of the Girl Guides, felt like crying as she went into the house"; Albert the gardener, with "his old khaki shirt open to the waist, revealing the throat and chest of an Apollo"; and Mrs. Prior, Alice, Shirley and the maids "Noranmaude", all of whose lives intertwine in intricate patterns during this one summer term.

SUMMER'S DAY

MARY BELL

Greyladies

Published by
Greyladies
an imprint of The Old Children's Bookshelf
175 Canongate, Edinburgh EH8 8BN

© Mary Bell 1951

This edition first published 2008
Design and layout © Shirley Neilson 2008
Preface © Shirley Neilson 2008

We have been unable to trace the copyright holder, the author or any heirs. If anyone can put us in touch with the rightful person, we will be delighted to be able to pay the royalties to them.

ISBN 978-0-9559413-2-0

All rights reserved. No part of this publication may be reproduced, stored in or introduced into a retrieval system, or transmitted, in any form or by any means (electronic, mechanical, photocopying, recording or otherwise) without the prior written permission of the above copyright owners and the above publisher of this book.

Set in Sylfaen / Perpetua
Printed in Great Britain by the MPG Books Group,
Bodmin and King's Lynn

Preface

Summer's Day is a beautifully written novel set in a girls' boarding school just after the Second World War. At this time school stories for girls were still at a peak of popularity with their tales of schoolgirl chums, games and the whole competitive hierarchy of school society. Adult novels view school and schooldays from an entirely different perspective (it would be odd if they did not), moving the spotlight from the girls to the staff; celebrating the individual both in and out of school.

This is a novel entirely of its time, in an England recovering from the War and before the social turbulence of the sixties.

There are clearly defined distinctions between social classes, and this community covers all classes, from the servants' hall to the headmistress's study. Pupils are "Miss Sophie" and "Miss Jasmine" to the domestic staff; Honor, the young assistant matron, is perhaps the loneliest person in the school, denied both the mistresses' common room and the servants' hall; the speech of domestic and ancillary staff is shown as more colloquial and less grammatically correct than that of "the school"; but there is, at least with the more sympathetic characters, a fair bit of intermingling and nowhere is there any suggestion of snobbery.

We are not yet in the age of the teenager and student revolt. School stories written for girls of this period are, with only a few exceptions (Antonia Forest, Josephine Elder . . .) novels of conformity, exhorting the young to abide by the rules, obey authority without question . . . to play up and play the game.

In the Chalet School series by E.M. Brent-Dyer, for example, the message in very many of the books is that if you don't obey and conform, something awful will happen to you. Only when you've hit bottom and learnt the error of your ways, and probably sustained a serious injury as well, will people like you, and only then will you be a real Chalet School girl. The School is all; individuals have to conform.

The women and girls, and the one or two men, in *Summer's Day,* are individuals for whom the school is *not* everything, and it is the intertwining of the separate strands of their lives in delicate counterpoint that gives the book its dynamic. There is no overt rebellion – even Jasmine and Sophie are discreet while blithely ignoring the rules - but they don't all pull together for the sake of the school.

In particular none of the main characters is keen on games. Sophie and Jasmine regularly and illicitly avoid them, Miss Cottingham, their house-mistress, admits she takes no interest in cricket, and Mr. Walker, the art master, thinks there are few spectacles more boring than young women knocking balls about. "At this heresy Honor gasped."

Instead of enthusiasm for "knocking balls about", these characters enjoy the more solitary pleasures of literature. Miss Meadows, persuaded out of retirement by the dire need of the Classics department, is packing; "As she dusted and moved her books lovingly she struggled to come to some compromise between the number she knew to be quite essential and the number which would go into her trunk." Miss Cottingham's mind is on the problem of the bloodstain below the viscount's window while the rest of her takes roll-call at prayers (causing her to overlook Jasmine's feat of ventriloquism answering *adsum* for Sophie as well as herself); a member of the Sixth reads Shelley behind the pavilion instead of watching the cricket match; Miss Truscott asks to borrow one of the confiscated copies of *Forever Amber* as her young man has accused her of becoming a blue-stocking and she thinks it might act as a sort of counter-irritant; Miss Bishop and Miss Meadows, after a trying day, discuss Sappho, for a rest.

My own favourite literary reference concerns Miss Meadows and Shirley, the second housemaid:

"[Shirley] produced a book from under her arm.

"I kept it so long," she added, "because I read it twice."

"There's another one," said Miss Meadows, at the shelves, "which goes on from there."

"You mean – the same people – and what happens next?"

"Yes," said Miss Meadows, handing her *Good Wives.*

Shirley ran her fingers softly over the edges of the book. Finally she held it against her apron, smiled, and said, "Good night."

The detail in this book is abundant, intricate and almost casually thrown in; the characters are finely drawn, with affectionate wit, pithy observation and gentle understatement. Perfect ingredients for a literary feast.

Shirley Neilson
Edinburgh 2008.

SUMMER'S DAY

CHAPTER 1

THE school, empty and expectant, waited within sound of the sea. During term time the sea could never be heard through its hygenically opened windows, nor when, as now, Alice opened one of them would the blown newspaper in the empty corridor sound loudly, or the water in the pipes of the heating arrangements pass with a cracking sound. The small echoes in the empty building seemed to Alice far more significant than the comfortable murmur with which it was filled all the term.

She opened the door of Miss Bishop's study, a room directly over the main entrance of the building and commanding an expansive view of terraces, playing-fields and sea. A room also furnished with liberality of taste, expense and regard for scholarship. Sunlight, books, one or two period pieces, and under her feet the most comfortable carpet; Alice always felt the room a little chill. She decided to air it for ten minutes before going down to tea at the gardener's cottage.

Miss Bishop, in essence, appeared before her as she moved round her Sheraton writing-table: fortyish, brilliant, controlled, handsome; in Alice's opinion, hardly human. Alice supposed that she must be the only person who remembered Unity Bishop's arrival as a frightened new girl, at the age of twelve, clinging to her father's hand, and, in this very study, in the process of being welcomed by the then headmistress, bursting into tears. The father was dead, the old headmistress in her dotage; Alice was quite certain that Miss Bishop herself did not remember it. The child, in her opinion, had done well to cry, might reasonably have increased her vehemence had she foreseen herself growing into the detached, successful woman who considered it her duty, to be calm and cheerful. Alice wasted no pity on the past self who had witnessed those tears; she had changed from a young, pretty parlour-maid to an old and stout one, with little difference in her state beyond an increase in her salary and her blood pressure. She decided that the study was aired sufficiently and went away.

In the room which was to be Miss Meadows' Alice lingered with a sense of comfort, deciding that she would try to change that rather cold green counterpane for a rose-coloured one she had seen in one of the linen cupboards and that she would put flowers on the table between the windows. Miss Meadows, who as senior classical mistress had retired ten years ago, was coming back at sixty-five to fill a breach made by the war. Alice remembered with gratitude her kind, rather fragile presence, and her attempt to become nothing beyond a gentle old maid. She patted her hair in front of the mirror, surprised for a moment to see no neat cap on it since she had only come up to the school for the afternoon.

On her way round to the back stairs she cut through one of the long dormitories, looking strangely naked where the cubicle curtains had been taken away to be washed. Passing beds lately occupied by girls whom she liked or disapproved of her expression changed subtly, softening to one of amused tolerance as she approached the two belonging to Sophie and Jasmine. Miss Sophie so gentle and Miss Jasmine so naughty: Miss Sophie perhaps her dear Miss Meadows in embryo, Miss Jasmine a female edition of the devil. A likely couple!

In the empty kitchen Alice collected her gloves and string bag where she had left them on the massive scrubbed table. The rag rug looked forsaken without Timoshenko who had migrated to the gardener's cottage. Mrs. Prior's lop-sided basket-chair creaked stealthily in her absence.

Rather thankfully Alice shut the back door on the school and its brooding emptiness. She would be glad to get down to the cottage and to hear from Mrs. Munnings, over a strong cup of tea, what that Albert of hers had been up to lately. No good, that was certain.

CHAPTER II

THE people who were soon returning to the school made their preparations or enjoyed their last days of freedom according to age and disposition.

Jasmine, lifting a receiver in Pimlico, heard Sophie's voice in Kensington saying "Is that you, Jay?"

"Yes! Sophie!"

"Yes. Are you alone? No uncle?"

"He's out."

"Good. Well, Mother says your aunt's bringing you with her to the cocktail party, that's right, isn't it?"

"Yes."

"We can't go to it, of course, though we might squeeze in at the end, but we can do what we like and can you stay the night?"

"Uh–*hum!* Of course! I'll tell Aunt May. And I'll bring things."

"No, don't, I'll lend you a nightie. And we can talk for ages - lights out at nine soon! Wonder how the One and Only's spending her holidays?"

"In the rain in Brittany."

"Doing what?"

"I shudder to think!"

They stopped talking to giggle.

"How's your Uncle Arthur?"

"Awful," said Jasmine. "But I got five bob out of him yesterday."

"What're you going to do with it?"

"Take Aunt May to the pictures . . . here she is - Aunt May, it's Sophie - can I stay the night? . . . She says, 'Of course, darling.' See you to-morrow."

"Lovely! Good-bye, Jay."

"Good-bye."

"You ought to keep that five shillings, darling," suggested Mrs. Tern. "It's only four days until school."

"Oh, *no*, Aunt May, so much the better - he can't in decency refuse me pocket-money. And if we go in the one-and-threes we can have tea as well. Be nice, ducky, I've only three more days and to-morrow I'll be at Sophie's."

Mrs. Tern suffered from a congenital inability to refuse her niece anything; they made their arrangements cautiously so as not to disturb the Reverend Arthur Tern and in a few minutes set off in the spring sunshine which gleamed on Jasmine's yellow hair and the sequins on Aunt May's hat.

On the outskirts of Lewes, Mrs. Prior prepared to leave her cottage. In spite of the outdoor sanitation to which she swayed heavily down a brick path, while the spring flowers surged against the black balloon of her skirt, she considered it a great deal cosier than the school basement. From one of her two bent apple trees a thrush serenaded her and she waited, chamber-pot in hand, to listen; returning, she slapped it down in the kitchen, gave her investigating cat a half-hearted kick and went on with her packing.

She hated leaving her own kitchen. The glowing range,

the red plush hanging from the mantelshelf, the warmly berugged floor, the greasy sink, the variously coloured china on the dresser and the pictures of Victorian little girls picking posies or smiling unnecessarily at cows, were intimately home. Her son, Jim, languishing in strange places with the Royal Navy, thought of his mother's kitchen with the same nostalgia.

Mrs. Prior took Jim's photograph from the place of honour over the plush drapery and smiled at the face which Jasmine and Sophie had declared to be the handsomest one they had seen. Young, blue eyed, sunburned, in his wide sailor collar, he smiled back at his mother. She put the picture in her trunk beside her next dearest treasures, two china spaniels, also from the mantelshelf, and wrapped them all securely in a large, artificial silk handkerchief which she took from under a jar of bluebells on the table; it was labelled "A Present from Italy. To My Sweetheart," and had been sent by Jim.

Slowly and sadly, her feet bulging over the tops of her shoes, she lumbered round the house. She looked into Jim's room and secured the window, to safeguard the cottage's peculiar odour of stuffiness which would greet her at the end of the term. She patted, in passing, the truckle bed from which she had such difficulty in persuading him to rouse his golden limbs in the mornings, limbs which now swung, far away, in a hammock over tropical seas.

In a remote corner of Sussex, at the end of a dank and muddy lane, Miss Meadows also fortified her cottage against her absence. It was considerably more refined and not nearly so comfortable as Mrs. Prior's dwelling. Her kitchen was a small, mouldy-smelling shrine dedicated to the evil spirit of a stove which smoked. The sitting-room with its pseudo Adam fireplace, willow pattern china and Persian carpet was dustier than she would have liked to know, but at sixty-five she did not see dust very well. The petals from the wild anemones on the piano made a little white drift on its rosewood surface.

As she dusted and moved her books lovingly she struggled to come to some compromise between the number she knew to be quite essential and the number which would go into her trunk. She picked up Catullus, crossed the room with him, sighed, shook her head and put him back on the shelf.

If poor dear Unity had not written so urgently requesting her assistance nothing would have induced her to go. Poor Unity, who had always been so sensible and so clever, and had been deserted by two classical mistresses simultaneously with no immediate prospect of relief. Miss Meadows, who had taught Miss Bishop her declensions, saw no help for it; she would have to go.

One or two of the rarely opened books had damp mould marks; she dreaded to think of the state of her home when she should return to it. Perhaps if it were to be only for the summer term it would not be too bad. She was old and comparatively useless and mustn't be selfish. Opening Catullus she read: "*Sed dicam vobis, vos porro dicite multis milibus et facite haec charta loquatur anus,*" [But to you I will tell it: do you hand on the tale to many thousands and let the paper speak this in its old age] and decided to take him after all.

"Margery!" called Nannie, "come up and let me see this tunic on you! Margery! Is there anything special to be saved for your little case? Margery! this is the way to pack a trunk!" Her voice seemed to fill the last of the holidays and Margery ran up from the garden or down from the nursery to satisfy her demands.

As Nannie knelt on the floor with her mouth full of pins Margery lolled against her shoulder and stroked the little hairs at the back of her neck.

"Give over, do, and stand up straight," said Nannie, briskly, feeling like a Roman matron. "You will enjoy being in the big school this term."

"Will I?" said Margery.

The Junior House, with its less than life-size white-painted beds, rose coloured matting and friendly animals climbing up the walls had been a very different proposition from the school itself. Nannie, on a tour of inspection, had liked the walls, though daddy had only said, "Well, if I woke up there in the morning I should sign the pledge." Nannie had known which was her bed because of Augustus taking his ease upon it, and Margery glanced sadly at him where he lay now, to be left behind, half hidden by underclothing awaiting her trunk.

"At least two inches," said Nannie, standing up. Margery lingered. "Run along now." Margery went slowly up to the nursery, dragging her feet.

There she brooded over her two small brothers with a

new abstraction. Lucky, careless little beggars! How many more years they would spend grovelling and squawking on the nursery floor. For her such days were done.

"I'll see to Augustus," Nannie said firmly, bustling round the room. "And put a stitch in his neck and scrub him, I will," she thought, "now I've got him!"

That evening Nannie, for reasons for which she despised herself, went up to Margery's room and touched the pillow. When she looked for Augustus he was gone.

She glanced from Margery's sleeping face to an untidy bulge in the trunk among her neat packing. Well! There it was.

She adjusted the blind and went downstairs.

Honor Christow threw the chicken feed into various receptacles, shooed a stray bird into the hen-house and closed it for the night. She strode down the rectory garden, swinging the pail, her round, rather plain face glistening in the sun. She was utterly wretched.

Instead of being able to stay at home and run the rectory, the village, and her vague amiable father, she was forced by his miserable stipend to earn her living as assistant matron at St. Helen's. She had completed two terms in the School House and knew that she would have to return for a third if she wanted a useful reference. In spite of her twenty-three years and the rather brassy heartiness she cultivated for the benefit of the Girl Guides she felt like crying as she went into the house.

As she prepared their uninteresting supper her mind went over the school and its afflictions: the interfering, dictatorial matron, cheeky girls, stupid servants, the stuck-up mistresses who thought, she supposed, that because their occupation was purely academic they belonged to a different world from hers. Certainly no one in their senses would want to do her job. The dreary sorting of endless linen, washing of the cheeky girls' hair, chivvying of dormitory maids: it was all so horrible that she salted the leathery omelette with tears. Perhaps one day she would get a job in a boys' school where it wouldn't all be so beastly, only there she would miss her one friend at St. Helen's, the games mistress, who slapped her on the back with affectionate if painful vigour and drank tea sitting on her bed at night. Perhaps next holidays she could afford to ask Celia to stay with them. Celia, living in London, would surely like a week in the country, and they could both do physical jerks on the lawn.

A little cheered by this prospect she tipped the omelette on to a cold plate and carried it off on the long journey to the dining-room, wondering as she did so why they didn't save themselves trouble by eating it in the kitchen.

The Briggs family were going to bed: or, rather, they were being persuaded into retirement by the eldest daughter, Shirley.

Tidying the small, squalid living-room, rolling hair ribbons, collecting a grubby nightgown from the floor, Shirley reflected sadly that she was doing so for the last time before returning to the school. She was happy enough as second housemaid on the staff side at St.

Helen's, but she missed the large, rowdy family she mothered at home.

Her pretty face flushed with exertion, she persuaded her sister Eileen to get undressed. Her sweet, friendly smile, which Miss Bishop had felt she should be trained not to administer so freely, caressed the children as she put them to bed. Miss Bishop was unaware that it had been the effect of Shirley's smile upon an important, but gouty, visiting cleric, as she arranged his footstool in front of the guest-room fire, which had caused him to decide that he could return to preach in the school chapel with the minimum of discomfort.

When two of the children fought over the possession of a towel Shirley parted them expertly and dried their tears.

"Must I wash?" asked Eileen.

"Yes," said Shirley.

"How much?"

"Hands, knees, and - boomps-a-daisy!"

"All that?"

"Yes."

When Shirley had tucked them up she continued an endless saga about a family of orphaned children who lived in a tree and subsisted, rather immorally, on the offerings of milk and cakes left out on their doorsteps for the pixies by trusting housewives. Because it was her last evening she had to bring the family to a situation in which they could be left, without causing undue anxiety, for an indefinite period.

She went from rickety bed to bed delivering kisses, then settled herself in the kitchen with her mother to mend her black uniform stockings. The trams rattling down the ugly street shook the little houses regularly. It was only three miles from the school but Shirley felt, herself, justly, in a different world.

Lady Berwick's cocktail party was in full swing. Guests, cigarette smoke, speared sausages, olives, conversation and black market gin were mingling very well. Catching sight of her daughter Sophie through an archway she told her to go away, darling - well, just one sausage - and perhaps she might look in for five minutes at the end. She watched her, with Jasmine, the yellow head and the brown one close together, nibbling sausages, descending the stairs.

Mrs. Tern, hemmed into a corner by a deaf old gentleman whom she vaguely concluded to be a girlhood flame of Sylvia's, rewarded his information about the state of the country with a sympathetic smile and listened to the scraps of conversation around her. Above a peroration on post-war chaos she heard Sylvia's clear voice exclaim: "Oh, Major Bluton, I've been dying to see you. You built the Burma Road - so wonderful. *Do* you think you could look at the kitchen sink? Yes, practically flood level."

On her left two ladies who had daughters at school with Jasmine had their heads together. "So obvious," thought May, "I must try not to do it, and yet I'm too proud of Jay to keep quiet about her. In another year or so I shall feel like a dowager." The two prospective dowagers raised their voices:

"I do hope Angela will marry - I can't imagine what to do about careers and George has *no* ideas beyond golf.

Then if she lived far enough away one could go and stay with her. So pleasant. Not that any one can get any houses these days, it would probably mean taking one's own newspaper to the Embankment."

After an interval:

"Poor Mary's getting so plain I think she'll have to be a lady doctor."

"Is she interested in medicine?"

"I shouldn't think so. Why?"

And behind her: "So clever of dear Sylvia to have cocktails. Though I can't think how she's done it. One does get so rebellious about carrying around little bottles of milk."

She suddenly caught such a libellous remark from the old gentleman about a cabinet minister that she stopped smiling and said she would like another olive.

A tall, dark young man apologised as he moved round her chair and she saw him making for the door. A moment later Sylvia dislodged the old gentleman.

"Dear May, it is so lovely to see you. I'm so glad you couldn't bring Arthur. Jasmine's looking radiant. They will keep appearing, I suppose they want a cocktail, so I've sent them down to the morning-room. That's my nephew Tom - I expect he's gone to join them."

"Mildred's boy?" asked Mrs. Tern, settling down for a good gossip.

"Yes, and so clever, and good-looking, too, I think. He's a civil servant - the old-fashioned sort," she added, hastily. "But Mildred says he'll never go far. Too much conscience. She means vertically, of course - in his career - it's already taken him twice round the earth. Perhaps that's why he looks so sunburnt, or it may be his Welsh blood. One can't tell." Catching sight of her husband sniffing thoughtfully at a cocktail she added quickly, "Do speak nicely to Roger, I've been using his Napoleon brandy and I believe he's found out. There'll be an awful upheaval but it's all so impossible - one can't *create* things and after all if it's there in the cellar - and it does seem to be going down rather well."

May, judging from the cheerful buzz around her, thought that it did. She arranged a nice opening remark but Sir Roger, twirling the fluid in his glass, edged his way down the room to his son.

"He's going to ask Algy," said Sylvia. "That won't help him." And she added affectionately, "Algy's such a fool he'll need all the Berwick money. I sometimes think how lucky it is - with a son like Algy - that I married money. On the other hand if I'd married someone else he might not have been such a dolt. Fate *is* rather wonderful."

"Yes, dear," said May.

"Tom's different though." Sylvia glanced at the doorway which had lately framed her handsome nephew. "Poor Mildred married a Welsh farmer so he has brains."

Tom, who had, as his aunt supposed, gone down to the morning-room, thought at first that it was empty. Then he heard stifled laughter from the window. He found all the cushions in the room packed on to the small veranda with Sophie and Jasmine making themselves very comfortable in the April sunshine with their sleeves rolled up and their stockings rolled down.

"Any luck?" asked his cousin.

He nodded and produced from his pockets five olives, nine sardines on toast and six anchovies, three of which had parted company with their pastry settings.

They thanked him graciously.

"Jay's staying the night."

"So am I," said Tom.

"But I thought – "

"Well, you were wrong, dear."

"Have you told Mother?"

"No, not yet."

"You didn't bring any cocktails?"

"I couldn't, Sophie," and squeezing his long legs between the cushions he proceeded to tell them about his job in West Africa. Red, dusty roads, endless miles of bush, frangipanni, little scarlet birds, black children, mangoes, monkeys, long stretches of silver sand with palm trees behind them, warm, inviting seas which hid treacherous currents and the stings of opalescent rose and purple jellyfish - the lovely Portuguese man-o'-war - passed in a bright procession over the little veranda. Jasmine asked him to go on. Since this was what he wanted he did so. He was quite certain she was the most beautiful girl he had ever seen.

In the drawing-room, fortified by her unwilling host's '48 brandy, Mrs. Tern continued to enjoy herself. She always enjoyed Sylvia's parties; it was odd to think that they had been at school together and now here were Jasmine and Sophie growing up.

She smiled at Algy who brought her something with a

cherry in it. When she refused it he sat on the arm of her chair and drank it himself.

As she chatted to him she remembered again to be thankful for an afternoon away from her husband. Roger might be dull but Arthur was depressing as well. To become the uncle of such a niece as Jasmine, and an orphaned niece at that, was, in Mrs. Tern's opinion, the best thing that her husband had ever done. When her doubts as to the wisdom of the union had become a certainty, and she could see the rest of her life stretching in front of her as a desert of dreary acquiescence, the two-year-old girl had been deposited upon her nearest relatives. Unlike Mrs. Tern, Jasmine appeared to fear no one; from the first she had bawled with a sturdy indifference to her uncle's comfort which had immediately endeared her to her aunt. At sixteen she had formed a bond of mutual resistance with that lady, which, if it could not defeat the Reverend Arthur Tern, could usually circumvent him. Together they preserved a façade of decorous obedience and enjoyed themselves immensely in his absence.

May roused herself from her reflections to consume Algy's cherry on its stick.

"Oh, I say, there are the girls," he said, and there they were, being given brandied cherries by Sir Roger, who appeared to have forgotten about his loss.

A moment later Algy introduced the clever Tom. May, left alone with him, was conscious of some trepidation lest he should burst into a dissertation on Eisteddfods and ethics - the Welsh, she knew, were very religious. Also she had an uneasy feeling that intellectuals did not wash.

But the young man turned out to be delightfully clean and his conversation no more intelligent than was comfortable on a warm afternoon, which meant that it consisted of complimentary remarks about the weather and her niece's person.

When she departed to see to her husband's dinner that niece rubbed her young cheek against May's and said that she and Sophie wanted to go to the theatre.

"With Algy," said Sophie.

"Yes," said Sylvia, "and Tom can keep an eye on her," glancing at Tom, from whose expression it was apparent that he would like to keep both eyes upon her, for as long as possible.

May kissed her niece, gave her permission, and departed for the quiet vicarage – which would seem so desolate for another term – where she relieved her feelings by pressing all Jasmine's school uniform.

When May was in bed Sophie and Jasmine leaned from their window looking at the stars.

"What a lovely evening, wasn't it, Jay?"

"Um. Your cousin's got what it takes."

"What, old Tom?"

"Yes."

After a moment: "Are you cold, Jay?"

"No."

"Have you done your holiday reading?"

"No, I haven't."

"I suppose it'd be too late to start now."

"Much."

"There will be a row."

"I know. Sophie, I do hate going back."

"You won't mind when you're there." Kicking the wainscot, she added: "He's not as handsome as Jim Prior."

"What, Tom? Well, no, if that picture's true he couldn't be. Dear old Priory. I think she's the only one I'll be really glad to see."

"There's one other for me," said Sophie.

"Who?"

"Never mind."

"Oh, *I* know," said Jasmine. "G. *Him!*"

"I don't care, you can laugh."

"Sweet Sophie! I won't. Or not very much."

"Don't let's go to bed for ages. Soon we'll be in a line saying '*Adsum*'."

"So terribly soon."

Wishing they were free of it they hung their soft faces out into the world. Brown hair and yellow hair on the window-sill lifted faintly in the April wind.

CHAPTER III

THE school was itself again. For two days Mrs. Prior, Alice, Shirley and a fleet of dormitory maids had been working to bring it to life.

The mistresses had arrived in the morning, and now, at tea-time, one or two new girls with their parents, having been refreshed from a silver teapot in Miss Bishop's drawing-room, wandered round the garden in disconsolate little groups. The real influx would arrive in the autumn and they were rather conscious of having done the wrong thing.

Miss Meadows' books were up on the shelves of her room, where Alice's narcissi greeted her with their starry stare.

On Honor Christow's wall a picture of the rectory garden, in oils, dispensed a little comfort. In the kitchen the range glowed, Timoshenko rubbed ecstatically around familiar legs, and from the mantelpiece, flanked by the china spaniels, the room received the benediction of Jim's blue smile.

Mrs. Prior's heavy footsteps seemed to shake the house as she swung enormous saucepans and called in her raucous, cheerful voice, upon "Noranmaude" to do her bidding; sisters, and much alike, they appeared simultaneously, like a Greek chorus, to repeat her orders and render assistance.

In the sunny attic under the sky Shirley had unpacked her scanty treasures. She sighed when she found she was to share it with Doris, for both Nora and Maude had been explicit about her feet. Partly for this reason and partly because of the view of the sea Shirley chose the bed by the window. On the dressing-table, in its metal Woolworth frame, she had set the picture of her united family, an impressive spectacle, going down in steps. Doris's young man, in a circle of shells, looked a little superciliously across at them. Recognising "The Fish" in sudden amusement she peered a little closer to see if the camera had included his spots.

Already, the room was possessed by the stale smell which emanated from Doris's possessions and with which she was to spend the term.

At six o'clock the girls from the London train arrived. In a confusion of pigtails, tennis rackets and laughter they spilled out of the school bus on to the drive. The games mistress, whose duty it had been to accompany them from town, bounced down behind them and told them not to dally about but to get themselves in an orderly fashion to the cloakroom. She added briskly that she could see she would have to smarten them up again after their lackadaisical holiday ways.

"Oh, God," said Jasmine, trudging up the gravel.

The girls' high voices filled the evening and from a may-tree a thrush joined madly in the noise.

In a navy-blue stream they surged into the house, but not even the school hats and regulation jackets could hide the brightness of their faces or the grace of their young limbs.

Albert, coming out of his cottage, passed the back of a

hand across, his face and raised his thick lashes to look appreciatively towards the school.

The main school building, which contained the School House and a large proportion of staff, was a grey, just pre-Victorian erection which if not beautiful was in no way ugly. It was wide and well proportioned and rested not without dignity upon its height of flowered terraces. The drive curved round steeply to the gravelled circle of the topmost terrace, before the front door. At the bottom of the drive, by the main gate, in its own bright patch of flowers that Albert liked best, stood the gardener's cottage.

Across the road were playing-fields and below that the town sloped sharply to the sea. The fields themselves, owing to the tendency of the land to precipitate itself towards sea-level, had disconcerting slopes at their farther end, thus assisting most unfairly in the destruction of visiting teams who were not used, like the school, to this idiosyncrasy.

The other houses, some four in number, were independent at the school end of the town. As the size of the school had increased, the Governors, realising that to build upon existing ground would cramp them impossibly, had bought up the large houses by the sea. This entailed upon their members more freedom of movement than Miss Bishop liked.

The school chapel rose, upon a luckily acquired potato plot, at the back of the grounds beside the sanitorium.

The original aim of the Founders, as stated in their

records, had been to train the daughters of poor gentlemen for the position of governess. A picture of the first few of these little maidens, in modest shawls, survived from the 1830's. They must have been much of an age with the future queen when they stood looking eagerly and quaintly from their group in the wooden frame, at a world which was to change so much. Sophie, crossing the hall in her brief gym tunic, was inclined to stop sometimes, peer at the hopeful faces and wish them well, as though their future still lay before them and they were captured for ever at the age in which the artist had set them there.

On the first day of term the school seemed to wake from its sleep, its dried veins dilating again with footsteps and chatter.

Prayers. Three hundred girls in the assembly-room on a May morning. Miss Bishop upon the dais. Behind her Miss Cottingham, senior music mistress and house mistress of School House, urging her organ zestfully on to the hymn "Lord Receive Us with Thy Blessing" sung dutifully and unenthusiastically by the School.

After a moment Miss Bishop lifted up her clear contralto and joined in. She felt that that hymn was too old a chestnut to fit into her painstakingly modern arrangement of the school. In five years she had improved the plumbing and directed the spare time attention of the girls to world politics rather than Zenana missions, while some beneficent fate had stopped the children saying "ripping". One day she would get down to the hymn.

Plain girls and pretty girls, but all, at least, in early

youth, they stood beneath Miss Bishop's watchful eye. At the back of the hall she could see the taller girls of the upper school and distinguish one or two who would be leaving that term. Charity Morgan! Her steel-rimmed glasses seemed to be reflecting the sun. Already, thought Miss Bishop, the child's face was set in the lines of a village spinster. If only she could be relied upon to keep up her music and not listen too much to that dreadful father. I must keep in touch with her, thought Miss Bishop, without fail.

The hymn ended and the school kneeled down. Miss Bishop led them in a prayer of her own composition while her gaze wandered to a shining head in one of the back rows and remained there.

" . . . Lord help us so to choose our vocations that we may use the gifts that Thou hast given us to Thy glory . . ." The shining head moved restlessly as though the full weight of its headmistress's and drawing-master's attentions were faintly irritating. Miss Bishop could see that Mr. Walker's eyes were fixed and glassy. Jasmine Tern! Art for art's sake, indeed! The prayer ended on a stifled snort.

The front row of the school said "Amen" in various trebles. They knelt on during the collect for the day.

Margery, kneeling with her nose almost on the platform, told herself that she would on no account begin to cry in this blessed respite because they would soon be standing up.

I won't think about Nannie, she thought, or Daddy or the boys. I won't . . .

Miss Bishop and Mr. Walker continued to observe Jasmine, one with irritation, the other with hopeless love.

She'll be leaving too early, mused Miss Bishop, and yet I don't know! Another year – seventeen. One can't pin oneself down to any definite fault in her character but I shall always look upon her as one of my failures. What will anything so wilful and so lovely make of her life? She glanced sternly at Mr. Walker and decided that part of her question was answered.

Poor Mr. Walker clasped his fingers until his knuckles grew white. With patient resignation he had guided unwilling children in the pursuit of art until Jasmine came to spoil his peace of mind. Always susceptible to beauty, his teaching had never been brilliant, for if at harsh words a cheek quivered or a pair of blue eyes was raised towards him dimmed with tears, Mr. Walker added marks, so that if while under his tuition nobody did very badly, neither did anyone do very well.

He continued to gaze at all that he could see of Jasmine while a stray breeze from the open window lifted and dropped a curl over her left ear. Mr. Walker's heart rose and fell with the curl. She was beautiful beyond dreams. For two drawing periods a week he would be able to rest his longing eyes upon her and in another year, he supposed, she would be gone. The love of his life and over so soon! He feigned deep prayer with a sigh.

A scraping of three hundred chairs. An address from the headmistress.

As Miss Bishop let fall her favourite maxim – Character is Destiny – Jasmine, her wide eyes upon the platform, her lovely face raised with a sweet attention, administered a sharp kick to Sophie's shin. Sophie, expressionless, moved her hand under cover of her school hymn book until it was within pinching distance of Jasmine's thigh. They sat in rapt, delicious agony, suppressing giggles.

Jasmine, who had no faith in destiny and much in herself, leaned back and stared dreamily at the platform through narrowed eyes. Life, with a capital "L" and all its implications, might begin next year. One day she wouldn't just be coming back to school. It was sure to be such fun! The little smile flickered over her mouth. The world, against which she had been warned in Miss Bishop's catechism classes, would soon be at her feet. Jasmine clasped her fingers round her knees and swayed gently in pleasurable excitement. It would be wonderful to be free! Free to wear grown-up clothes (already Aunt May was saving up for them) and to dazzle every man she met - how easy it had been with Tom; free to say "I will" or "I won't," instead of "Do you think" or "Please, Miss Cottingham." She met Miss Bishop's eyes and lowered her own.

The address over, Jasmine stood slackly against her chair, waiting for the little ones to file past. Her attitude, in an athletic school, was frowned on by the seniors, and not quite under her breath she was humming a little tune. Mr. Walker's anguish rose to its height. Once again he observed the long legs, hair the colour of yellow leaves and a smile like a fallen angel; not even her indolence or the school clothes could disguise these facts. She went on humming with irritating cheerfulness as the school marched out.

The little girls, their faces pink with suppressed energy, jostled each other as decorously as possible and as soon as they were outside the hall began to scamper.

Mr. Walker, waiting patiently at the gangway beside Miss Stebbing (modern languages), watched the children as they passed. Charming they were! and which of the moderns could catch their youth? There was one standing plumb in front of him who needed a Sir Joshua to do her justice. A solemn, radiant little face it was, with Jasmine's grace but without that haunting naughtiness: an angel proper. And that pathetic gold band round the teeth! He would like to paint her against a background of darkened scenery and call it simply "Girl with a Plate." The procession had come to a standstill round, him and he became conscious of an unwavering stare.

"Pleath, Mithter Walker," said the vision, "you're thtandin' on my toeth."

He stepped back, sighed, and continued to wait amongst the staff. Jasmine passed him with her secret smile. He despaired quietly. For him no angels, fallen or otherwise, would give a flick of their silver wings.

He passed the downstairs recreation room. Happy, glorious confusion. Chairs pushed to one end and rows of trunks against the walls; girls kneeling on the floor.

Miss Bishop went through with her eyes averted: how shockingly those children unpacked.

Jasmine, waltzing in time to her song, her arms full of vests, sleeveless, summer weight (three), knickers, navy, with elastic legs (four pairs), and petticoats, princess (two) came down the centre.

"Steady, now, Jasmine dear, steady," said Miss Cottingham, kindly. "There's a good girl."

Miss Bishop, hearing, hurried by. That was one thing she was certain Jasmine emphatically was not.

Margery unpacked Augustus furtively, and carried him up the stairs. Outside the dormitory, overcome by his familiar presence, she stopped.

Honor, turning the corner and coming upon a strange little girl clutching a grey and shapeless animal asked kindly, "Where are you going, dear?"

The little girl, who had decided to cry in the lavatory, looked balefully over Augustus' head. "Can't he even be excused?" she said.

In the break period Sophie sacrificed her lemonade and biscuits and ran down the drive to see her first love.

She gave a swift glance over her shoulder, hoping her defection had not been noticed before she doubled round the science building on a less frequented route to the gardener's cottage.

At the door she paused to get her breath and replace her pigtail, her face bright with love and exertion. She stood in Albert's porch thinking, "I wonder if he'll have changed, I wonder if he'll be pleased to see me," before she knocked.

Albert opened the door and let her in.

With a swift greeting she ran down the passage and into Mrs. Munnings, who opened the kitchen door.

"Is he - ?" said Sophie. "May I - ?" and stood and stared.

"Shut that door, Albert," called Mrs. Munnings, and: "Come in, Miss Sophie. There 'e is."

Sophie went into the kitchen and there he was.

Sitting on a rather damp portion of the carpet, his small hands clasping two spoons and a rattle, he raised wide eyes to the doorway, dried tears on his cheeks.

"Darling!" said Sophie and went on her knees.

She picked him up, moist and dribbling, and held him tightly against her school tunic. His small features broke into rapturous smiles.

"There now," said Mrs. Munnings, "sit down, my duck."

Sophie subsided on to a chair. "He knows me! He remembers perfectly, doesn't he?" She moved the boneless little body about in her arms. "How sweet you are!" She laughed and the baby laughed too.

" 'Ave a cupper tea, dear," said Mrs. Munnings at the hearth.

"No, I daren't," said Sophie. "I'll have to get back. But I'm so glad I've seen him. I thought he might have forgotten me. Four weeks is a long time." She handed the baby to his mother, looked at him fondly, leaned over and kissed his damp cheek.

"*Darling* Geoffrey! Good-bye, my sweet." In the doorway she said: "D'you still bath him at six?"

"Thereabouts, Miss."

"And if I - if I come one night - can - "

"Any time you like, dear," said Mrs. Munnings, "but don't get into trouble on his account."

"I won't - but it would be worth it. I must run."

Stumbling over Albert in the porch she gasped. "Thanks

awfully - I'm awfully late."

Albert, lolling in the doorway, watched her flying feet on the gravel. He thought how pretty she was and wondered what she saw in his son.

Miss Bishop sat in her study. Her brown hair, drawn away from a high forehead, enhanced the sensible serenity of her face; her dress, shapeless, dateless and very expensive, toned with the panelling and old rose curtains. So, she felt, she would have her portrait painted, and not as her predecessor (M.A. Oxon) in mortar-board and gown, who smiled benignly from the common-room wall.

She flicked a pencil between her fingers and wondered, as always, if she did as much as was possible for her girls. Girls were such strange, dear creatures, so defenceless in their youth! The world waiting to receive them was unexpectedly different from the rows of dormitories with their neatly curtained beds.

There was a knock on the door.

"Come in, Jasmine," called Miss Bishop.

Jasmine closed the door behind her and came up to the desk.

"Sit down, dear."

Jasmine sat.

"I sent for you, as you know," said her headmistress, who had been listening for that casual step, "to ask about your plans for the future. Have you any plans?"

Jasmine, who had so many that they would take an hour to tell, and would not, in any case, appeal to Miss Bishop, shook her head.

"No, Miss Bishop," she said.

"Your uncle," said the headmistress, fingering a letter on her desk, "has no suggestions. I only gather that you intend to earn your own living."

"Not so much intend as must," thought Jasmine, and held her peace. The reflection that "earn" in her sense was probably a good deal more elastic than in Miss Bishop's caused her to smile.

Miss Bishop leaned over her desk. "I do want you to remember, dear, that we really wish to help. I could suggest a number of careers – but you know them. The initiative must come from you. And then, when you have decided we will do what we can."

Jasmine's abstracted gaze wandered towards the window, her lovely profile lifted against the light. Watching her, Miss Bishop decided that she was what her soldier nephew would have called a flighty piece. She sighed.

Jasmine retrieved her straying attention, " . . . more work into your last four terms. To have passed matric, become a left-handed bowler and learned to behave like a lady are not in themselves sufficient equipment with which to face the world."

Jasmine sat up. Fancy the One and Only Unity talking like that! "I must tell Sophie," she thought.

"I suppose you don't favour a university?" asked Miss Bishop.

"No," said Jasmine. Three more years of grind and supervision! What an idea.

"I think that is just as well. You have the brains but not

40

the industry for scholarship standard."

"Too true I haven't," she thought. Realising that Miss Bishop was waiting she sat up and said desperately, "I might be secretary to an M.P. I'd like that, I think."

Much heartened, Miss Bishop started to mention some gentlemen of Liberal persuasions when she realised that, in her own phraseology, Jasmine couldn't care less about their politics. She wanted admiration, comfort, and very little work.

That she would get what she wanted, Miss Bishop had no doubt. She felt suddenly sour and defeated. Such hours of work she put in on behalf of deserving girls like Charity Morgan and they needed it all. But Jasmine would use her yellow hair and her golden eyes and need trouble no more. She tried to be just.

"See if you cannot work harder this term, my child, and try to cultivate some of that team spirit which appears to be completely lacking in your make-up. I should like to feel," she continued, bending her grave, kind eyes on her pupil "that St. Helen's has done all that was in her power to do for you. I need not add that I should wish you to have done your best for St. Helen's."

The soft May wind blew the rose curtains into the room. Within a few feet of each other they shared a momentary silence, divided by the widest, most impassable gulfs which separate women. Miss Bishop was conscious of that constriction in her vitals sometimes experienced by good women when they realise the potentialities of a bad one. Each, to spare the other's feelings, wished to hide her knowledge of the gulf.

"You may go now, dear," said Miss Bishop, "and think over what I have said."

Jasmine went politely out of the room. Turning a corner where carpet ended and parquet began she started to slide. A door opened and a grey, rather dowdy figure emerged. There was a collision.

Jasmine apologised, disentangled herself and her victim and waited for the blow to fall. Miss Meadows peered short-sightedly and put her hand on a shining head.

"Have you hurt yourself, my dear child?"

Jasmine stared: "Oh, no," she said. "Of course not. And I'm terribly sorry. But you - "

"Quite all right, dear. I'm afraid I don't always look where I'm going. I don't think - ?"

"I'm Jasmine Tern."

"Jasmine," said Miss Meadows, and added irrelevantly, "what beautiful hair."

Jasmine collected Miss Meadows' books and asked where she was going.

"To the Upper Sixth, dear. Thank you very much. I haven't been here for ten years, you know, and I'm still a little confused."

Smoothing the shattered Homer, Jasmine took her down the stairs. Outside the Upper Sixth she raised her tawny eyes with her sweetest smile. A real honest to goodness old lady! A thing that, in what she considered the studied artificiality of St. Helen's, she hadn't expected to find. Already the exasperation occasioned by Miss Bishop was fading from her mind.

"I must tell Sophie," she thought, running again. "What

with her Geoffrey and my old lady the school is looking up!"

In her study Miss Bishop looked thoughtfully at the door through which Jasmine had left. She murmured, to comfort herself, her favourite quotation:

> "Golden lads and girls all must
> As chimney sweepers, come to dust."

In one of the long dormitories Sophie's lips just moved. "Jay!"

"Yes?"

"What's bitten our Unity about you?"

"Thinks I'm lazy."

"But you always were."

"She's had enough of me, I suppose. Well, she won't have very much more. It's going to be a ghastly term."

"May not. I like your old lady."

"Uh, huh."

"Is that you talking, Sophie Berwick?"

"Yes."

"Who were you talking to?"

No answer.

"Who?"

"It was me, Charity, and well you know it."

"I do think you Fifth Form girls might set a better example. You can both report yourselves to Miss Cottingham in the morning."

"Yes, all right."

The dormitory was quiet.

Margery, who had been remembering Nannie's nightlight, pulled the sheet a little down from her swollen eyes to see what was going on. Then, feeling another explosion welling upwards, she stuffed Augustus' feet into her mouth.

In the attic Shirley watched Doris get into bed in her vest. Then she turned down a corner of *Her Only Lover,* opened the window as wide as possible and cleared the patch of moonlight in a jump.

In another attic Alice shuffled the texts into her Bible, inspected the screw of her hot-water bottle, pinched the gophers in her starched cap, gave another tweak to her curlers and put out the light.

Under a shaded lamp, Miss Bishop, with quiet efficiency, massaged skin food into her face.

The kitchen range still glowed in the darkness and the porridge bubbled to itself. Timoshenko stretched, scratched the hearthrug, yawned, and went to sleep.

In the gardener's cottage Mrs. Munnings looked at the clock again; and the landlord at the local persuaded Albert to go home.

The moon looked full into Miss Meadows' bedroom where she knelt in a white flannel nightgown, saying her prayers.

CHAPTER IV

THE time-tables were organised, bells rang at forty-minute intervals, well oiled bats drove cricket balls into the nets, Albert whitened the lines on the grass courts. His wallflowers glowed on the terrace below Miss Meadows' room and she breathed their warm scent with a grateful heart.

Miss Meadows was not finding her lot as difficult as she had feared. The grave courtesy of the Sixth made her lessons easy, and they actually appeared to be interested in Euripides.

The Upper Fifth, whom Miss Bishop had warned her were a godless and ignorant crowd, wished her good morning as though they meant it when she smiled at them over her spectacles, picked up the books that she dropped, and, if they showed no enthusiasm for Latin, at least they kept quiet while she taught.

She wondered why Unity disapproved so strongly of Jasmine Tern. She was no fool though she might be lazy, and it was a pleasure to look at the child. The lesson went on.

None of the girls read brilliantly, few were so much as attending, but they all paid Miss Meadows the civility of pretence, which was much for the Fifth. Angela Cunningham was reading a novel, Grace Wiley completed an overdue Algebra prep, Jasmine stared into space and Sophie, beside her, her white brow puckered intently, was carving her name on her desk.

Miss Meadows recalled Sophie's attention to Cicero's "De Senectute" and Jasmine's head went up.

She tried to visualise old age and failed. Impossible to imagine her long legs moving slowly, in woollen stockings, like the old lady's in front of her. She half-closed her eyes until the print swam, trying to experience short sight. She couldn't really convince herself that these things would happen to her. Looking round the classroom she had a sudden feeling that it was a tableau suspended in time: the open window, through which the scents and sounds of summer came; a bee buzzing past Miss Meadows' ear; the sun on the oak panelling; the half intelligible phrases hung as if for ever on the blackboard; the rows of bent heads above white blouses and school ties. Years later, she supposed, she would remember it. Looking at her contemporaries she reminded herself that one day they too would be old. It seemed so strange! And there was old Cicero, God knew from how many years away, catching up on them, and the future stretching in front of her into distances when they would be dust - Sophie dropped the penknife with a clatter and cut short her wanderings in time.

The old lady continued to dispense fragments of her classical treasure, which the girls made every effort to withstand. From generation to generation the paradox that the results of learning were admirable but that the process was humiliating had been passed down through the school. Miss Meadows, who had learned to take life as she found it, went on teaching as best she could. Hesitating uncertainly between the coloured chalks, manipulating her spectacles on their chain which ended in a little black case pinned to her worsted draped bosom, she tried to drag the class along with her. When the bell rang they stood up with relief.

Released into the sunshine they ran and shouted to disperse their pent-up energy. Pursued by Sophie, Jasmine's golden beauty flashed past Albert, who usually managed to be at hand when the older girls were out of doors. Watching the wind and their exertions reveal their contours he thought with disfavour of his tired wife and muling child.

Albert, since his release from the army, sometimes found life a little dull. Though he did not regret the exigencies of the Service he remembered his gay adventures in France and Italy with the sad reflection that here indiscriminate peccadilloes would cost him his job.

As he leant on the mower, his old khaki shirt open to the waist, revealing the throat and chest of an Apollo, the wind lifting his brown curls, he was not unconscious of the fact that though the beauty he admired was forbidden, at least he was among his peers.

Honor Christow, crossing the grass on her detestable duty of supervising recreation, noticed Albert and drew in her breath.

Turning lazily against the mower he favoured her with a long look between his sleepy lashes before stooping to collect the grass.

After break the Upper Fifth trooped into the studio with much unnecessary noise. Told to collect drawing-boards, somebody dropped one, and, as if this disaster were catching, twenty-five more clattered to the ground. Informed that the grouping from the last class would not do for them, they expressed themselves eager to help and rearranged the room with such vigour that not a piece of furniture was still. In vain Mr. Walker waved his arms and called upon them to desist while they interpreted his frantic mouthings as further exhortations to toil. When some ten minutes of the period had been wasted they consented to sit down.

Hot and wretched, Mr. Walker attempted to explain the nature of their work. The sun in his eyes, he longed to adjust one of the blinds of the ceiling window, but dared not touch it as he knew that at the first movement twenty-six willing bodies would hurl themselves to his aid. He set them a still life picture, a group after the manner of Cézanne, and wondered if one or two might get any life into the result. As their heads bent over the boards he wended his way between the chairs.

About ten per cent of the girls had an inkling, of whom Sophie was one. Behind these chairs Mr. Walker waited longer and his criticisms were more harsh. Wherever he saw a gleam he strove desperately to fan it into a blaze. The girls who were bad remained bad because he gave most of his attention where there was hope; for this, since he was an artist before he was a schoolmaster, he could not blame himself.

They dropped and broke their pencils, asked permission to sharpen them, mislaid their rubbers, spilled their paint water and generally plagued him to death. With dogged, unhappy persistence he went from chair to chair. He looked at Jasmine's efforts with disfavour and at her face with a sigh. Once he stopped to inform them that the hallmark of the true artist was his inability to spare any effort which would make his work as perfect as lay in his power. Sophie, licking the lead of her pencil, digested this; she decided that he was right.

He had acquired, on his way to the school, a boiled, pink lobster, to complete the group for which he wished. Before the lesson was half over he wished it at the bottom of the sea. Once comment upon the wretched thing had started nothing would persuade them to be quiet. Was he quite certain it was dead? Wasn't that just the slightest movement? Might not the poor thing be in pain? Surely there was something the matter - a slight cast - with one of its eyes? It had the identical expression of someone's maternal aunt. It was unkind, it was positively wicked (in several indignant voices) of the last speaker to mock the dead. If it *was* dead. Wasn't there a peculiar smell? Mr. Walker was dubbed "Fishy" from that moment and the name spread throughout the school.

Jasmine, who was tired of drawing, championed the cause of the aunt. Several of her acquaintances - looking round her she named them - resembled animals that she knew. Between Mr. Walker's complexion and his dead protégé's there was very little to choose.

Sophie was uneasy and sad. This sort of thing was the cause of the only rift that sometimes arose between Jasmine and herself. She had outgrown her pleasure in half unconscious cruelty while Jasmine, apparently, had not. She wanted to soothe Mr. Walker and tell him not to mind. She had a suspicion of the way in which Jasmine's beauty affected him and wished that she, of all people, would be quiet.

With some dim idea of ranging herself upon his side she asked, before the bell rang, if she might return to finish her picture in the half-hour after lunch. He was surprised and pleased. He wouldn't be there to help her, but she might come and work by herself.

That, said Sophie, was all that she wanted. She knew it wasn't much of a picture but she would like to finish it off.

The herd commented gaily, as herds will.

Was Sophie ill?

Had she turned over a new leaf?

Lent was last term.

Was it just a mean, greedy subterfuge to get the lobster to herself?

Would she save them just a claw?

Jasmine sat back with a faint, amused smile, while Sophie, glad to have drawn their fire, went placidly on with her work. But catching Jasmine's eye she felt suddenly cross. "She always manages to stay in the audience," she thought, indignantly, "and all of us only amuse her, even when it's me." She turned a scowl upon her friend, all the more angry for being well aware that if the Form's humour became a nuisance Jasmine would take her part: whatever their private differences, against the world they were one.

In the afternoon the Fifth played cricket. In the evening they did more lessons and went through the motions of prep.

Mr. Walker, occupied with special coaching and examination statistics, contrived to forget his grief. But strolling later in the garden and then through the little beech wood where a few late bluebells strayed, he derived no comfort from his surroundings, and was overcome again with the difficulties of his task. He knew he would never teach successfully except those who were willing to learn. He wished for the hundredth time that he could support his irritable widowed mother solely upon his art. As he could not he gazed bitterly up into the green shadows, cursed himself for an idiot, and retraced his steps to the school.

On his way home he looked into the playing-field where Albert, silhouetted against the sky, was arranging one of the nets.

Mr. Walker went up and asked him to sit for him.

Albert, who set a good value upon his appearance, promptly asked him what it was worth.

"Half a crown an hour," said Mr. Walker, shortly. "Take it or leave it."

Unoffended, Albert gave a final shake to the net and wiped his hands on his trousers.

"All right," he said, amiably. "I'll come."

The girls' recreation times were organised and supervised with such quiet, tactful persistence, that it irritated them a good deal. When it was fine and they had the run of the grounds, Honor or one of the junior mistresses read or walked in the gardens too. When it was not they were herded, as far as possible, into the large recreation rooms. Studious girls sought the library, a favoured few - the Upper Sixth - shared studies. As they came into neither of these categories, Sophie and Jasmine, like soldiers on foreign soil, immediately spied out the land to see what comfort it would yield.

It did not take Jasmine long to discover a disused attic, where traces of occupation still remained. The soldiers who had been billeted at St. Helen's during its wartime period of evacuation had departed long ago, and only a few isolated groups in the town stayed on to plague the mistresses with hopeful whistles after school crocodiles. In this attic she and Sophie settled down.

There was a great deal of dust, an enamel cup, a piece of newspaper, a boot, and a small photograph upon the floor. The photograph, which was of a round-faced young soldier and labelled "To Mother from Ronnie" they collected and pinned on the wall. The boot, which Sophie said was lucky, was also reserved for ornament. The cup would come in very useful when they had anything to drink. From home they smuggled two cushions and an old coat of Sir Roger's; he missed it frequently and blamed Sylvia in his heart. Mrs. Prior, upon Sophie's birthday, which occurred in April, had given her a calendar with a picture of Mr. Pickwick warming his toes at a huge log fire. This they considered very cosy, and for a year he and Ronnie had surveyed each other across the room. There was also a library of four books, and a pile of strictly secret correspondence, intended to consist mainly of letters from admirers. The letters, necessarily from the opposite sex, contained one from Jasmine's Uncle Arthur, not at all admiring in tone. It was little enough time that they ever managed to spend there but it made a wonderful retreat.

Here they retired, and quarrelled, on the day of the lobster's début.

When the storm had subsided, Sophie extracted some toffees from her pocket and threw one, rather sourly, across the room. Jasmine caught it and put it in her mouth.

"All the same, Jay," said Sophie, "you are rather awful."

"It's not my fault he's so hopeless. I don't wish him any harm."

"Poor fish."

"I didn't say that."

"But you think it."

"I can't help what I think," said Jasmine reasonably.

"No," said Sophie, " I suppose you can't."

Mr. Walker, whose ears should have been burning, took Albert home with him. Telling his mother, who immediately took offence, that he did not want any tea, he led Albert down the garden to the large light shed he had fixed up as a studio. "Take your things off," he said.

"What?" said Albert.

"Take your clothes off, man." At sight of his startled countenance he said: "Here, take this," and threw him a triangular bandage. "Put that on and I'll turn it into a leopard skin afterwards."

"Here, what is this?" said Albert. "Sort of cave man?"

"No," said Mr. Walker, suddenly laughing, "sort of god," and he fussed happily with furniture and blinds.

After half an hour he tossed Albert a cigarette and told him to walk about.

"That's a damned awkward position, isn't it?"

"It is that," said Albert.

"But it's what I want."

Albert, inhaling luxuriously, did as he was told, and Mr. Walker was reminded of the careless grace of panthers he had watched patrolling in the zoo. Strolling to the front of the easel Albert was confronted with the preliminary sketches of a young man arrested, apparently, in flight.

"What's the hurry?" he asked.

Mr. Walker laughed.

"He'll only be at one side of the canvas, the rest I can finish later on."

"Well, what's on the other side?"

"It's a tree - bush - a shrub as a matter of fact."

"A *shrub?*"

"Yes. You see, this god was chasing a girl and she got herself turned into a laurel to escape from him."

Albert's jaw dropped and he looked so genuinely taken aback as he expressed his opinion of the girl's intelligence that Mr. Walker wanted to shout "Hold it!" He determined to get that expression into his picture, for so, he felt, might the original Apollo have looked at the laurel, and he wondered if Daphne herself, if she still retained the ability to see and feel, might not, upon observing her charmingly baffled swain, have felt that she had been a little hasty.

When Albert climbed into his grass-stained trousers and laced his boots Mr. Walker arranged for him to come again. Until the light failed he continued in a blissful dream to plot out his picture; the school, the girls and his uncomfortable home so far receded that his mother, fighting her way over piles of old canvases, had to ask him twice if he intended combining both tea and supper with breakfast.

Margery, vainly seeking privacy to cry, crept into the long badly lit cloak-room which smelt of shoes and dust. Her own garments hung conspicuously in the centre so she edged her way down to the darkest corner by the lavatories and sobbed wildly into a prefect's coat.

Sophie and Jasmine had a rare half-hour to themselves before bedtime. They crept past the mistresses' common-room into the main hall, looked guiltily around them, caught sight of Honor on the landing and effaced themselves, then, with caution, slipped down to the basement. Very slowly they opened the kitchen door.

Mrs. Prior, singing loudly and tunelessly, her feet on the fender, her spectacles on her forehead, the cat on her lap, was gazing at a picture paper. Without turning round she called "Come in, now!"

"How did you know it was us?" asked Jasmine, shutting the door.

"Hinsink," said the old lady. " 'Ungry?"

"Golly, yes."

She threw the cat to Sophie and struggled to her feet to produce tarts with jam on them. "You'll be gettin' me the sack an' no mistake."

They sat on the kitchen table, munching and swinging

their legs.

"Timoshenko likes jam," said Sophie, giving him a portion.

"More fool he," said Mrs. Prior.

"How's Jim?" asked Jasmine, nodding at the mantelpiece.

Mrs. Prior's broad countenance creased to a smile. "May be gettin' leave soon."

"*Really?*"

" 'E says so. An' being as I'm 'ere 'e'll 'ave to 'ang around like - won't be no comfort for 'im goin' 'ome alone. I bin wonderin' if Mrs. Munnings might put 'im up. But 'er ladyship might not like that."

"If he's half as handsome as his picture her ladyship will lock him up."

Mrs. Prior laughed, looking up at it. " 'E's better'n that," she said. "I suppose 'e'd better get a room in the town."

"But we'll see him?"

"I've no doubt o' that."

"Tell us about when he was on that submarine."

Mrs. Prior told them. They sat on in the firelight while, from his scraps of information, she conjured up desperate adventures and they held their breath. Moonlight on the South Atlantic, misty islands, the depths of the ocean, filled the kitchen, and Sophie so far forgot herself as to clasp Timoshenko until he squeaked.

"Oh," said Jasmine on a sigh, with complete sincerity, "isn't he wonderful!"

CHAPTER V

MATRON finished her fourth cup of tea, straightened her high cap above a pair of piercing black eyes and went down to the linen-room to see how Honor was getting on. She had the lowest opinion of her assistant's capabilities, which, to do her justice, Honor had done little to dispel.

She found her in the basement, dispiritedly looking through piles of linen and putting it, as she suspected, on the wrong shelves. The high windows revealed at the bottom a narrow area and at the top a cabbage patch. Among the cabbages was a pair of legs and down through the bars of the window floated something that sounded suspiciously like a serenade. Matron's eyes darted from the window to Honor's expressionless face: was there a slight flush upon it? and her nose twitched.

"Haven't you nearly finished?" she asked.

"No," said Honor.

Albert's silver notes showered into the room. He whistled high and cheerily, like a blackbird, as though his tune were an overflow from the pleasure he took in the sunlight and himself.

"I'll shut the window," said Matron, reaching for a long pole.

"Don't you think it's stuffy enough for me in here already?" asked Honor.

Matron's face reddened. "Miss Christow," she said, "rudeness is one thing I will not have."

"Nor I suffocation," rose to Honor's lips but she

swallowed the words and, with tears smarting her eyes, turned back towards the shelves.

Matron looked hard at her bent back and finally put away the pole. With her eyes on Honor and her ear on the window she brooded in silence. Of course the girl did come from a rectory, and was plain enough, in all conscience, to be able to behave, but that young man was immoderately handsome and far too uppish. She knew perfectly that Albert sometimes took flowers to the front hall with a melting charm which caused Miss Bishop and even the redoubtable Alice to feel how nice it was to be served by such an efficient, polite young man; but she knew, she felt, a thing or two more than Miss Bishop, and a vast experience of the slipping of others had taught her that you never can tell.

With a last look at her assistant she told her to hurry up now and slammed the door. She bustled smartly up the stairs with her mind running over the docketed pigeon-holes it kept neatly stored: arrangements about mending; a possible change over among her spotless medicine shelves; a few well-chosen words to the dormitory maids and a few to Miss Bishop about stricter supervision by the prefects of changing down after games. With everything thus arranged tidily her mind closed up in discomfort at the thought of the disorderliness of such a thing as a love affair.

Honor pulled the steps against the shelves and climbed up them. She had failed to adjust them properly and when she was half-way up she fell, with a considerable clatter, to the ground. The whistling stopped, the legs came nearer and Albert's interested face looked down between the bars.

"Hurt yourself?" he inquired.

Honor looked up and her mouth, which had started to quiver, suddenly smiled. "Not unduly - and it was my own fault."

"Should I come an' fix 'em for you?" asked Albert.

"Oh, no!" She scrambled to her feet and arranged the steps again while Albert, since it appeared to be the only course open to him, gave her advice.

"Dull job yours, isn't it?"

"Very!" said Honor with a sigh.

"Yes, I like the great open spaces myself," and he jerked his head, laughing, towards the cabbages. Honor laughed too. " 'Arf a mo'," he said.

He disappeared and when Honor was forlornly counting pillow-cases his low whistle made her jump. He was peering down at her and waving a bunch of roses below the ceiling.

"What on earth - " she began, craning her neck awkwardly to stare at her unorthodox Romeo.

"I thought you might like 'em—it's a bit musty down there. Catch!"

He threw them and she jumped and missed them. Tied together by a piece of raffia they glowed at her feet.

"But really – "

"Don't you like 'em?"

"Oh, yes - but – "

"That's all right, then," said Albert, smiling down.

She picked them up and suddenly it was all right. He

was the first young man who had given her flowers so that his smile and their scent after her miserable tussle with the Matron warmed her heart.

Someone called to Albert across the cabbages and he said, "So long!" and turned away. His face suddenly reappeared to say, "Be seeing you!" before his legs went out of sight.

Honor stood in the middle of the linen-room with the roses against her face.

Jasmine lay on her back while her fingers plucked vaguely at the long grass. She was alone since Sophie, for her sins, had been kept in to disentangle a passage from *Les Miserables*; dictionary in hand, ink on her face, the tantalising outer world beyond the window, she thought that they had been well named.

A ladybird climbed up one of the long stalks beside Jasmine's nose, from the wood behind her a cuckoo called and from far away on her left came the regular click of a cricket ball. The fact that she ought to have been watching her House defeat Wortley Montagu's made her wriggle more deeply into her retreat; she settled her hands comfortably behind her head.

The blue arc above her face grew nearer and warmer, the cuckoo's voice fainter; finally she slept. She woke to hear voices at the edge of the wood. Recognising Honor's she flattened herself against the ground; the wretched girl would report her for not being at the match.

"Why aren't you watching the cricket, Mr. Walker?" she heard Honor ask.

"For the same reason, I suspect, that you are not. There are few spectacles more boring than young women knocking balls about."

At this heresy Honor gasped: "But surely it's necessary - and so healthy?"

"So are lots of dull things. But that's no reason why I should go out of my way to be distressed by them."

"Well, well!" thought Jasmine. "The man's got sense!"

"But surely – well - Celia Warrender says that games keep girls' minds - I mean - " Jasmine could almost hear her blushing. "She says a healthy body means a healthy mind."

Mr. Walker laughed aloud. "Tripe! Since what she means is an empty one. See that?"

"What?"

"That handsome hind netting the strawberries. You'd go a long way before you'd see anything more healthy - or more beautiful. And his mind? His mind," said Mr. Walker, thankfully, "contains a good deal more than is dreamed of in your games mistress's philosophy!" After a moment he added: "Thank God."

Honor made no answer.

"Young woman," said Mr. Walker earnestly, "don't let them turn you into a schoolmarm. You see - I'm fast becoming one myself and I don't like it at all. And now I must go and coach two horrible children for their school certificate." Jasmine heard him walk away. She reflected deeply on the astonishing revelation that he had a life beyond his futility in the school studio. Faintly, from beyond the strawberries she heard him call: "Half-past five, Albert – don't be late."

She did not have time to wonder what Albert and Mr. Walker might be up to for almost at once she heard his boots quite close at hand.

"Lovely day!" he said, and without seeing his face Jasmine knew that the warmth in his voice was a caress.

"Yes," said Honor, and added, "I have to go in."

"Well," said Albert, "the garden's big enough. If I'm spoilin' it for you I could go somewhere else."

"No, no – I really must."

"On a day like this?"

"I've a lot of work to do."

"Too bad."

His expression must have been quizzical for Honor laughed.

"You've been gettin' beech leaves – I like to see 'em indoors – young an' green. I'll get you some more."

"This'll be enough – "

"Go on – I'd like to. Come along."

Their steps retreated towards the wood.

A moment later Sophie joined Jasmine, breathless, and flopped down at her side. "Thought you'd be here. I've just dodged the Christow. What a life!"

"You've missed a treat, my pet," said Jasmine, and told her tale.

Sophie's whistle was soft and long. "The hind and the maiden," she murmured. "The plot thickens!"

"Yes," said Jasmine, "I think it does."

Miss Bishop's catholic taste for information embraced a wide field; her modern views had caused her to arrange for the Matron to give hygiene lectures to each class in the Upper School. Since soon, no doubt, they would be running homes of their own she saw no reason why they should not be able to run them well.

Matron and those of the Upper Fifth who were School House girls were old enemies. She cast her bright gaze over faces she knew and disliked as she took her place that evening in the unfamiliar room. Any airs from that young Jasmine would soon be stopped.

She lectured graphically and to the point upon the dangers of improperly disposed refuse, on the look-out for those flickering smiles which changed to irritating blankness directly she watched a particular face. To-night they were wonderfully quiet. When she finally turned to the blackboard behind her she found that instead of the expected virgin surface there was much writing in many colours. The Form watched her back grow rigid.

The subject for discussion at the next meeting of the School Debating Society was announced to be "Should Your Feet Smell?" (Upon the care of these features she had lectured the Lower Sixth.) Beneath this was a question: "Those in Favour?" Those in favour were evidently the entire Form for twenty-six various signatures appeared.

Someone had written; "Since public opinion is so unanimous there will be, after all, no need for this discussion."

"Which of you impudent, vulgar girls – "

"But all of us," said Jasmine gently. "Don't you see - ?"

"That's enough! I shall report the whole Form to Miss Truscott. Jasmine Tern - go and stand outside."

Jasmine graced the corridor until the bell rang.

Matron knew that she would not enjoy reporting the Form to Miss Truscott for she considered that lady both frivolous and a fool. Miss Truscott, as Upper Fifth Form mistress, was frankly tired of hearing that her girls were the worst in the school; for some reason that she could not quite explain, she liked them all. Matron handed two girls the board rubbers and grimly set them to work. She enlarged upon the necessity for initiative and a practical turn of mind. Finally she asked if any of them had the intelligence to think of a way of disposing of organic refuse in the country, say, far from the dustman's route. None of them, apparently, had. She told them that the merest child might have thought of the neighbours' pigs. They sighed, for this was true. And now, she asked them, what about tins?

They stared hopelessly. With rising irritation she pointed to the girl beside Jasmine's empty desk. Directly she had done so she realised her mistake, for those two were as thick as thieves. Vengeance was swift.

"The neighbour's ostrich, Matron," said Sophie, getting politely to her feet.

Celia Warrender accepted her tea-cup and tucked her legs more comfortably upon the foot of Honor's bed. She wore a checked and corded dressing-gown which had belonged to her brother and leather slippers. Her face shone honestly from an admixture of natural good humour and a liberal application of soap. Honor threw her a lump of sugar which she caught without upsetting the cup.

"Well, old girl," she asked, "how's things?"

"I had a dreadful morning - Matron's temper ran riot. I'm afraid one day I'll really say what I think."

"That woman drinks too much tea," said Celia, stirring hers. "Indigestion's her trouble. And lack of fresh air. I'd like to tell her so."

"Would you?" asked Honor.

"Well, when she's not here I would." They both laughed. "I say, I like your roses."

"Yes."

"They're early. Daylight robbery?"

"No."

"I suppose they're from an admirer," and Celia threw back her head in a hearty laugh. Honor's faintly heightened colour might have been caused by hot tea; she knew that what Celia dismissed as All That could never come within the scope of their confidences.

Celia proceeded to give her details of the match, accepting pressure of work as Honor's excuse for her absence. "But seriously, you know," she complained, "some of those Upper School girls are awful slackers - a miserable crew - I can't make it out. D'you know only about five of them take cold baths! I can't think why Matron doesn't make it compulsory in the summer term. Why when *I* was at school I was up before the bell rang and turning out the slackers - girls had some energy in those days. Is there any more tea?" She clasped her hands round her knees. "Believe it or not, but one of the Sixth supposed to be watching the match was half-way round the pavilion and reading a book. And guess what it was?"

From her expression Honor was about to hazard *No Orchids for Miss Blandish* but Celia said, "Poetry!" and taking a draught of tea she added profoundly, "Shelley" as if that made it worse.

Honor looked at Celia's puzzled frown - dear, honest Celia whose schooldays were no farther distant than her own - and from her to Albert's roses.

She wondered for which of those contrasting worlds she was really intended, for she felt that she belonged to neither. It was very confusing; she sighed.

Margery lay quietly looking at the dormitory curtains, waiting for the tears to come. All day she was on view to the public and at each of the worst moments she told herself: "I'll be able to cry when I'm in bed." Now here she was wasting her time. She blinked at the ceiling in surprise. She recalled the worries which had gripped her since she had climbed into the train. Mothers went away and died, with no more than a kiss and a wave; how easy, then, for Nannie, when one's back was turned, to be careless crossing the street. Or even for her to fulfil that promise to better herself and go up to the box room for her trunk. But to-night she remembered how Daddy had said - horrified - "Holy Moses! I'd marry her first!" and smiled before she went to sleep.

The windows of the mistresses' common-room were open to the sky. It was a large room, supremely untidy; textbooks cascaded from the shelves, sheets of paper littered the floor, ink pots and two coffee cups sprouted from the mantelpiece, a pair of tennis shoes and a jar of irises huddled behind the door. Miss Truscott, although the room contained five ash-trays, threw her cigarette end out into the night.

"Was Lenin born in Georgia?" asked the English mistress, blue pencilling an essay.

"You're thinking of Stalin," Miss Truscott informed her, ruffling up her bright hair.

Miss Crowther threw that essay on the pile beside her and picked up the next. After a moment she sighed. "I do wish they wouldn't keep referring to Elizabeth as the Virgin Queen."

"What extraordinary things your girls write about," said Miss Truscott, with a ruler absently poised before her nose.

"The subject," said Miss Crowther coldly, "was 'An Admirable Character'."

Miss Stebbing laughed.

"Then you might tell them," said Miss Truscott, whose subject was history, "that among Elizabeth's many admirable virtues her virginity has no place. She had 'a *membrana* on her'," she explained, pointing the ruler at Miss Crowther, "she had no choice."

"A *what?*"

"A *membrana.*"

"Who says so?"

"Ben Jonson."

"And how did he know?"

"Ah, there," said Miss Truscott, "you have me. But in the interests of accuracy you should point it out."

"I shall do no such thing." After a while she said: "Your Form may be evil but their essays are the best in the school. Here's Jasmine Tern discoursing with accuracy and charm upon St. Teresa of Avila. D'you think that's odd?"

"Not necessarily. That lady had a remarkable fund of dispassionate common sense. Were they given her for holiday reading?"

"Never, as far as I know."

"Then that is odd. They must actually read on their own."

"I confiscated *Forever Amber* from three girls' trunks," said Miss Cottingham, looking up from her book. They all laughed.

At half-past ten Shirley, since it was Alice's evening out, brought in a tray of tea. She managed to clear a space at Miss Cottingham's elbow and then, looking round the room, she drew the curtains and put the irises up on the table. She did this, not reproachfully, but as though they were nice, rather clever children who deserved a tidy nursery. From Miss Cottingham she took a cup of tea and wished them good night.

Shirley knocked at Miss Meadows' door.

"I thought you'd like a cup of tea, Madam," she said as she went in and, setting the cup carefully down, she produced a book from under her arm. "I kept it so long," she added, "because I read it twice."

"There's another one," said Miss Meadows, at the shelves, "which goes on from there."

"You mean - the same people - and what happens next?"

"Yes," said Miss Meadows, handing her *Good Wives.*

Shirley ran her fingers softly over the edges of the book. Finally she held it against her apron, smiled, and said, "Good night."

When she had gone Miss Meadows adjusted her spectacles and returned to the Aegean Isles from which Shirley had brought her back.

Matron paused outside Honor's door on her way to bed; she, too, had had a trying day. Neither Honor nor Celia were pleased to see her but they were too kind to show it at such an hour.

Over her third cup Matron expanded sufficiently to tell them about that Berwick girl and the ostrich. Celia coughed so violently that she said she thought she had a cold.

When they had gone Honor undressed in a happier frame of mind than she had known that term. There were a young man's roses on her dressing-table and there was definitely one girl in the school whom she liked.

CHAPTER VI

THE fathers' match, which occurred during the first half of the term, caused a good deal of heart-burning among the twelve fathers - eleven team and one reserve - detailed to represent their kind.

On a hazy morning in early June eleven gentlemen looked anxiously at their flannels and their barometers, while the twelfth, Sir Roger, turned his face to the wall. His wife and nephew, summoned to his bedside for a consultation upon a painful stiffness in his back, had been sympathetic, the nephew going so far as to assert that lumbago, if not treated with care at the first symptoms would continue with increasing agony through life.

Sylvia, hat in hand, was lost in a day-dream before her mirror when she answered Tom's knock upon her door.

"You were unkind to poor Roger," she said, frowning at him, "he thinks he's going to die."

But Tom, instead of looking contrite, explained simply, "I want to go in his place."

"*What?*"

"Yes, seriously, sweet. Another month doesn't give me much chance to look at the girl."

"Jasmine?"

"Yes." He picked up one of the bottles from her dressing-table and sniffed it. "That's nice."

"There'll be half-term," said Sylvia, choosing another hat.

"So there will. Bless you! But I'd like this as well. And I

look so nice in flannels."

"I dare say. But how do you expect me to explain you?"

"It's quite easy. You know you can manage headmistresses. Your usual vague and trusting charm. And it's necessary, too. We can't let down the side."

"There's a reserve," she said, severely.

"But one of the others may be ill."

"They may have pushing nephews too."

"Then how nice that would be for the girls. Please, darling." Tom rubbed his lean cheek against hers. Sylvia's cheek curved softly and sweetly like a child's. "How long, with her aid and the beauty parlour's, would it continue to do so?" she asked the face in the mirror. And: "For ever" Tom's eyes assured her, reflected beside her own. He had that trick, known to some men - and at no time to Sir Roger - of making women sure they have enchantment.

"Very well, darling," said Sylvia, thinking a little enviously of Jasmine, "I'll do my best," and she turned up her face to be kissed.

As the day increased it grew hotter. A few more flakes of paint were blistered from the pavilion; the pitch, rolled by Albert, was sweet and true, girls arranged deck-chairs for the visitors. Miss Bishop, regal in flowered linen, gratified each parent by real or assumed recognition.

Jasmine strolled past the pavilion and twelve pairs of eyes, one pair of Tom's and eleven pairs of fathers', followed her out of sight.

The fathers won the toss. They played well considering they were a scratch team and out of practice, and better than the first eleven. Tom, whose offer to resign in favour of the reserve had been rejected, since that gentleman preferred the safety of his deck chair, was afraid to knock their balls about, they looked so pretty scattered round the field. He blocked unhappily; it would be just his luck to give that poor little thing at point a black eye.

May and Sylvia gossiped merrily without paying much attention to the cricket and Sophie and Jasmine sat on the grass at their feet.

"What have you done with Arthur, May?"

"Funeral," said May, with as much simple pride as if she had ordered the victim herself.

"You *are* clever, darling," said Jasmine, endorsing this.

The first few of the fathers to be out settled themselves comfortably in the sun, their caps over their eyes, and hoped the rest of the side would be in a long time. This was really the way to spend an afternoon. They observed their clever daughters and the surprising youth of some of the mistresses with gratification. They had chosen the right school.

"Who's that chap?" asked a small girl's father as Mr. Walker went by, liking the look of him. "I don't remember - "

"Oh, that's Fishy Walker," his daughter informed him. "He's not anybody's father. As far as I know," she added with intent - a failure - to shock.

"Fish?"

"Yes. The drawing master."

"And what do you draw?"

"Fish," she explained patiently. "Do watch the bowling,

dear."

He did so, taking furtive glances at his daughter during runs. Did they really draw fish? he wondered. It seemed an odd reason for him to be scrounging for those fees. Perhaps it was a prelude to one of those modern careers, like girls looking after animals in the zoo, and he had a vision of himself creeping through the dim shades of some future aquarium to an assignation with his daughter among the octopuses.

During the interval, while Matron presided over the urns in the pavilion, prefects handed out cups of tea. Tom, taking one of the plates of sandwiches offered to him by Charity Morgan, and insisting upon following her round with it, displaced the curate for ever from his pedestal in her heart.

He had had very little opportunity to talk to Jasmine so he decided that the best thing to do when he went in again would be to send up a good catch. At the first opportunity he did so and sat down on the grass beside her. May smiled so kindly at him that he leant his dark head against her chair while he tried, successfully, to distract Jasmine's attention from the field.

But this did not last long for very soon the fathers reached their century and generously retired. The girls played gallantly, but in spite of Tom and a father in the slips, carefully but not obviously dropping catches, they had only made sixty runs before they were all out and stumps were drawn.

Celia, who with other enthusiasts, had been calling, "Played, oh, well played!" and "No - go back!" across the field, listened to the cheers changing from treble and soprano to tenor and baritone and congratulated her pupils on their brave effort.

The end of the game was a signal which released the visitors across the road and into the grounds, except those who were catching immediate trains. When they reached the little wood Tom cast such an imploring look at Sophie that she announced that she simply must show her mother and Mrs. Tern her garden, adding that she knew Jasmine was sick to death of it and as Tom was no doubt more interested in food what about the raspberry canes? Sylvia and May, looking quite deceived by this artless diplomacy, allowed her to lead them away.

Tom fingered the leaves nervously, not quite sure how to take his opportunity now it had come.

"We're not allowed to eat them," said Jasmine, gazing at the green fruit, and, indeed, the kitchen garden was out of bounds. This being so they were alone in it and she thought that had been an astute move of Sophie's.

Tom longed to kiss her and she was wishing he would do so, but her youthful air and the school tunic were too much for him. Instead he said: "Will you write to me, Jay?"

"When you go back to West Africa?"

"Yes."

"It's a long way," she said, imagining her letter embarking at - would it be Southampton? - and cruising off over the Atlantic, a touch of Mediterranean at Gibraltar, the Atlantic again. . .

"Will you?" asked Tom, hoping she saw him as a rather

heroic figure in a topee, scanning the horizon for the mail.

"Oh, yes!" said Jasmine. Her letter had arrived, it was being taken from the mail bag by - would it be black hands or white? - black, she was certain. "I should love to," she said. Tom received the smile that was intended for the enormous negro who went bounding up the hill with her letter in his hand.

"I thought I might come and see your aunt at half-term. I'll be staying with Aunt Sylvia."

"We should be so pleased," she murmured sedately, discounting Uncle Arthur, who would be no such thing. Into the silence she dropped a suitably admiring comment on his cricket. Since she had been chattering to May during most of his innings she knew nothing of the blockings or the catch.

Her cheerful indifference to the game pleased him vastly. "When will you be leaving school?"

"Another year," she sighed, "another year at the end of this term." She wriggled her shoulders and threw back her head, as though, thought Tom, she were prepared even now to slough off the three R's with her school uniform and go out into the world unencumbered; like something small and bright, he thought, like a candle flame.

She peeped at him under her lashes. "Will you write to me, too?"

"I should think I will."

"And send me pictures of - of mangoes and monkeys?"

"Of every one!"

"I should love that!"

"I'll be away a year," he told her, as they retraced their

steps to find their aunts. "About a year."

He hoped, without much conviction, as he opened the wicket gate, that she would keep some memory of him in her young dreams of romance. And, indeed, he would have much to live up to, for in her mind's eye, as he closed the gate behind her, she saw the Emperor raise Eugenie's fingers to his lips, Browning ardently pace the sick room and Bothwell ride out into a windy night.

CHAPTER VII

WHEN Honor washed the little girls' hair - a task she disliked only less than performing the same office for the bigger ones - she was pleased and surprised to find Shirley at her elbow with offers of assistance. The little girls - who had just left the Junior House where they had been the big girls - hopped and chirruped round the large wash-room on the first landing while Honor waded among them with jugs of water and shampoo. This particular room was invariably a subject for ribald comment because of the frequency and ease with which it changed its sex. When the first eleven were not playing the fathers or any of the neighbouring boys' prep schools the large label saying "Gentlemen" was kept, with its face turned primly to the wall, in the bottom of Matron's cupboard among the bandages. To-day the room was strictly feminine as the black ribbons, combs, pools of soapy water and the drone of the electric dryer proclaimed.

The little girls, of twelve or thereabouts, seemed young and sweet to Shirley from her distance of eighteen. She put two of the children close together to share one dryer and watched the sudden streams of brown and auburn fan out above her hand. They kicked and poked each other without malice and tied Shirley's apron strings to the chair. She continued happily to smooth back the hair from the round foreheads, and Honor, passing and ordering them to untie her, wished she had Shirley's patience.

Shirley was happy so she sang, and when "*I* don't want her, *You* can have her, *She's* too fat for me" rose above the dryer they demanded an encore. As they swung round to talk to her or peered suddenly between their flying manes they were as nice, she thought, as her little sisters.

Shirley's desires were few but definite. Her home, which contained both poverty and domestic bliss, seemed to her perfect, and she hoped to spend as much time there as possible until she left it for one just like it of her own. When her father, tired and dirty, returned from the small local dockyard in the evening, saying, "Well, old girl," as her mother held up her face to be kissed and their youngest daughter bawled upon the floor, Shirley knew that that was what she wanted. She told the children of her family as she worked.

When Matron came to inspect Honor's efforts, which she did audibly and tactlessly in front of the girls, she packed Shirley off and reproved Honor for enlisting her assistance. Shirley opened her mouth to explain but Honor frowned her away; she was not likely to convince Matron that any one would seek the company of those exasperating children when they might reasonably be somewhere else. Matron's black eyes darted from Honor's downcast face to Shirley's confused and pretty one, and taking hold of two little girls' plaits she pronounced them to be damp.

Sophie and Jasmine, drifting through to the lavatories, raised a speculative eyebrow across the room. They thought Matron's temper might be due less to Honor's misdemeanours with the dryer than to the fact that she had disappeared among the beeches with Apollo.

The warmth of Honor's smile, reminiscent of ostriches, surprised Sophie but she returned it with interest for she had just discovered that Matron, on a tour of inspection, had unearthed the store of sample make-up which she and Jasmine had hidden beneath the paper of her drawer. They did not use it, but liked to feel that it waited, a tryst with the future. Now it would arrive in her trunk with a note to Sylvia who would say, "Good God, darling, I should think they're poisonous; try my Elizabeth Arden."

When Honor released the little girls they sped thankfully away.

In the garden Margery danced along the paths for a precious twenty minutes before tea. Her newly washed head glinted in the sunshine and the bow which Honor had tied slipped off. She removed a bag of toffees from the leg of her knickers and remembered Shirley's song. "Time is a great healer," she thought.

Shirley took herself and her troubles down to the kitchen.

Mrs. Prior said: "Silly old sod," and threw Timoshenko a piece of fish.

Timoshenko did not make much effort to catch it for he was, at the moment, exhausted by his love life and between a succession of passionate nights he passed the warm, sleepy days in a dream. He took a couple of mouthfuls of the fish then popped into Mrs. Prior's chair.

The peace of the kitchen was suddenly disturbed by Noranmaude who shot in with their eyes bolting. Behind them came a young sailor.

Mrs. Prior dropped a plate and a saucepan and flung herself into his arms.

The young sailor swam up laughing from her vast embrace and planted a succession of kisses on her face. He saw Shirley slipping out of the door and said, quickly, "Introduce me!" Proudly, Mrs. Prior did so.

She also introduced him to Noranmaude, "Me son Jim!" It was the sweetest music.

Shirley, too shy to intrude, suffered Jim's blue and frankly admiring gaze then whisked the other two girls from the room. He watched the last flick of her print dress at the door.

Mrs. Prior spun round the kitchen like a top. Suddenly it was the most beautiful place in the world. The rows of blackened saucepans unaccountably shone, the flags beneath her feet were buoyant, the tap, to which she rushed for refreshment, filled the kettle with a silver stream.

She called questions over her shoulder as she flung the largest cups on the table, then, when the tea was brewing, she went and kissed him again. The brown hands held her shoulders in the grip that was so reassuring and the blue eyes looked into her own.

Mrs. Prior produced a cake she had made for Miss Bishop's tea and carved enormous slices.

"Blowed if you ain't better-lookin', love."

"Speak for yourself," said Jim, blowing his tea. He smiled over the cup.

"Where's yer ship?"

"Greenock. 'Avin' 'er bottom scraped. We orter get six weeks after all these months."

"Six weeks." She sighed. "Sorry it ain't in the 'olidays. We'll go 'ome on me 'arf day?"

"We will that."

She smoothed his round hat with "H.M.S. *Indestructible*" upon it between her wrinkled hands.

Timoshenko was sniffing round the strange kit-bag. Jim said, "Hey, old boy," and stroked his chops for him before he produced his mother's presents from the circular depths.

She received a pair of ear-rings, some nylon stockings (Christ knows when I'll be wearin' them, she thought) and a glorious silken night-gown about the size of a tent. (Extravagance! That'll be seein' me into me grave.) They were both delighted.

Jim fastened the kit-bag, hung it on his shoulder and swung off down the drive to his room at the pub with that slender grace with which His Majesty's naval uniform clothes all his ratings.

Shirley wandered round the garden in a golden dream. She had laughed gaily and reassuringly at her father's jokes about the trouble her pretty face would be to him, only to be plunged into love at first sight.

Sophie and Jasmine, on their way down from an illicit appointment with the strawberries, noticed her and smiled. Sophie, who had developed a social conscience, thought: "She's as pretty as Jay and only a little older, yet she spends her days turning out rooms." Jasmine, who had none, merely registered the fact that she was her only worthy rival in the school.

As they inspected the stains on each other's faces they uttered their gratitude that the garden, when Shirley had gone, appeared deserted.

And so it was, except for Albert, who, considering it too far to go down to the cottage was buttoning his trousers behind the tool shed.

At the Silver Herring Mr. Jones and Poppy leaned their elbows on the bar. When the customers bought - or tried to buy - a drink for Poppy Mr. Jones always said: "That'll do, Poppy," before the third. When Albert arrived Poppy had had her ration so she shook her head as she handed him his tankard.

Albert said: "Here's how," and turned his back upon her. Their relations, which had once been amorous, had dwindled to the bestowal of a drink and a rather bored kiss when the bar was empty.

Mrs. Prior and Jim came off the brilliant pier - he had some difficulty in wedging his mother into the turnstile - and set off arm in arm, towards the pub. In the late summer dusk Mrs. Prior was conscious of the glances cast at the handsome sailor and her step became lighter as her head went up. They peered into one of the noisy amusement alleys, at the pin tables and the fortune teller: "Madame Romano Will Tell You All," they read. Mrs. Prior could have told her a thing or two, and said so. At the next batch of fairy lights they stopped for ice-creams.

Jim ushered his mother into the pub and smiled at Poppy as he ordered port and lemon. "I'll ruin 'im," thought Mrs. Prior, but it was nicer than her usual bitter. She hailed Albert who joined them and soon they were immersed in a pleasant round of drinks.

Poppy made eyes at Jim while she polished the glasses, and Albert told him bawdy stories of his life in the army, which Mrs. Prior capped with gusto. She approved of the way Albert took life as he found it - and he found a good deal - but she would not have exchanged all the Alberts in the world for the straight, bronzed young figure at her side. While Jim collected further refreshment from Poppy she heard the wind rising and thanked her Maker that her mind, instead of travelling anxiously out to sea as was its wont on such occasions, could rest between Poppy's lace curtains and the gleam of brass and pewter, for neither wind nor waves at the moment could touch the sailor who trod the sanded floor.

Doris turned her collar inside out in readiness for the morning and peeled her stockings from her stout legs. Shirley, cooling her steamed face at the window, said gently that it was something to be able to get hot water— not like home where she and her mother were always filling the copper.

Doris, disinterested, breathed loudly as she dug her broken corsets from the folds of her stomach, dropped them on the mat and clambered into bed.

"I see James Mason's at the Regal," she said, "Cor!"

But Shirley, averting her eyes from the corsets, had forgotten James Mason. She, too, was listening to the wind rising and wondering what it would be like at sea. Her mind went down to the Silver Herring as she balanced herself on the window-sill.

That night a storm blew up and the sea could be heard through the open windows.

The wind blew round the dormitories, lifting hair from pillows; then banged open a window Sophie had left unfastened in the empty attic. Mr. Pickwick flapped loose from his moorings and Ronnie rattled across the boards. And over Matron's door, hoisted to this eminence by an unknown hand, there danced a notice saying: "Gentlemen."

CHAPTER VIII

SUNDAY was always rather a depressing day at the school, the depression being due partly to the interruption of the normal routine and partly to the consumption of rations bought at the tuck shop on Saturday.

In the morning those who had not been confirmed stayed in bed for an extra hour and developed headaches, while those who had, rustled behind their curtains in a manner which they supposed would not disturb the sleepers. They then slipped forth to join one of the two distinctive camps: the High who crept along the corridors with their stomachs rattling and the Low who queued decorously outside Matron's little surgery for cups of tea. Some of the former sometimes contemplated themselves having their hair cut off like Lilian Gish in a revival of *The White Sister.*

The School House settled down to their breakfast with a great clattering of chairs after singing their Latin grace.

The sky wore that washed and driven look which had been imparted to it by two days of rain, and Jasmine, watching the little clouds flying past at the tops of the high windows, longed to have the day for her own. She informed Sophie that it was electricity and not iron which had entered into her soul, and for the rest of her life she was sure she would never hear an electric bell without conscious gratitude that it held no summons for her.

"Then don't become a bus driver or a nurse," said Sophie.

"Like hell I will."

Rather miserably they consumed the large pieces of heavy toast which Noranmaude produced as a tribute to the Sabbath.

They attended matins in the school chapel and sat with what patience they could muster through a sermon by the local curate, lent for the occasion. During his twenty minutes they managed to school their ears against any external impression and to use their eyes. Three hundred Sunday blouses shifted rhythmically with the impatient wrigglings of young shoulders. A few heads bent unaccountably over books were studiously absorbing the marriage service. Matron wore a cap and bow so stiff it looked as if it would cut her head off. A few of the mistresses had gowns - relics of their college days - and Jasmine thought they looked extremely foolish. She pushed her panama hat a little farther back and fingered the soft, bright curtain of hair. She was just piling it on top of her head for a party, a party to which she would sail down a broad and circular staircase while several young men elbowed each other out of the way at the bottom, when Sophie jerked her funny bone with more accuracy than she had intended to remind her that they were standing up for the hymn. "You've broken my arm," shouted Jasmine above the music, in great pain. She saw Miss Truscott's frivolous hat quiver and held her book before her face.

As they crossed the damp and springy grass they encountered Albert in a new suit on his way to the pub and envied him his freedom with sad hearts. Honor saw him, too, with his eyes shining and his curls darkened by hair-oil, and her heart turned over at the gaiety of his smile.

From the School House a long crocodile, with Celia and Honor at its tail, wound its way into the street. Girls from the Lower Fifth downwards were forced into this form of exercise between chapel and Sunday dinner, those in higher forms being allowed the comparative freedom of the parade, along a specified route, in parties of three: Miss Bishop's study of psychology having informed her, correctly, that while two will agree upon most species of devilment, a third will usually have a sobering influence.

Sophie and Jasmine, who had no wish to join the crocodile, accepted Angela Cunningham's offer to make a third. They had abandoned the course of locking themselves into the lavatories since Matron, having learned of the habit, inspected these apartments after chapel and banged upon the doors.

They walked sedately past the playing-field towards the sea, through a world from which they were as rigidly divided by their school hat bands and the necessity to be back by one o'clock as if, they felt, they were in purdah.

They strolled along the upper promenade, sharpening their pace a little when they caught sight of the crocodile across the road. When it turned a corner they slowed down and sniffed the air.

They looked around them at the families spread out upon the beach, the couples arm in arm along the sun-warmed pavement, the stalls offering ices and winkles; it was all so bright and gay that they forgot for the moment that it was not for them. They climbed upon the railings and leaned over, looking out to sea. With a sudden defiant gesture Jasmine removed her hat and let her hair blow back inland. She felt as if she were a figure on the prow of a ship, ignoring the crowds and the shingle below her, seeing only the crested waves and the gulls above her head.

The wind was so cool and kind against her cheeks, the motion of the galleon beneath her so smooth; unconsciously she thrust her bosom a little forward, her head a little back: the *Cutty Sark*, perhaps? The galley slaves sweated and cursed at their oars behind her, the bearded captain, who wore ear-rings, a knotted scarf around his brow, had just remarked upon the beauty of their figurehead to the mate when Sophie nudged her and pointed out Jim Prior where he walked upon the beach alone. His mother was cooking the Sunday joints. Three pairs of eyes observed his every movement with delight.

Sophie and Jasmine, who had glimpsed him from afar, had asked Mrs. Prior for an introduction but they were too wise to remark upon this to Angela. They watched him push back his round hat and, leaning his elbows on the winkle stall, start a conversation with the tattooed proprietor.

"We ought not to stay here," said Angela.

Sophie and Jasmine leaned farther over the rail.

Angela repeated herself.

"I heard you the first time," said Jasmine coldly.

It was Angela's private opinion, for she was naturally law abiding, that both Jasmine and Sophie would come to a bad end. However, since they had to stay together and it was physically impossible to march the two of them away, she decided not to waste her time.

"What sort would you like to marry?" she asked them. "Jim Prior," said Jasmine without turning her head, and thinking, unexpectedly, of Tom.

"And you?" inquired Sophie politely, aware that for this opportunity Angela had instigated the inquisition. "Heathcliffe!" she said deeply, remembering him.

"What about our Soph?" asked Jasmine, looking over her shoulder.

"Mr. Knightley," said Sophie sorrowfully, for she reflected that she could not amuse him as Emma had done.

Jasmine put her knife and fork down beside Mrs. Prior's Yorkshire pudding and let the noise of eighty people eating break over her. The sunlight fell in long warm bars over the raised table at which Miss Bishop dispensed hospitality to the curate; he looked nervously over Miss Truscott's head at the rows of polished tables and femininity, as though, thought Jasmine, he found his exalted position a little frightening. Then she saw Miss Meadows lean towards him with the bread as solicitously as if he were a little boy - in another minute, she thought, she'll tuck his napkin into his stock for him - but she must have said something to cheer him for he looked relieved and laughed. "I suppose we are rather awesome in the mass," she thought, and looking round her she felt suddenly sickened by the smell of beef and the chattering crowd. They would be herded from the dining-hall to dormitories and gardens, from there to tea, from there to letter writing, from there to evening prayers. It was too ghastly. She saw a swallow fly past the window - going where? at least wherever he wished to go. And leaning back she let her mind wander in the impossible place she wanted. There was a stream and a sun-dappled wood, banks of eternally blue and scented violets; oddly, between the trees, the white gleam of a statue, and sometimes, on the sward above the water, there appeared a nymph or shepherd; it was so quiet that she could hear the stream splash on the stones and one of the shepherds singing; far back in the wood there were suddenly notes as clear as water and the leaves rustled: it was not a shepherd because whoever moved there had hairy legs and hooves.

Honor called down the table a request to hurry up, please, and Sophie, jogging her gently, said, "Come back. Where were you?"

The little stream crashed to a waterfall and ended in a roar of conversation. "In heaven," she said, helping herself to custard, "Arcadia."

No sooner had Miss Cottingham settled herself with a nice murder and her feet up than there was a knock upon her door. She called wearily to the visitor to come in.

"It's only me," said Miss Truscott, doing so, "but I hoped you'd lend me - as you say you have it - *Forever Amber.*"

"*I?*" said Miss Cottingham, appalled.

"Yes, you know you collected three copies. They can't all be out."

"Out!" echoed Miss Cottingham. "Heaven forbid. And I

really don't think - "

"Oh, but please. My young man accuses me of becoming a blue stocking and I thought perhaps if I absorbed that - well - it might act as a sort of counter irritant."

"In my young days we called it something different." Miss Cottingham burrowed in her cupboard.

Miss Truscott laughed.

"Then take it," said Miss Cottingham, getting up again. "But it seems to me a curious route to take to marital bliss. And don't tell your young man I gave it you. And put it under your arm." Miss Truscott did so. "And don't lose it," she called down the corridor. "I don't wish to be considered a thief."

Miss Meadows adjusted her unfashionable hat, flicked a clothes brush vaguely over the collar of her aged coat and skirt, smoothed on a pair of still older wash leather gloves. Quite satisfied with the result she looked into the common-room on her way out, to adjust her watch. She was of that school which, when it is invited out to tea, asks at what time it is expected to arrive and acts upon the answer.

"You ought to be out of doors, you know," she said kindly to Miss Truscott, who dropped the *News of the World* over her book.

"I'm just taking an afternoon catching up on myself. Where are you off to when everyone else is asleep?"

"I'm going out to tea - and I mustn't be late. My hosts," she added gravely, "are five young men."

As Miss Meadows turned the corner into the High Street

there was a low whistle from a few yards down the road and a young man who had been leaning from a window in one of the side turnings looked back into the room. "She's 'ere. That'll be Ginger. Tea up?"

"Kettle's bilin'," said the corporal, shovelling ten spoonfuls into the pot.

Of the three other soldiers in the room one flicked a particle of dust from the aspidistra, one inspected his shining countenance in the cracked mirror, one sprang to open the door. Ginger, who had gone down the road to meet her, escorted their guest into the room. They smoothed the sergeant's pillow, swathed delicately in an antimacassar, in the only arm-chair, and placed Miss Meadows against it.

The corporal set his black and scalding brew on the table in front of her and asked her to pour it out. Miss Meadows, wading her way through tea with tinned milk which tasted like sweetened senna, enormous buns whose creamy contents burst upon her face, and lumps of very good gingerbread made, they informed her, by Ginger's mother, enjoyed herself with a will.

She had made their acquaintance upon a gusty day on a little beach outside the town which was still littered with the aftermath of hostilities. The soldiers were clearing the barbed wire away, Miss Meadows was looking for fossils. Suddenly the corporal had used a word to which she was not accustomed and when he apologised she saw that his hand was running with blood. Miss Meadows had assured them that sea water was a good disinfectant, had bound the hand in her handkerchief and had extracted a promise, since she was sure the rust was dirty, that he would present himself at the next sick parade. When she saw them again, she said, she would expect to be told that he had done so. She did see them again. She was reassured as to the corporal's welfare, and when, looking sadly at the evidences of destruction around her, she said it was a pity that people did not attend less to politicians and more to Sir Thomas More and Plato, they asked her to tea.

When they had finished the gingerbread she relaxed upon the sergeant's pillow, puffing resolutely at a cigarette. They told her funny stories about their unit and long after she had meant to be back at the school her sudden, gentle laughter floated out into the street.

In the deserted common-room Miss Truscott yawned, sighed, and threw *Forever Amber* on the floor. She looked up her horoscope in the *News of the World.*

The original and the picture looked thoughtfully at each other in the school kitchen and Mrs. Prior offered her son one of the mangled cigarettes from her pocket. But Jim, who had been rubbing Timoshenko's cosy cheek against his own, shook his head as he made for the door. He was just in time to catch Shirley before she left the cool flagged passage.

"It's your afternoon out, isn't it?"

"Yes." Shirley prepared to run.

"Are you - doin' anything?" he asked humbly, over Timoshenko's head.

"I go 'ome," said Shirley, turning pink.

"Is it far?"

"Three miles."

"D'you walk?"

"No. Tram."

"Well, couldn't you walk to-day?"

Shirley hesitated.

"Please. Sun's beautiful. Let me take you, Shirley."

Shirley jumped. Suddenly aware of the embarrassment it would be to present Jim to her family, who would be certain to draw only one conclusion, she looked wildly round.

"I c'd just take you to the end of the road," said Jim, looking away from her and back to Timoshenko.

"All right - all right - thanks." She turned away.

"I'll meet you at the back door in - how long?"

"Ten minutes," said Shirley, and ran.

Disregarding Doris, who snored upon her bed, her mouth full of toffee, three toes protruding from the holes in her stockings, Shirley changed her cotton dress for an artificial silk one and touched her childish lips with coral. She smiled happily at her reflection as she crowned it with a six and elevenpenny hat.

The girls twisted at their desks, chewed their pens and gazed continually round the unresponsive recreation-room for inspiration. What satisfaction the recipients could derive from remarks which had been almost literally squeezed from their offspring was a wonder to Charity Morgan, who, as House prefect, surveyed the girls from the mistresses' desk. Her own letter to a widowed parent had so little connection with the expression of her feelings that the two ran concurrently. "Dear Father," she wrote: *that was an overstatement.* "I'm sorry you feel Miss Bishop's views are too modern" - *Why the hell did you send me here, then?* "How unfortunate that Mrs. St. George has been pursuing you so pointedly" - *You must be mad if you really believe that but if it's true then she is.* "What a pity you don't wish me to make more use of my music when you have, as you say, spent so much money on it " - *That ought to fetch him.* "Yes, of course, I realise that you know best" - *What a lie.* "But I do share Miss Bishop's views about my future . . ." She looked up just too late to see Sophie passing a note to Jasmine.

"Will you say *adsum* for me if I skip prayers?" she had written.

During the next communication between Charity and her parent Jasmine scribbled: "O.K., who's your boy friend?"

Sophie made a large "G" on the desk with her finger and Jasmine grinned, for she had known the answer.

At prayers Jasmine's ingenuity was taxed to its utmost. To say *adsum* twice, once during the B's in Sophie's voice and once later in her own was no difficult matter, but to ventriloquise so that Sophie's answer appeared to be coming from beside a girl called Bernard instead of from down the line beside one called Sully was very hard indeed. Not until the Lower Fifth were throwing back their *adsums* did Jasmine breathe again. Had she known it, she had preserved her anonymity only because Miss Cottingham's mind still worked upon the problem of the bloodstain below the viscount's window.

Sophie took a stick of barley-sugar from her

handkerchief and wrapped it in a piece of graph paper. An uncanny quiet hung over the building with all the rest of the House at prayers. Sophie sent up a prayer of her own against discovery and dashed down beside the wall until she was hidden from the school. She rose out of Albert's hedge like a banshee, to tap with the barley-sugar on the kitchen window. He was so startled that he nearly drowned himself in his tea but Mrs. Munnings, saying briefly, "For God's sake, Albert," admitted Sophie to a full view of his blackened face. She made no comment upon his appearance and Albert, annoyed that she should apparently take it for granted that this was his usual manner of imbibing, explained what she had done to him as soon as he recovered his breath. Sophie giggled. Albert gave up looking cross and laughed, too.

Mrs. Munnings poured Sophie a cup of black, syrupy tea, which was just as she liked it, and settled her with the baby on her lap and the cup in her hand while she got his bath ready. Sophie sipped alternately at the tea and the baby's downy cheek.

Sophie and Mrs. Munnings exchanged remarks upon the beneficial effects of barley-sugar and then discussed the rival merits of napkins folded to an oblong or a triangle. Albert groaned and cut himself another slice of bread.

The untidy table, the fire, the cosy gossip, were just to Sophie's liking. This is what I shall have, she thought comfortably, as she pulled the barley-sugar back from the baby's uvula. A kitchen filled with crockery, firelight, half-dried garments and a canary, and a nice chat with a friend - over cups of tea - about the best type of food for children. It will be fun. She jogged the baby gently while he pulled her pigtail.

When the bath was ready Mrs. Munnings enthroned Sophie and the baby beside it and cheerfully ignored the perilous angle at which they arranged themselves as Sophie tested the water with her elbow. She and Geoffrey exchanged an endless and unintelligible conversation. Albert continued audibly to chew.

Sophie folded the baby's rather dirty little garments neatly beside her and soaped him carefully upon her lap. He was a little large for this treatment, or her lap was a little small, and as the slippery areas increased they both found it difficult to balance. When he was safely in the water Albert said, "Good for you," to all that he could see of her flushed face. Sophie grunted.

The bath took a long time, partly because Sophie was inexpert, partly because they both wanted to prolong the business.

"You won't 'arf cop it if they catch you 'ere," said Albert, watching her smooth powder with meticulous care upon his son's behind.

"I know," she said, sighing, "but I don't care now."

Indeed, as she kissed the pale, clean little face she felt the force which would presently drag her back to the school peculiarly irksome. She hoped vaguely that Jasmine had been successful but if she had not - well, she had had her pleasure and nothing authority could do or say would now detract from it.

"Could I just tuck him in?" she asked Mrs. Munnings.

Albert sat on with his elbows among the cups, listening

to the footsteps overhead and brooding on the strangeness of women. Though the two upstairs were of the opinion that he could not compete with his baby there was one, at least, in the school who was not. He remembered with pleasure the expression upon Honor's face in the drive that morning, which had made her for the moment almost pretty.

Sophie hung Albert's shirt, which she found in the baby's cot, over the rail behind his head to shield him from the light. He closed his eyes with a touching obedience so she and Mrs. Munnings leaned out of the window with their faces among the wistaria and talked.

Upon the Briggs' doorstep Shirley kissed her father. "Good-bye, Dad, it's been ever so nice."

"You 'adn't orter brought so much to your Mum, duck," he said, worrying. "The kids can manage an' you've got your position to keep up, an' that, in that smart place."

Shirley caught sight of a navy-blue figure beside the tram stop. "I've got all I want, Dad," she said with truth.

"Ah, but there's pretty things you'll be needin'. Not but what," he added, looking at his daughter, "there's anythink I c'd see as'd make you prettier."

Shirley laughed and straightened his collar. "See you next week, Dad."

" 'Bye, dear."

" 'Bye."

She climbed up the swaying stairs of the tram with one hand holding on to her dress. Suddenly she found Jim helpfully anchoring it about her knees and herself looking down on a sailor hat.

"That your Dad?" he asked at the top.

"Yes."

"D'you think he'd forgive me if I took your 'arf day up?"

"I - " began Shirley.

But Jim, raising the bluest of eyes, said simply, "I ain't got very long. Six weeks at most." When Shirley said nothing he added: "I thought the country."

Shirley nodded. The tram rattled and shook through the mean little streets, jerked over the points. When it hurled itself round a corner to a view of the sea with a shadow of rose on the horizon, Shirley felt that if Jim had not been holding her hand she might have floated off the wooden seat into heaven.

CHAPTER IX

ON Mrs. Prior's half-day she and Jim went down to the cottage.

He caught sight of Shirley through the window of the servants' hall as he passed and blew her a kiss. This gesture so affected her that she spent the rest of the afternoon turning out Miss Meadows' room in great disorder and wondering what it would be like when he kissed her himself.

Mrs. Prior sailed into the bus station and towed Jim on to a front seat. They opened the window and as they left the London road she began to sniff appreciatively. The sweet, thatched cottages in the down country were bright with stocks and lilies, the children who stared or hung on gates had changed very little from the companions who played in summer gardens when she was a girl. When the bus dropped them at the end of the lane she breathed deeply. The downs were scattered with thyme and hawk-weed, a lark rose over her head, sheep cropped drowsily on the skyline. Jim had a vision of all the tropical shores he had visited which, however beautiful, telescoped inevitably to this.

The little old house, settled at an unlikely angle, looked as if it had risen from the earth itself, and even with its closed windows and untidy garden had a welcoming air. Pansies and groundsel overflowed on to the path, roses scrambled above the long grass, delphiniums rose majestically beneath the bedroom casements. When they opened the door a bee flew in ahead of them.

Jim made a fire in the kitchen and Mrs. Prior produced from a large black bag the supplies which she considered her due. These were adequate and had been collected from the school kitchen. When the kettle was boiling, their cat, who had been boarded out next door, strolled in to tea.

After tea they smoked and pottered in the garden. Mrs. Prior leaned her elbows on the fence and gave her neighbour an exaggerated account of Jim's exploits while he boarded up a broken window.

Jim wandered into every room. Before they left he slipped down amongst the long grass at the back of the cottage, beside the apple trees. He threw away his cigarette and stretching his arms on each side of him he closed his eyes. Touching as large an area as possible he could almost feel the earth rocking. He breathed sorrel and clover and turned his cheek against the grass. This was better than the sea. This was land.

On the terrace Albert clipped the grass borders round the roses. From time to time he stopped to wipe the sweat from behind his ears with a purple handkerchief. In the cool hall, which smelt of ink and furniture polish, and framed through its wide oak and nail-studded door the flowers, the grey roofs of the town and the sea, Alice moved a jar of lupins on the floor and straightened a card tray (in which no one left cards). Albert, catching sight of her neat, respectable person, plucked a rose, held it out to her and went down on one knee. Alice said, "Get along with your foolishness," and went away, but she smiled, in spite of herself, all the way down to the basement.

As he turned back to the shears Albert saw Shirley, motionless, leaning from Miss Meadows' window with a duster in one hand and a book in the other.

"That's not what you're paid for," he called softly. Shirley, taking her eyes from the sea, closed the book, frowned at him and shook the duster on his head. She found love a great deterrent to order and method, for Jim came between her and each article she dusted, and she replaced the furniture in such an unusual and haphazard fashion that Miss Meadows was later surprised to find a little bust of Dante wearing her most disreputable hat.

Albert, whistling and swinging the shears, encountered Mr. Walker in the drive, coming out of school. They set off together. Mr. Walker, to his own surprise, was beginning to enjoy Albert's company. As they walked the half-mile to his house he mentioned that he had had a shocking afternoon with the restless, talkative members of the Upper Third, and when Albert replied simply, "Them bloody kids," he found the remark a comfort. From tormenting, terrifying little devils it immediately slipped the Upper Third into their proper perspective in the universe. Them bloody kids! And then forget them. It was fair enough.

He shepherded Albert round the house and into the shed without, he hoped, disturbing his mother. If he had been alone he would never have begun work without excusing his absence, but Albert, who, after her third appearance in the studio had once told him in one brief and ruthless sentence what he would do with the old lady, was a great support to him. As he painted the beautiful, indolent creature, he envied him his cheerful self-absorption.

The picture was growing, it seemed to Mr. Walker, with a power of its own. Light and shade seemed to suggest themselves and the tan over the tensed muscles was perfect. When Albert could not come he added touches to the sunny glade in which the figures stood. The plural seemed correct to him, for the little laurel was assuming a strangely human grace beneath his fingers.

While Albert, stretching and smoking, stark naked, commented upon a Degas reproduction of a lady at her ablutions - "Too bloody like my old woman" - Mr. Walker found himself unable to rest. He painted the undersides of some leaves he wished disturbed by a breeze and to the laurel he gave a little twist which was like the way that Jasmine turned her head. To him as (he supposed) to Apollo the laurel represented the unattainable; though at the back of his mind there was a cynical little doubt as to whether Jasmine, in the same situation, would have appealed to Zeus.

He cherished his brief and infrequent meetings with her as an insurance against the barren future. He had observed her on the afternoons when the Upper Fifth played cricket, lolling idly in a corner of the field she hoped least likely to be visited by the ball, and later bowling left-handed breaks with an efficiency by which she seemed surprised. He had seen her on her way out of the gates for a walk, uneclipsed, he considered, by the depressing panama hat. He passed her sometimes in the garden with her yellow head bent sideways towards Sophie's and between them the low giggle he could recognise from three hundred others. Week by week she wasted all of her own time and some of his in the drawing periods. A little savagely, as he coloured Albert's curls, he thought that they were well matched.

Albert, after the sitting, fastened his belt before his portrait - "Christ! me own mother wouldn't know me!" - passed a comb with five teeth in it through his hair, said, "O.K., thanks! So long!" in the doorway and whistled up the path jingling two half-crowns in his pocket. In a happy mood, he said " 'Evenin' Madam!" to the old lady at the window and accompanied it with a smile that sweetened her temper. He went home by way of the Silver Herring.

After three glasses he came out into the summer dusk, feeling very pleased. He stood balancing himself on the curb, humming softly, wondering which way to go. The faint throb of a band called him from the pier, the mingled smells of dust, spilled petrol and a freshness which might have been the sea were in the air. Albert, who was sensitive to smells, had planted night flowering stocks outside his bedroom window and sometimes when he came home late and sober he would wake Mrs. Munnings to enjoy them with him. Her usual reply was, "For cryin' out loud, Albert! That kid'll wet if he's woke," at which Albert would laugh and remove his boots with care. He swayed back on to his heels, thinking that they had had more fun before the baby came. Two girls, tipped forward by their high shoes, their shoulders raised as if to keep their balance, laughed past him with a strong gust of ashes of violets. "Very nasty," thought Albert, who had tired of it on Poppy. He whistled after them as they turned the corner, looking back.

He went to the school gates. Outside his cottage he was assailed by a bellow from his son, and breathing the sweet air he turned back into the drive. He sauntered round the deserted gardens, deciding, if he met one of the mistresses, to say he had forgotten to close the tool shed.

Below the terraces he paused to look up at the school, one or two of the windows already filled with light. The building seemed to be alive with a gentle, busy murmur, indistinguishable until from the wide french windows of the mistresses' common-room laughter suddenly dropped over the flowers. Above it, on the first floor, he could see Miss Meadows arranging a reading lamp and a heap of books. Over the front door Miss Bishop's stately shadow appeared on the soft curtains then moved away. A comb dancing on the end of a string, from one of the top dormitories, proclaimed that the little girls were supposed to be asleep. In one of the music-rooms an enthusiastic maiden was making a disaster of Schubert's serenade.

Albert found himself humming an accompaniment as he went across the grass. He leaned against a fence beside several unfortunate little plots, divided by shells and stones, belonging to the Lower Fourth. He remained there a long time, wishing for - God knew what. Something sweeter than Poppy, younger than his wife, more mysterious than his child. He remembered another summer dusk when, not quite tipsy, he had dared to go alone through the narrow lanes of the Casbah. The Algiers that he knew had seemed cut off behind him as he wandered through the old streets, so tiny he could touch the houses on both sides and sometimes the sky had been shut out above his head. He had known that the white figures of women on the roofs were peering down at him and that he would be ill advised to look up, but he had hardly cared to, so enchanted had he been by the spicy smells of dirt and cooking as he stumbled past Arabs smoking, gossiping, selling sweets thick with flies. The seeds of adventure which lay, he supposed, in every one, had been fostered for five years to a green growth and did not wither because he had come home. The easy routine, the soft spoken employer, the bells on Sunday, the tea in the kitchen, the wife to sew buttons, the pub from which one did not rush for fear of a sergeant major, the shops in which no one bargained - how sweet they had been in retrospect, how dull when he had settled down! A girls' school! he thought, turning his back upon it, and spat over the fence.

Someone else had taken the burden of youth and dissatisfaction into the garden. Honor, her tiring but uninteresting tasks finished, wandered along beside the lawn, plucking a leaf to pieces as she walked. She was, perhaps, the loneliest person in the school. Denied the freedom of the mistresses' common-room or the ease of the servants' hall, there was no company besides her own to which she might naturally turn, except for Celia's, and even Celia palled. She disliked and avoided the Matron, and although both Miss Cottingham and Miss Meadows remembered, since she might be lonely, to request her company sometimes in the evenings, she feared that none of them enjoyed such sessions very much. There were times when Honor watched the companionable couples at recreation, and heard their giggles, with a desire for the crowded hours of her own schooldays which would have surprised them very much. They considered her rather sad face a dim one and dismissed her from their minds.

She thought of her father, his shabby cassock thrown over a chair, the jug of black coffee, which he hoped would keep him awake half the night, placed vaguely on the floor, writing away in a study invaded by the spirits of hay and honeysuckle. If only any one were ever likely to pay for those dissertations upon the journeys of St. Paul! If only she were at home.

As she turned a corner she came upon Albert by the fence. She would have gone back but hearing her footsteps he straightened up and hailed her softly. "Lovely evenin'!"

"Yes," she said.

"Don't go," he murmured, seeing her retreat. He made room for her beside him at the fence. "Lonely?"

"I - "

"I know. 'Tisn't quite my cup o' tea, either," and he indicated the school. He took one of her hands, smoothing it in his work-roughened fingers and suddenly, with instinctive gallantry, laid a little kiss in the palm. Honor, for whom the world was rocking, looked at the shadow of his bent head. She knew that she ought to go and that she would have to stay. Albert, after a swift glance at her face, drew her to him and kissed her with admirable restraint. Directly she tried to move he let her go. "I'm sorry," he said, looking down at her, and thinking that was just the tone which would appeal to her most. It was.

The shy curates to whom she gave tea at the rectory, the village schoolmaster, her rather boorish cousins, faded to a milk and water memory beside this possessed young god who kissed her warmly and calmly because, apparently, they shared a summer dusk. The fact that he was married and not what her aunts called One's Own Class increased, to her romantic mind, his charm and daring.

"I must go," she whispered, "please!"

"Don't forget me!" said Albert against her face. "Good night!" He watched her dim figure in its unbecoming cotton dress disappear into the shadows near the school.

At the Silver Herring Jim, remembering the country, looked so long into his glass that Mrs. Prior asked him what he saw there. He shook his head, laughed over the rim and said, "Nothing! Drink up, Mum!" but Mrs. Prior was as certain that Shirley's face lay among the bubbles as if she had seen it there herself. She was quite satisfied for she was fond of Shirley and already in her mind they made a Lovely Couple.

" 'Ave one on me, now, duck," she said.

Albert leaned on against the fence with a cigarette suspended from his lips. Honor, Mr. Walker, Poppy and Mrs. Munnings each had a different vision of his face before they slept.

CHAPTER X

JASMINE grovelled and swore among the dusty racks in the basement. They contained a communal collection of discarded or unclaimed paraphernalia for the pursuit of games. In winter the hockey sticks - now cast into a dim recess - adorned the racks in which, this term, cricket bats leaned drunkenly together. Girls scuffled and chattered round the room.

"For goodness' sake hurry," said Angela. "You're terribly late. Aren't you ready?"

"No."

Sophie offered her two pads, for the same leg, from the pile on the floor.

"One's got no straps."

Angela said desperately, "Well, come without, then. You're always last."

"So I am."

"Then do come on."

"If you think," said Jasmine, fanning herself with a pad, "that I'm exposing my shins to your onslaughts - "

"Then I'm going."

"There's nothing to stop you."

"Come on, Sophie - "

Sophie shook her head.

Another girl said seriously: "I shall have to report you if you're late."

"You're very welcome."

They had the littered room to themselves.

"If people go on offering me left-handed pads and advice I shall have a seizure," said Jasmine, turning over the pad in her hand. "This is marked Cozens. Wasn't she - ?"

Sophie sat down in the dust. "Yes. Last Speech Day with that enormous baby and looking like nothing on earth. Hands all over potatoes. It makes you think."

"It ought to make you think, with your baby farming," said Jasmine twisting round to look at the backs of her legs.

"They're still there."

Jasmine laughed and picked up another pad. "Tiverton," she said.

"Killed in that plane crash."

Jasmine threw it swiftly behind the racks.

"Some day," murmured Sophie, dreamily, "people will pick up pads labelled Tern or Berwick."

Jasmine visualised this odd possibility. People would rise from one Form to another, would shout through the dormitories, would scuffle among the dust in the basement - and they would be free. "God help them," she muttered, "shut in here - and thinking of us."

"Thinking what?"

"Oh - 'That's the one in Hollywood.' Let's go and see Priory."

"Don't you think - ?"

"We've had it in any case."

"I suppose we have."

They dribbled a cricket ball round the room then set off for the kitchen.

Mrs. Prior was crooning to herself as she wallowed in a

mound of heaving pastry. She waved a sticky, hospitable hand. " 'Allo, my ducks."

"We won't be missed for a bit - how's Jim?"

"Lovely, 'e is. Keep yer fingers out o' that. An' when you do get missed?"

"Trouble again," said Jasmine with a sigh.

"I see it round yer like a 'alo."

"So we thought perhaps - ?"

" 'E'll be back in a minute. 'E was lookin' for Shirley." She winked.

"You mean - ?" asked Sophie cosily, sitting on the table.

"Proper case it is."

"What fun! When'll they be married?"

"Give 'em a chance dear! - let go o' that jam - 'ow you do run on. Not but what," she said, reaching for the rolling pin, "young folks did orter be kept waitin' too long!" and she gave a bawdy chuckle in which the girls joined. As she bent again to her pastry, her bosom heaving with exertion and laughter, Jasmine had a vision of countless fat old women spreading flowers and canopies and whispering to the bride. She murmured "Juliet's nurse!" in Sophie's ear.

" 'Ere they come," said Mrs. Prior as the door opened.

Shirley and Jim stopped shyly at sight of the girls.

"Come on in now." Mrs. Prior wiped her hands and drew them forward. "Me son, Jim. Miss Sophie - Miss Jasmine."

They shook hands and both the girls, glancing from Jim to his picture, thought that it hardly did him justice. The candid admiration in their wide eyes left him silently twisting his hat.

"Well, my ducks," asked his mother, "what d'you think of 'im?"

"Wonderful!" they said together.

Jim, taken aback, caught Shirley's little smile where she waited in the window, and laughed. "Whatever 'ave you been up to, Mum?" he asked.

"I tell 'em where you been."

"Everywhere," said Sophie, "it's been such fun!"

"We've been to all those places with you," Jasmine told him. "Plymouth - Naples - Gibraltar - Durban - and round the Cape - "

"We saw the pictures of Naples!"

"The time you missed your ship - "

"Yes, we worried about that!"

"And the time you played centre forward in Shanghai."

"And shot three goals!"

"Sakes alive!" said Jim. He looked at the ardent faces raised towards him, unaware that for the rest of their lives he would be used as a touchstone by which they would appraise man.

"We'll 'ave a cupper tea," said Mrs. Prior, beaming round. She swept one end of the table clear of pans and bowls.

None of them ever forgot that tea. Mrs. Prior, observing the three prettiest girls of her acquaintance taking her son for a hero, wheezed and smiled and let them talk. It amused her to reflect that this bronzed young man sat there laughing and cutting slices of cake because years ago she had slipped with old Prior into the heather. "It's a rum world and no mistake!" she thought, reaching for the milk.

Jim, whose head might have been turned if he had not been in love, watched Shirley where she sat, shy and silent, while he told tales of storms and sunsets, porpoises and flying-fish. Shirley, a little startled to find herself at a table with the two young ladies - they were two cautions - slipped back into the happy dream in which she had drifted since the first day Jim came into the kitchen.

The girls, enchanted, left cake upon their plates. Years afterwards, Sophie, meeting a celebrity, thought, "Ah, once - in the school kitchen - there was no disappointment!"

They all moved the cups to the draining-board. "Leave 'em there!" said Mrs. Prior, with a magnificent gesture.

Jim stood beside Shirley at the open window. She caught his look, then glanced down swiftly at her fingers twisting a corner of her apron, her small head beneath its starched cap bent shyly away.

The sun shone down through the area. Mrs. Prior opened one of the ovens. Sophie, watching them, thought, "So this is it!" and Jasmine, ever afterwards, connected a summer afternoon and the smell of hot pastry with love.

"We'll have to go, Priory," said Sophie, "thank you awfully for the tea."

Jasmine held out her hand to Jim. "I hope we'll see you again. And you won't forget?"

"It's a promise," said Jim. "First port I gets to. A postcard each."

"We'll keep them always," called Sophie. "Good-bye!"

They banged the door, their running feet sounding loudly then faintly, along the passage.

Jim and Shirley stood at the end of the table, each wrapped in a strange cocoon of enchantment, each wishing they were together and alone.

"Gawd 'elp them!" thought Mrs. Prior. Aloud she said, "You goin' out, Jim? I got work to do."

High on the downs the ox-eye daisies fluttered and lay sideways in the wind. On the road below, the green bus, growing smaller, wound its way back to the still visible sea. Jim and Shirley watched with gratitude the disappearance of their last link with the town.

Jim took Shirley's transparent hat with its bunch of heavy, glazed cherries off her head and out of his way. He kissed her with a combination of love and skill and passion which made her feel that she was going to faint. When he held her away and looked humbly and searchingly at the fair, flushed young face tilted towards him he did not know that his own wore a reflection of the cloudless certainty which held him like a spell. "Oh, Shirley," he said, "Oh, Shirley!" moving his lips along her cheek.

They sat on the firm turf-covered chalk and Shirley smiled to remember Doris's reminiscences of her warning to The Fish: "Never set down, my Mum tells me - keep walkin' all the time."

"What is it, my darlin' " asked Jim.

"Nothing," said Shirley, Doris forgotten. She lay back with helpless docility beneath his hands.

Jim murmured against her parted lips all the love and

loneliness that had accumulated during six years at sea. With his mouth on her throat and the small hands, ingrained with the floor polish of staff bedrooms, against his hair, he realised she would have as little defence as the daisy leaning against her head. He lay with his cheek on the cheap dress, trying to still the raging in his blood.

When he raised his head again he said, "Let me look at you a moment an' then we'll go." He watched, half smiling, the lines of chin and nose and cheek, the childish curve of temple below her hair. Shirley looked back at him, trying to memorise the face above her for the years ahead. "I'm what's so wonderful!" she thought: "What the two young ladies thinks the world of! to look like that for me!" She kissed him tenderly and softly before he pulled her to her feet.

"Better keep clear until tea," said Sophie. "What about the attic?"

"Uh huh," said Jasmine.

They took a long and circuitous route which included dormitories, bathrooms, the upper reaches of a fire escape and the corridor past the maids' bedrooms. They passed Matron's door singly, like Indians; Jasmine melting among cubicle curtains until she saw Sophie disappear at the far end of the passage.

On the fire escape they were arrested by a hiccough and gurgle from a bathroom window. They peered inside.

Two little girls, their tunics soaking, bedroom jugs at their feet, sat on the edge of the bath. Their eyes bulged.

"What on earth?" said Jasmine.

"Oh, Lord, what a fright!" A bloated countenance was raised towards her.

"What are you doing?"

"We've done it now. And I've won. I've drunk a whole jugful. Margery had to leave about a pint in hers."

"She's going to be sick," said Sophie, looking down.

"She has been."

"Oh."

"Better leave them to it."

"Well - have fun."

"Little pigs," said Jasmine, running again.

When they closed the attic door they felt safe.

"Hallo, Ronnie," said Sophie, collecting him from the floor.

"He looks pretty dreary after Jim, poor boy."

"Yes, I'll just stick him up." She did so and smiled at Mr. Pickwick.

Jasmine knelt on Sir Roger's coat with her elbows on the window, looking out to sea. "We'll get hell if we're caught."

"I should think we will be."

"Yes. Oh, well - don't let's think about it now."

They wiped it from their minds.

"Half-term soon," said Jasmine, watching a yacht against the horizon, making out to sea. "Freedom for two days." She wondered who hoisted the white sails, turned the tiller as they chose. How enviable they were!

Sophie was busy reorganising last year's calendar to bring it up to date, changing each figure to fit the days of the week. "There," she said, "that's right until the end of term."

"A world away," sighed Jasmine. "Eight more Saturday lectures." She ticked them off on her fingers. "Careers - as if they can't finish with us when we do get away. That M.P. with the false teeth: do I care whether he's in or out? The Cave Man as an Artist - carefully censored. Modern treatment of diseases of the mind - really I think our Unity's overreaching herself a bit there." Sophie giggled. "But perhaps they have a waiting list? We could find out. And at least two missionaries - fancy showing us a picture of a crowd of fortunate natives sitting in the sun and expecting us to put our pocket-money towards changing their happy lot for ours; now, if it were the other way round - "

Sophie said, "Do shut up, Jay," and going through the pile of letters added: "We'll put Jim's cards with these."

"Yes, that will be something." She leaned from the window again. Somewhere out there Jim and Shirley wandered, free. She remembered the way they had appeared in the kitchen. It was as if they had seen love at the source.

She tried to say something of this to Sophie.

"Ye-es," said Sophie, tightening a bow, the end of her pigtail between her teeth. She flung it over her shoulder and sighed. Jasmine's metaphor made her see love as a river, bursting through the first thaw of winter snow, increasing and widening, falling over precipices, slowing down, running between summer fields and at last, spread thinly and muddily, into the sea. "*Où sont les neiges d'anton*," she murmured with an aptness which would have surprised Miss Stebbing. "What about Tom?" she asked.

"Tom?" echoed Jasmine who had not connected his gratifying passion with whatever they had seen in the faces of Shirley and Jim. "So little," she said. "Tom's just - Tom loving me and me enjoying him doing it."

"Have you no heart, Jay?" wondered Sophie, unappalled by such chilling honesty.

"Why yes," said Jasmine, putting her hand over the school tunic where she could feel that organ pumping her blood. It was, she supposed, wound up like clockwork and no doubt would go on until it ran down again unless some accident should happen to stop it. How odd it was! She looked at her young, thin hands on the window-sill, at her legs with ink spots on the stockings - extremities kept going by the heart whose existence Sophie thought so speculative; and not only kept going but kept sufficiently beautiful to annoy Miss Bishop and to make Mr. Walker's heart turn over. A curious thing!

A clock striking half-past three reminded her that she must take the body in question to the dormitory and clothe it suitably for tea. She got up, stretched and yawned, her arms above her head. "Better get in before the crowd, old Soph."

Sophie said to Ronnie and Mr. Pickwick: "So sorry we have to leave you. But we'll be back very soon, dears. Don't fall down again."

They jumped the uncarpeted flight of stairs to the maids' corridor and Sophie wrenched her ankle. She swore quietly and fluently while Jasmine bound it, without material improvement, with two inkstained handkerchiefs and a tunic girdle.

In the dormitory, which should still have been empty, there was a shadow across one of the warm, window-shaped patches on the boards, a movement among the curtains. Matron's door opened an inch.

Margery, still pale from her contest, considered that any moment might be her last. She remembered Joan of Arc, Nelson coolly displaying his medals, Charles the First marching smartly to his doom. She walked boldly down between the beds. Matron's door opened wide. Charles the First stood like a rabbit in a trap while she entered the dormitory.

"What are you doing here?"

"I - "

"You look very pasty. Are you ill?"

"No," said Margery, her martyr's pride stung.

"Have you missed games?"

Could she get away with it? But that was unworthy - the king didn't run before the rabble.

Margery rubbed one shoe on her stocking, seeing the crowded streets, the winter day.

"What are you thinking of?"

"Charles the First," she answered, surprised into truthfulness.

"And I want no impudence. You can go to bed an hour early. Go downstairs at once."

Charles the First shivered with awful dignity as he crossed the sunny room. He felt sick again and wished to make it quite clear that it was the January weather and not his fear which caused the tremors.

When Sophie and Jasmine tried to sidle past her door, Matron, who had tasted blood, bounced out like a jack-in-a-box and drew them in.

"You've been missing games!"

They stood side by side on her oasis of terra cotta hearth-rug, stricken dumb.

"Where have you been?"

Since they would both have died before implicating Mrs. Prior or disclosing the blessed sanctuary of the attic they remained silent, staring into space. Matron drew the blind to half-mast to keep the sun off the carpet. "When did you last see your father?" muttered Jasmine, below her breath.

Sophie thought: "I wonder if one good hearty lie – " then decided against it. Her head appeared to be swelling and Matron's potted ferns, orange cushions, lithographed Virgin and Child and row of neatly treed and polished shoes seemed to be swinging round the room. As the pain in her ankle became excruciating she leant forward and was sick.

Matron had Sophie in a chair, cold water on her forehead and newspaper on the floor while Jasmine was still thinking: "This really is the end."

Sophie opened her eyes and they both started to apologise at once but Matron, that astonishing person, accepted this behaviour very kindly, only remarking with unconscious accuracy that worse things happened at sea.

In the sanatorium Sophie lay back on her pillows with a

sigh of content. She had her foot on a cushion, magazines and lemonade at her side, a rather ominous-looking basin (just in case) well within reach, some soft wool of an almost heavenly blue and some needles upon her lap, with which Sister had said she might do as she liked and which already she had mentally metamorphised into something for Geoffrey. A lovely patch of sunlight in which, if she wriggled to the left and undid her pyjama jacket - she did so - she might hope to get a little brown, made happiness complete.

"I wish I was ill oftener," she thought. She approved heartily of Sister's taste in literature and turned the pages of the magazines. "A really useful vest for Baby," her fingers smoothed the blue wool. "Some Simple Rules for the Mother-to-Be." She relaxed blissfully as she read.

The sunlight moved across the bed, the lemonade sank to the bottom of the jug, the jar of roses filled the air (just as if she was a real invalid), the blue wool became three inches of uneven ribbing, the Mother-to-Be, it grew obvious, was in for a hectic nine months. The sounds of bells, of people calling, of running footsteps, came faintly over the garden from the school. All those poor girls hurrying to prep and supper and she idle and alone! The print began to swim before her: "Knit one purl one . . . Plenty of water for the kidneys." Sophie slept.

Jasmine waited outside Miss Cottingham's door. That section of blue carpeted passage, with its white-painted doors and two pictures within her line of vision of Florence Nightingale and the Mona Lisa - Jasmine considered them strange companions - was painfully familiar. Here she had come regularly, term after term, to await what Miss Cottingham optimistically styled correction, for each time uncorrected - she returned. Her young shoulder, which had once reached the bottom of the Mona Lisa's frame now touched her chin, while the crown of her fair head, she noted, had topped Miss Nightingale's cap. She nodded genially to the two ladies as she measured herself against them.

Three ill-mannered little girls went past and grinned at her; Jasmine looked coldly over their heads. Matron, passing with a glance of quiet satisfaction, received a malevolent glare. Miss Meadows went by with her lips moving, her eyes on the ground; as she put a pile of translations on her table she distinctly remembered seeing someone close at hand. She looked into the corridor and asked kindly, "Can I do anything for you, dear?" Jasmine thanked her and shook her head. Miss Meadows realised she had been tactless and went away looking as if she thought Jasmine was paying a social call.

"The old sweet!" Jasmine murmured, comforted, turning to the pictures again.

She was engaged in trying to stare the Gioconda out of countenance when Miss Cottingham, who had not, as Jasmine supposed, been keeping her waiting because she had taken a tip from a dictator but because she had been hastily putting three detective stories and nine undarned stockings behind the cushions, opened the door and beckoned her in.

They looked a little nervously at each other, both

disliking the interview.

"Well, Jasmine?" said Miss Cottingham, knowing perfectly why she had come, but determined that a personal aversion to Matron should not lessen the upholding of her authority.

"Matron told me to report myself to you for missing games."

Miss Cottingham remembered the shawled little girls in the frame in the hall, the record of whose curriculum had revealed a sad amount of physical inactivity, and thought that justice had come full circle.

"Do you take no interest in cricket, dear?"

"I can't say I do, Miss Cottingham," said Jasmine in a tone which made the words polite.

Her housemistress sighed, for she took none herself and saw the force of this. She looked from the graceful young creature at her side to the plump and ageing hands in her lap. "I suppose Sophie Berwick was with you?" she asked; and added, "I hear she is unwell?"

"She was unwell on Matron's carpet," said Jasmine with content.

Miss Cottingham clicked her tongue but whether in sympathy with Matron or Sophie or annoyance with Jasmine she did not say. She was silent for a long time during which Jasmine supposed her to be thinking out some unspeakable punishment, but in reality she was remembering that she had sat in this room for fifteen years, plump and rather dowdy, reproving generations of girls for the mistakes they had committed. Those very girls who had all gone away and become dons, mothers, actresses, doctors, schoolmistresses, even lawyers, and whether she had ever been the slightest use to them she couldn't say. They wrote, they sometimes called with difficulties, they came to tea - she recollected, smiling, that her predecessor once removed had obtained two suffragettes' release from prison - but at other times they rarely thought of her, and indeed, she told herself, there was little reason why they should. Might she not, she wondered, just as well have accepted the offer of a young man to accompany him to Africa, whither, upon her decision that her work lay at St. Helen's, he had proceeded in solitude, to take his revenge upon the local carnivora, which was the fashion for rejected suitors in those days. She returned Jasmine's golden cheerful gaze, wondering if perhaps those martyred tigers had died in vain.

Finally she took the poems of Victor Hugo from the shelf and handed them to Jasmine. "You will translate one of these into English verse during recreation. Don't choose one of less than fourteen lines. And I mean verse," she added, "not doggerel."

"Yes, Miss Cottingham." Jasmine moved towards the door.

Miss Cottingham said desperately, "Wait a moment, dear."

Jasmine waited, looking startled.

"You remember the Foundation Girls, in the picture in the hall?"

"Why, yes," she said, surprised.

"When those little girls came to St. Helen's they rose at

half-past six, with their governesses, to tidy the classrooms. They had little recreation and poor food but they considered themselves privileged, as indeed they were, for they studied mathematics and Greek. When they in their turn became governesses they earned perhaps sixteen pounds a year and if they had saved any of this when they married they were not legally entitled to spend it as they chose. It is owing to the efforts of those little girls and their contemporaries - "

"The Bronte's," murmured Jasmine.

"And their daughters, that you - "

Miss Cottingham stopped herself, a little taken aback by this unusual flow of rhetoric. "Does that impress you?"

"Why yes," said Jasmine, her nose wrinkling in astonishment, "it does."

"Sufficiently to make you conform to a curriculum which has been so dearly won?"

"Perhaps not actually to conform," said Jasmine, with honesty. "But sufficiently" - she hesitated and gave Miss Cottingham her brilliant smile - "sufficiently to make me see some reason why I should."

"That was worth two lions and a tiger," said her housemistress and laughed.

"I beg your pardon, Miss Cottingham?"

"Nothing, dear. You may go."

When Sophie woke she found that Margery was being assisted by Doris, as sanatorium maid, into the other bed. She allowed Doris to put away her clothes but held firmly to a brown paper parcel which she pushed behind the sheets. When Doris had gone she unwrapped it furtively, out of sight.

"What's that?" asked Sophie.

"You won't tell?"

"Not a soul."

"It's Augustus," said Margery, producing his greyish and love-worn form. "It was all right at the Junior House, and now we've come here - I can't tell him he's silly in School House, can I?"

"Dear me, no."

"Is that something for a baby brother?" asked Margery, her eye on Geoffrey's vest.

"Yes," said Sophie, wishing it was.

Margery was silent until she asked, "Do you want that basin?"

"No. Take it if you like."

She did so and settled herself comfortably with Augustus on one arm and the basin on the other. "Now, I've got everything," she said.

Sophie pitched a magazine on to her lap.

"Thank you," said Margery, turning the pages politely. After an interval she pushed it away with a sigh. "They all seem to be about love."

In the silence Sophie counted stitches.

"Sophie."

"Yes?"

"I only lost because I was sick."

"I dare say. Whatever made you think of it?"

"It came in a flash. And - Sophie - in case we're bored in here I've got another one."

"What's that?"

Margery smiled and wriggled her toes. "See who can wait longest to be excused."

When the school was quiet the moon rose late and flooded the seaward rooms. It swept into the dormitory and turned Jasmine's yellow hair to silver, exposing with fine impartiality her sleeping features and Charity's button nose. It dropped on Matron's countenance, who pulled the sheet over her head. Honor dreamed that Albert was coming towards her over gold and silver flowers. Miss Bishop stepped firmly from her couch and drew down the blind. In Miss Meadows' room the moving flood lit up an open Theocritus upon a pair of cotton interlock combinations; in Alice's it received a welcoming grin from a tumbler containing her teeth. It fell upon the reverberating mound that was Doris and caught a gleam from Shirley's open eyes.

Sophie knelt at the foot of her bed, brooding upon the moon-washed roofs of the town. Grey and blue and silver they slipped down to the sea, and, as Margery moved in her sleep to cover Augustus, she leaned from the window to people the quiet town. Who tossed and turned down there, she wondered, who drew their lovers to them, who came home late and carried up their boots, who stole down to throw stones into the sea. She sent a blessing out to the strange, adult people, of whom in a year or so she would be one.

Jim leaned over the rail on the deserted promenade. The moonlit sea sucked up the little stones and returned upon them; sucked and crept back. In the school above the town he imagined Shirley sleeping, her hair about her face. Suddenly he ran down to the beach, flung off his clothes around him and plunged into the small, soft waves.

Mr. Walker paraded the garden and the studio. The silver light reminded him of Jasmine and he could not sleep. His mother, requiring her shutters closed, beat uselessly with her shoe upon the wall.

Albert, to let in the moonlight, climbed over his wife and woke Geoffrey, who, startled by the radiance, wet his bed.

CHAPTER XI

JASMINE kicked at last year's twigs, rubbed her shoulder against the warm bark of a tree. She was, by this time, so used to the feeling that she ought to have been somewhere else that it scarcely intruded.

Idly she turned the leaves of More's *Utopia* to observe that Erasmus, on returning from a visit to England, had recorded as noteworthy the fact that Sir Thomas treated his wife with as much courtesy as if she were a maid of fifteen. Fifteen! thought Jasmine, looking down at the childish shoes supporting a slim instep, a white heel protruding from a hole in her stocking. How old was the wife? she wondered. And did girls grow up sooner in those days or did the school system deliberately try to retard their development? To do the school justice she thought not; that it was probably she who was a misfit in the system.

She saw Timoshenko sidle round the trunk of a tree, arch his magnificent back, his tail waving. He patted softly at a fallen leaf. She picked him up and cuddled him gently. "You and I," she said, "are a pair, darling!" He turned up amber eyes very like her own, rubbing his nose beneath her chin.

Mr. Walker, stepping into the wood, stopped abruptly at sight of the two golden, sensuous creatures rubbing together. If he approached Jasmine would doubtless greet him politely, she might even give him the smile she was giving Timoshenko, for fear he would report her for not being at the school. Further than that, he felt, her thoughts would not stay with him. She was as aloof, as casual, as the cat in her arms.

The dried wood beneath his feet betrayed him. The golden eyes over the cat's back were so thoughtful, were almost appealing, that he stopped dead in his tracks. He could not know that she had been taking stock of herself, that the questions in her mind, half formulated, were ones which he could, in part, have answered. He said, "Good afternoon," and because she continued to stare at him began to feel a fool.

"Were you happy at school?" she asked him, voicing the most coherent question.

He was so surprised that he stepped backwards and sat down on a log.

"Happy?" he said stupidly. It seemed a ridiculous question. And looking back he thought perhaps he never had been. Certainly not at school, certainly not at home - not with his mother. At school he had always been an outcast because he preferred drawing to energetic pastimes, lacking Jasmine's protection of detachment. Watching the frown on her clear forehead he wondered if it were that very detachment which worried her now. "Aren't you happy?" he returned. "You always seem - "

"Yes," she said artlessly, "I always am. Or I should be, if they'd leave me alone."

"Alone?"

"Well - you know - being driven or fussed."

"Ah. Yes," he said.

It was the first personal conversation he had ever had

with her and as unexpected as her appearance in the wood. That she had haunted his waking hours and disturbed his dreams he forgave fully, for she had not, he imagined, arranged to do so. But from the face he found so lovely he would have liked to remove that worried frown. Yet it was impossible, he felt, to guess what disturbed her. Her mind must move in distances as remote from his as anything he could imagine. What vagrant thoughts did young girls, beautiful and alone, wandering in summer woods, keep close for company? He would never know.

Jasmine removed her hand from Timoshenko to smooth the bark of a tree. Her gaze wandered from Mr. Walker to the wood behind him and feeling superfluous he got up and went away.

She put Timoshenko on the ground and leaned back against the trunk.

She thought of Sophie who worried kindly about people, who bathed Albert's baby and hoped for others of her own; of Mr. Walker who, though he said he was not happy, lived, she was sure, when he was painting, in a daze as near happiness as made no difference. She thought of herself who had no external worries, no art to practice, who cared for nothing but to collect experience, wished only to live. If she had asked Mr. Walker he would have told her that was a career in itself. She was half certain of the things which would happen to her when at last she was free. "I expect I shall marry," she thought, "because one doesn't avoid it - more than once, perhaps, and there will be others. That will be sad for them but what can I do?" The leaves above her rustled as if stirred by the spirits of her forgotten lovers. "I'm sorry," she said, looking up into the shadows. At this strange apology for the way she was made, as though it were her fault, she looked positively startled. "It isn't like me," she thought, "to be worrying!" Experience, perhaps, would just go on, and at the end of her life, when she had absorbed the love and homage, and the colour from the grass and flowers around her, she would go out, she supposed, and there would be nothing.

But there also Mr. Walker could have reassured her for she would continue in the minds of those she had not loved.

CHAPTER XII

ALICE collected the House letters from the rack outside Miss Cottingham's door, Miss Bishop's from her table and the staff ones from the common-room mantelpiece. She put them in a canvas bag and gave them to Albert to post.

Albert, swinging the bag in time to his song, made off towards the town. The birds sang among the leaves which, heavy with midsummer, shaded his curly head. He kicked up the dust in the gravel and spat neatly on to the grass. How many love letters did the bag contain, he wondered, and answered himself, "Precious few, I reckon!" He reflected that if his calligraphy had been more efficient he would have written one to Honor. He imagined her turning the pages as she read what he would say.

In the post office where he poured the letters on to the counter the girl wore a pink voile blouse of which he approved. He said so and the girl, opening her mouth to tell him to mind his own business, caught the soft gleam from beneath his lashes and blushed and smiled instead. The letters were swept away.

Miss Meadows' epistle ran:

DEAR GINGER,

I have spoken, as I suggested, to Miss Stebbing about our conversation last week, for, as you know, modern languages are not quite in my line. However she strongly endorses my advice to leave the Russian, *it is* most complicated, *but thinks you should do well with the German when you will soon be hearing it around you. I explained that you have indeed, as you say, a gift for "picking up lingo" but she tells me that she started, this term, a Russian class consisting of two of the Upper Sixth and Miss Bishop - and that Miss Bishop has had to give up the lessons because the girls are getting ahead of her since she finds no time to do her preparation! There will probably be German classes open to your unit; do avail yourself of these. I do wish you a not too uncomfortable journey and as much happiness as may be found in that tragic country. I enclose a small dictionary and German grammar which I hope you will accept with kindest regards from your sincere friend.*

EMMELINE MEADOWS

PS.—My nephew tells me that German gin is quite disastrous. Take tea with grammar! E.M.

Margery had written to Nanny.

MY DEAREST NANNY,

I am ill in bed. I am enjoying myself. I am not as bad as you might fear but only sick from having too much to drink. There is a very nice dull girl aged 16 called Sophie Berwick. She tells me stories at night but she is dull all day because she is busy knitting vests for a baby brother she says is the child of her Parents Declining Years and they are too feeble to clothe him themselves. I made four runs not out last week. I hate Matron she is a hag. Miss Cottingham is a funny old girl. I am knitting a scarf for

Augustus. Tell Daddy he might write clearer so that I can read his letters. Miss Stebbing says she cannot think why I am always bottom in French. I can it is because I cannot learn it.

Please ask Daddy if I can leave school at fifteen.

Hoping this finds you as it leaves me, with Affectionate Respect.
MARGERY STILL

Aunt May was addressed by Miss Bishop.

DEAR MRS. TERN,

I regret to say I see very little improvement in Jasmine. Both Matron and her Form mistress report persistent breaches of rules and lack of attention to her work. Miss Cottingham, on the other hand, insists that Jasmine will settle down shortly, but I see no signs of her doing so. I only write thus harshly because her uncle insists that school discipline is lax - perhaps you could speak to Jasmine at half-term? If she would apply herself seriously to work for her last year she could do very well.

Believe me,

Yours sincerely,

UNITY BISHOP

"I believe her," thought May sadly, reaching for the telephone. "Is that Sylvia?" she said.

"Yes! Dear May!"

May read the letter over the line, since Arthur was out. "Do you think she'll mention it to him?" she asked.

"No, I don't," said Sylvia. "Answer it and tear it up. Better still say I've heard from the school that she and Sophie are both doing well."

"Sylvia, you're wonderful!"

"Not at all. I've a lot to forgive him - turning the other cheek for years. Which reminds me, do you ever take Turkish baths?"

"In this weather?"

"The dirt rolls out. You'll enjoy it. Come along and we'll have face packs and a cosy lunch afterwards. Lobster and ice-cream."

May put the letter beneath her handkerchiefs, a straw hat on her head and a note on Arthur's desk:

"Seeing the Woman's Guild. Don't wait lunch. May."

Shirley had written home.

MY DEAR MUM AND DAD,

I am walking out. I tell you so sudden because Jim has to join his ship direckly & we have only just begun. He is Mrs. Priors son what has always been so good to me. All thinks the world & all of him. I would like to bring him home on my day off so as you could meet. He says he is not half scared. Could we have the pink china. Do not worry dear Mum & Dad I love him very dearly & so will you. He is tall & has blue eyes & a lovely laugh.
Your aff daughter,
SHIRLEY

When this latter arrived Mrs. Briggs wiped her eyes.

"D'you think it's all right, Dad?" she asked.

" 'Course it is! Our girl can pick em!" He fingered the letter. "Would that be the Navy, Mum?"

"I'll believe all that when I see 'im. This room'll need a turn out!"

"All 'ands on deck, old girl! Well, they all loves a sailor." He leaned over the sink. "Give us a kiss, Grannie!"

Mrs. Briggs kissed him. "You've no call to go so fast, Dad," she said.

CHAPTER XIII

SOPHIE and Margery sang part songs while they knitted.

"Now my favourite," Margery said.

Sophie told her: "You stick to the tune and I'll make up a descant."

Matron, since it was Sister's day off, brought the Doctor up the stairs. Hearing the varying strains of "You can have her - I don't want her - she's too fat for me - " she opened the door with dramatic horror as though she were revealing the scene of a crime.

"Stand up for the Doctor," she said sharply to Margery, where she lolled, in gym tunic and bedroom slippers, upon the foot of her bed.

Margery climbed on to the floor.

The Doctor, who, rumour had it, was employed by Miss Bishop because he was the oldest and ugliest in the town, turned Margery's face to the light. "Better now?"

"Yes, thank you. It was just a bilious attack, really. I often get them," she lied.

"I see. Well - like to go back to-day?"

"Yes, thank you," she said with a sigh.

"I think you might."

Matron revealed Sophie's ankle and about nine inches of leg. As the Doctor lifted her foot and twisted it Matron kept leaning over and making little grabs at the sheet.

"Really she is awful," thought Sophie, wanting to giggle.

Jasmine, receiving a résumé of the scene later, said, "Yes, she's like the description 'Awful Purity' in the hymn."

"If Heaven's like *that* - " muttered Sophie.

But Jasmine had assured her humbly: "*We've* no need to worry. I fear the uncongeniality of heaven will never be a cause of concern to me."

The Doctor said: "Let me see you walk on it."

"Put your dressing-gown on," Matron hissed.

Sophie limped round the bed.

"Yes - well - perhaps to-morrow. But this young lady can go." At sight of Sophie's sad face he said to Matron: "Let her sit in the garden this afternoon." Matron grunted. They went downstairs.

"Good-bye, Sophie," said Margery, "it has been fun." She folded up her things.

"Do you think you could take the crusts?"

"All right." She collected their combined leavings from the cupboard and put them inside her pyjamas.

"Scatter them over the grass."

"Yes, I will."

"And don't drop them in front of that old bitch."

"No, I won't, Sophie. Good-bye."

"Good-bye."

Margery slipped into her Form room and up to her desk. She consulted the time-table pinned inside the lid.

"History," said the girl at her side.

"Where are we?"

"Bloody Mary."

"Oh!" As Miss Truscott discussed the Tudor Queen she turned her bright head from the Form to the blackboard, smiling at them, carrying them along.

"Isn't she lovely?" thought the little girls, watching her.

"Beautiful. Like a dream."

"That's what they mean," thought Margery, "all those poems about love."

"You aren't half as much in love with me as the Upper Third are," said Miss Truscott by the sea that evening, laughing at her young man's startled face.

"*Left* right, *left* right," called Celia. "*Left* - Jasmine Tern you're out of step."

Jasmine gave an obliging little skip. The line halted at the end of the gymnasium.

"Oh dear, oh dear," thought Jasmine. "I wasn't made for this!" She looked disapprovingly at Celia who swayed back on her heels, like a sergeant major, calling out commands. She looked like a bolster in her short tunic which, although pleated, was not designed to contain a large bust. Jasmine turned away her eyes. Little clouds of dust rose from the vaulting horses and a faint smell of rubber from their shoes.

A row of five girls, seated on a bench, their hands in their laps, watched the rest of the Form exerting themselves. Girls who were what Matron described as poorly - an expression which made Celia grind her teeth - were by her edict excused from active gym. Celia reflected bitterly that there was not one subject upon which she and Matron could be said to agree.

Jasmine caught Angela's eye where she sat against the wall. "Third time running," she thought, unable to repress a start of admiration. "Of all the bloody nerve!" She jumped, ran, stretched her arms, bent her knees, touched the floor at Celia's command. They hung upside down upon the bars like bats, hair and bows sweeping the ground.

When they were allowed to stand the right way up again Jasmine smoothed back her fair hair, shook the dust from her skirt. Celia thought irritably, "That girl's too vain to live!" And: "Put down the ropes!" she called.

Miss Meadows, passing the glass doors, peered shortsightedly through and smiled. How clever they all were! She watched the flushed faces, the display of youthful arms and legs. Someone stopped beside her and she turned to see Mr. Walker with a smear of paint on his face. He smiled at her absorption.

"You approve of them?" he said.

"Oh, yes!" she pulled her spectacles out on their chain. "It seems to me that we were so - " She looked back through the glass. "They have more confidence, I think."

"Too much!" he sighed.

"Too - ?"

"They rag me!" He had never meant to say it and looked surprised and foolish now he had.

"I'm sorry," she murmured, reabsorbed. "All the same," she said, turning from the glass again, "one feels perhaps the world may be safer in their hands."

"Perhaps," said Mr. Walker, doubting it. He watched Celia prancing up and down.

Jasmine swarmed up her rope with ease. This was worth doing, she thought. She rose above the blue figures, the neatly brushed heads; Celia, oddly foreshortened, looking square. This might be useful any day; seeking cocoa-nuts on a desert island, or even sanctuary from danger, impotent tigers and crocodiles yawning below. One carried, of necessity, a knife between one's teeth, and as the waving fronds above grew nearer, so the landscape beyond the screening bush sprang into view: soft and silver sand upon which, in all probability, no human foot had passed; the open, glittering sea; green glades down which elephants moved. She touched the beam on the roof and sighed. The view through the window before her consisted of weeds and Albert leaning on a spade. He pursed his lips in a soundless whistle, admiration widening his eyes. Jasmine nodded amiably and slid down. "Back to the treadmill," she thought with her toes on the ground.

Miss Meadows and Mr. Walker walked away together with a picture of Jasmine in their minds. He considered her elusive, beautiful, absent-mindedly unkind. She would give no thought to him he was certain, beyond the studio doors, and he could hardly blame her for not remembering where there was nothing to forget. Years later children would say, "Can't you do better than *that*? didn't you learn to draw at school?" and Jasmine, absently pushing back her hair would answer, "Oh, yes - yes we did." "Who taught you?" "Oh, rather an ineffectual little man - Fishy - I think he was called. Perhaps that's why I'm so bad." Why do I torture myself like this, he thought, looking round at Miss Meadows' kind face.

But she too had her own thoughts. Fifty years ago, she wondered, were we as charming, as sensible? I doubt it, she decided, but one forgets.

She was still brooding upon forgetfulness as she said goodbye to Mr. Walker and strolled out on to the grass. It was very nice to have a free period and although she knew there were more things she ought to be doing than she cared to think about she felt that she needed a rest. The familiar work, which she found absorbing, had been exhausting as well, and perhaps she had tried to do too much. It had been impossible not to offer extra coaching at odd hours which suited the Upper Sixth - no University gates should slam in young faces if there were anything she could do. Impossible, also, to resist Shirley's grey eyes sliding towards her bookshelves, or Ginger's thirst to understand the people with whom he would work. I'll go home at half-term and put my feet up, she thought.

And if the stove doesn't work, she decided recklessly, I'll go out to lunch and supper, too. The sun warmed her dry skin through her shapeless cardigan and striped cotton dress. She could feel the little pebbles of the gravel through the soles of her thin, old shoes. She could hear an unidentified bird from beyond the tennis-courts and from the long grass where girls were wont to sprawl in the sun rose a scent that reminded her of hay. "But scent and sound are fainter than they used to be," she thought sadly, "the grass isn't quite as green now, the summers are never so long." She saw two girls wave and greet each other, one of them walking with a limp. She reflected how the flowers in the borders retained, for them, a brighter hue. Their laughter came across the grass to her and suddenly she had a ridiculous urge to go over and tell them that in fifty years outlines would be dimmed a little at the edges, music would not be so sharp and sweet, there would be less sparkle on the snow; the only thing they could be certain of feeling more acutely would be the wind. She was standing still and blinking as they passed her and she valued Jasmine's courteous greeting the more because she was certain that they knew that *she* knew that Jasmine had no business to be out of doors.

The girls slid round a corner and dropped down on to the ground. Sophie withdrew two vests, each one grey at the beginning and blue at the end, from her pockets and spread them on the grass.

"Well, they are nice!" said Jasmine, thinking, "Rather him than me!"

"I've brought this Algebra for you," she added, "if you do it now I could copy it later - it's got to go in tonight."

Sophie smoothed the book, sucked the pencil and dotted X's and Y's across the page.

"Leave plenty of working so that I can show how I did it, Soph."

"Yes, all right. Do keep quiet."

Into the silence Jasmine dropped the information.

"There's an essay on Parrots for next week. I've done two very tasteful ones but I think I like the anti-parrot best so you can have the pro. And don't forget to improve the spelling and muck the punctuation up a bit."

"No, I won't. Thanks . . . I'll do one of these wrong now. That'll be more convincing, don't you think?"

Albert left the weeds to the winds of heaven and strolled down to the lawn. He thought it might be the break period shortly and that Honor might be on duty out of doors. Since obtaining her was going to be difficult he decided it would be worth while. Events slipped along all too easily and the effort of pursuing Honor would make a change. What he would do when his efforts were crowned with success he did not think; the procedure of taking thought for the morrow had never been one of Albert's faults. The Hand which fed the birds and clothed the grass performed the same offices for him and he accepted them with a whistle and a smile.

His brown throat swelled and contracted with the tune which it dispelled; he brushed back sweat and curls with an earthy hand. Miss Meadows, returning his greeting, was reminded of a visit to the Louvre. As he disappeared from view she thought: he's so very - I wonder if Unity quite! - but the next moment remembered that it should hardly be a crime to be beautiful and dear Unity was always so wise! There's one sense, she thought, smiling gently, that one doesn't lose. She retraced her steps to the school.

Sophie and Jasmine, arguing amiably in the long grass, saw Albert lingering with intent. They craned their necks and were quiet. The little girls appeared, noisy and scampering, with Honor following rather distastefully in the rear. She looked younger than some of the girls, thought Albert, with her awkward, rather coltish gait. When she saw him she gave him a hasty good morning and went to a garden seat. Albert took some raffia from his pocket and strolled over to where she sat.

She was far from beautiful, he decided, but she was young, she was feminine, and the sun was shining in the school garden.

The cheek that he could see bent away from him and over the stocking she darned, quivered at the sound of his voice.

"Are you angry with me?" he said.

Angry with herself, perhaps, but not with him!

He moved round to face her, saying, "Well?" and stretched out a hand towards her chin.

"Don't!" said Honor, thinking of the children, so that he withdrew it, but the gesture was not lost upon the girls in the grass.

"I don't want to worry you," said Albert, who did, preparing to move away. Honor looked up and, encouraged, he asked her, "Will you be goin' for 'arf-term?"

She shook her head dumbly for since Matron was going she could not.

"I'm that glad," said Albert simply and took himself away.

Honor answered the little girls' questions distractedly, letting them do as they chose. They became so rowdy that Matron rushed down from one of the terraces and handed out reproofs all round. Honor went into the house smarting with humiliation and remembering the soft tones of Albert's voice.

She met Celia on the stairs. "You look a bit fed up, old thing," her friend told her, glancing kindly at her flushed cheeks.

Suddenly Honor looked gratefully and a little enviously at Celia's open, friendly countenance; no such worries would be hers: it was safer to be like that! She linked her arm through Celia's firm, goosefleshed one and gave it a little squeeze against her side. "Where am I going?" she wondered, feeling her heart and senses, drawn by Albert's enchantment, washed away on some outgoing tide. "It's only Matron," she murmured, "and now I can tell you about it I don't mind. Are you free to-night?"

"Yes," said Celia. "We'll go for a swim. It'll do you good."

As they slipped into their mackintoshes in the last warm rays of the sun Honor reflected that the silken water which had lately lapped round her as she swam, and the wind which dried the salt on her legs, were not more concrete than her feelings for Albert, with which she seemed to be possessed. And like the sea and the wind those feelings were older than the ties which bound Albert to Mrs. Munnings and herself to a social class.

CHAPTER XIV

HALF-TERM dawned wet and gusty, with scuds of sea-blown rain disintegrating against the glass. No one's spirits however were dampened by this except Honor's, since Matron had promised the smaller girls remaining in the House that Honor should take them on the pier; and the little girls themselves awaited their treat rather gloomily for neither enjoyed each other's company particularly and still less in the rain.

Jasmine and Sophie stepped from the train at Victoria and into May's and Sylvia's arms.

May shepherded Jasmine into a taxi and she sank back in her corner with a sigh. "Can we afford this?" she asked.

"No," said May, "but we won't tell Arthur."

"Good Lord, no!" Jasmine murmured. "But it is nice." She rubbed her cheek against the comfortable shoulder and they gossiped all the way home.

In the vicarage they flung Jasmine's school hat into a corner and clattered up the stairs. May sat on the bed while her niece stripped off the neat clothes as though they stifled her and wriggled into a flimsy cotton dress. She shook her hair over her shoulders and fetched May's powder from her room.

When they reached the kitchen, "He'll be out until four," said May thoughtfully to Jasmine, who was lavishing hugs and kisses alternately upon her person and the cat. She picked up some fat clouded mince which had been intended for their lunch. Suddenly their eyes met over the dish and May bent down and gave it to the cat. "We'll go to a Corner House and then on the river," she said.

Margery touched the clock on the nursery mantelpiece, the rocking-horse, the old curtains, Nannie's hat behind the door. She ran her fingers over the tiles in the bathroom then flicked the church calendar which Nannie considered suitable for the lavatory and explained the freedom with which Daddy quoted texts at meals. She walked slowly down to the garden and seated herself in the swing. "Two days," she thought, "two days!" It was so short a time to lavish all the affection which accumulated in half a term.

Sir Roger brushed some imaginary dust from his lapel, smoothed his eyebrows and picked up a soft hat. He drew himself up to an inch above his usual height before the mirror and thrust his shoulders back.

"Very nice," said Tom, appearing behind him in the hall.

Sir Roger cleared his throat in some embarrassment and waited for his daughter to come down. So, once, a little anxious about his appearance, he had been wont to wait for Sylvia's step upon the stair. How short a while ago that seemed and how odd that he should now be waiting with as much trepidation for the approval of the young creature who came running towards him with her pigtail slapping her shoulders.

"You do look nice," she told him, tucking her arm in his.

"Where are we going?" he asked.

"Kew and then the pictures, and ices in between."

Sophie and Sir Roger wandered through the glades of Kew. Sir Roger, with his pretty daughter beside him, felt that many heads must be turned in their direction as, indeed, some few were. Glancing covertly at her face as they wandered from sunlight to shadow he was glad that it was high summer and not the almost unbearable blossoming of May as it had been when he followed Sylvia along these very paths. Sylvia, who he had known considered him a kind and dear little man with lots of useful money and a lovely title, had laughed and swayed beneath the blossoms and held her gloved fingers to the ducks. What she had gained from her kindness to him he found it hard to imagine; true she wore a large part of the money and half the title with equal distinction, but another man might have paid her bills in Bond Street and housed her just as well. What he had gained, he thought, gazing at the daughter who, declaiming beneath a tree, was giving him her repertoire of voices, was beyond his wildest dreams.

"Listen," said Sophie, "this is Miss Bishop. And Matron. And Mr. Walker. And poor Christow." Sir Roger laughed and glared at a young man who peered interestedly at this artless exhibition beneath the trees. In a year or so, he supposed, she would want to come here with a man younger than himself. But not yet! Surely, he thought, taking her arm again and tightening her pigtail bow, this must be the nicest age of all. And yet Sylvia a few years later had been - ! Well! He patted her hand.

Sophie was thinking that one day she would bring her

young man here; but earlier: in the spring.

Sir Roger glanced at the face beside him. "What are you thinking, my darling?"

She smiled sweetly. "That I would like another ice!"

When Jasmine was a little girl she and May had played a game called Avoiding Arthur. May's timid doubts as to the propriety of such a pastime had melted before the strength of her own feelings and Jasmine's frank dislike. During half-term their ingenuity was not taxed unduly and Jasmine, skipping along the road to the vicarage, thought that they were doing very well.

The drab vista of Pimlico did not seem dull to her. It was part of that delightful world from which, she felt, she had been prematurely snatched by Miss Bishop and to which she would in time return. She peered into people's basements where she could see tables being laid for dinner and occasionally an unmade bed. The open doors of frowsy little shops invited inspection and she lingered to scrutinise their wares. She wanted to sing and greet the people on the pavements and explain that for two days she too was free. She tilted her head from which the fair hair flowed like water and screwed up her eyes in the dust and the sun. She was no longer bound by restrictions and uniform, a prisoner on parole. Temporarily at least she was free of the world which was her heritage, as free as Arthur's shabby parishoners who passed her in the street. Forgetful of her years she gave a little kick to an empty carton and stopped to stroke a passing cat.

When she reached the dusty, nearly paintless railings of

the vicarage she looked upon them with love. The chipped façade behind them appeared warm and friendly and on the small patch above the basement windows May's eschscholtzias battled bravely with the smuts. She saw a cassock at the study window and dived round to the side door.

May, who was chasing caterpillars out of the lettuce, received her hug with a smile. She moved the salt from a kitchen chair and Jasmine sat down.

Even the kitchen was delightful, she thought, glancing at the blue and white striped china and May's little pudding cloths hanging over the stove. Here, if one were awakened in the night by toothache or other ailments, one might descend, as though it were daylight, for a few words with the cat and a hot drink, and warm one's toes at the stove - home was so nice! "No institutions for me," she murmured, nibbling a lettuce leaf.

"I had a letter from Miss Bishop," said May, reminded of it by this reference to the school.

"And what does our Unity say?"

"She wanted me to speak to you."

"Speak?" asked Jasmine, the lettuce suspended in mid-air. "Does Uncle Arthur know about this?"

"No, dear, I threw it away."

"Ah!" As May said nothing she added wickedly; "Well, darling, do give tongue."

"She thinks you ought to work harder."

"So I should. But I don't, and I never will."

"Well, I don't know much about it myself, of course. I learnt very little at school. It's just" - May reached for a salad bowl - "that I'd like your life to end differently from mine."

"God forbid that it should end in Uncle Arthur," said Jasmine, listening to the footsteps overhead.

May opened her mouth to expostulate but Jasmine's expression made her laugh.

"Come along," she said, kissing her aunt over the salad, "let's go and give him his lunch."

Thus abortively, May supposed, would end any speaking to Jasmine, and perhaps it was just as well. Arthur himself, by all accounts - as Jasmine reminded her - had been reared like Oliver Twist and much good it had done.

After lunch they played in May's bedroom with lengths of turquoise-coloured chiffon and their mouths full of pins.

"When will I wear it, do you think?" asked Jasmine, bowing to the slim young lady in the mirror.

"Sylvia's sure to give a party in the holidays."

"What a blessing her money is! Or rather Sir Roger's."

"What indeed."

"I don't get any more like the Rokeby Venus," she said as she peered over her shoulder, wishing her contours would increase.

"You'll do very well as you are."

"I suppose I will. Aunt May?"

"Yes?"

"What did you want most at my age?"

May sat back on her heels. It was hard to remember - certainly not what she had got! She and Sylvia had whispered confidences on twilight evenings but she had forgotten what they had said.

"I wanted children," she said eventually, "and - it sounds ridiculous! - fame."

"What sort of fame?"

"I was very vague. And Sylvia wanted romance."

"And she's got Sir Roger."

"Well, darling, he does very well."

"Yes. Is that all it comes to?"

"What, dear?"

"Wanting things, and not getting them, and then - doing very well?"

At this appalling suggestion May, arrested with her arms full of chiffon, simply stared. "I think one finds that later one doesn't so much mind."

"That makes it worse."

"Perhaps," said May, "perhaps," and watching Jasmine where she leaned from the window, thought, "I would like her to get what she wants!"

Jasmine, staring above the grubby little garden, with the soft air on her cheeks, felt that she would. Experience - life itself - she could feel them rising towards her in the noise of the traffic and the shapes of Arthur's stunted trees. She pressed her soft young person and the softer chiffon against May's window sill; she would squeeze more joy and enchantment from the years allotted to her than the others had done!

Tom, stepping on to the pavement below the vicarage, saw a splash of yellow hair at one of the windows and ran up the steps. A tall, sour looking gentleman in a cassock opened the door and asked him what he wanted. Tom wondered what would happen if he answered truthfully, "Your niece!"

The cassock, the glare, and the open doorway waited in unfriendly silence. Definitely intimidated, but determined, with that flash of yellow in his mind, to show that the Church, however militant, held no fears for him, Tom stood his ground.

"Is Mrs. Tern at home?" he asked.

He was told that she was and having, if anything, increased his unpopularity by explaining that he was Sylvia's nephew, he was left to kick his heels in May's drawing-room until she had removed Jasmine from the chiffon and the pins from her mouth.

He was peering at photographs and wondering how Jasmine got on with her uncle when May came in and greeted him with both hands outstretched. She had none of Sylvia's grace and beauty, having, in fact, a figure connected in his mind with the word matronly, but he approved of her heartily for she was comfortable and kind.

"I've been cutting out a dress for Jay," she said, "that's why we've been so long."

"Yes," murmured Jasmine, "and I look - " she smiled and threw out her hands.

Tom could believe that she did. He thought despondently of the frocks she would wear and the people who would see her in them while he was wilting in the White Man's Grave. "But she'll be at school most of the time," he consoled himself.

"And when do you go back?" asked May.

"Next month - about two weeks now. I shall miss - " he paused, glancing at Jasmine, who was looking, he felt, altogether too complacent " - London - very much."

"Ah!" she said, smiling secretly. "And which part most?"

"The lake in the park - and Whitehall - and the river - and the Mall. It isn't Piccadilly, as they always say in the novels, to which one's heart returns."

"But aren't there rivers there?"

"Rivers? Yes," said Tom, remembering crocodile infested reaches, "but not like this."

Jasmine's wide eyes fixed on him intently did not quite blind Tom to the fact that it was not him at which she stared. "It's as if I were a window," he thought sadly, "through which to see the world."

"Go on," she said.

"No, dear, don't," May interrupted, for it worried her to think of poor Tom surrounded by cannibals and mosquitoes and striding - she was sure he strode - through endless tracts of heat and dust. "Tell me about your mother and Sylvia and what poor Algy's going to do. Sylvia says there must be some profession he could follow without exerting himself too much, which he says he wouldn't like at all - I believe Algy is wiser than he would have one suppose - of course when we were girls it was so easy, they just went into the Guards or sat back in the country and collected dogs and rents."

"Uncle Roger thinks he ought to stand for Parliament."

"Of course, dear, how nice! There's still that."

Tom tilted back his dark head to laugh and Jasmine thought, "He *is* attractive! Well, one day - perhaps!"

"What are *you* going to do?" he asked. He laid one arm along the mantelpiece, disarranging two small shepherds and a clock.

"I? Uncle Arthur and Miss Bishop keep asking me - but how am I to tell?"

"I think you ought to do just what Miss Bishop tells you," said May, "in fact I don't know how you dare not. She frightens both Sylvia and me very much."

"Does she really?" asked Tom.

"Oh, yes. Much more than the girls, I think. There's still a chance, I suppose, that they may develop differently but Sylvia and I have already failed. All the time and trouble those intelligent people wasted on us and now Sylvia has to ask her children general knowledge questions and I forget to pay the milkman and can't even add up points. I always feel when I turn up on Speech Day that they must be thinking - and how justly - that their time might have been better employed."

"But surely Sylvia - ?" asked Tom.

"Sylvia brazens it out by looking beautiful but we both know Miss Bishop thinks that Bond Street can't fill empty heads. Yet the extraordinary part is," she said, looking round the room as though she expected to see lost Latin tags and mathematics floating above her in the air, "that we both *knew* the things they taught us once. They just *go* - and one can't imagine where."

The things that May had forgotten settled on the room like dust. Jasmine shook her head impatiently; it couldn't matter very much!

They had tea in comparative silence under the shadow

of the Reverend Arthur's frown. May, looking politely interested in his remarks, wondered if he knew how much time people spent waiting for him to go away. Tom accepted his advice for the rearrangement of West Africa with polite murmurs and nods and Jasmine treated him with such charming deference that May decided she had spent her pocket-money for the term. She was half ashamed of reflecting that if Jasmine continued to manage him so gracefully she would be able to have the dining-room distempered and a new carpet on the stairs. What will I do, a voice like a little cold wind asked her, when Jasmine leaves us alone?

Tom, watching them, certain that Mr. Tern was a trial both to Jasmine and her aunt, decided he was the sort who would like to be called Father and addressed him as sir. He ate May's rather crumbly wafers of bread and margarine with his eyes on Jasmine's face.

He would see that face, he was certain, through rains and droughts, for a year. He would open his eyes upon it smiling above a gym tunic in the school garden and close them upon that yellow head bent thoughtfully over a lump of heavy cake.

Well, there it was!

When he went it was Jasmine, by some kind manoeuvre of May's, who saw him to the steps. He closed the door firmly behind them and stood looking at the way that he should go: the first move he would make towards putting the sea, a good part of two continents and a year of time between Jasmine and himself. Once he had got as far as the road, even, it would be as inevitable as if he had already sailed.

"Dear Tom, don't stand there looking like a Celtic twilight!" said a little voice at his side.

He laughed, turned towards her and touched her hand. The fair face, with the brow a little puckered, looked at him intently, then over his shoulder, at the road, the houses, the sky. "That's just it," he thought sadly, "I'm the beginning - and I would like to be the end!"

He released her hand. "Don't forget to write, Jay. And - good-bye!"

"I will - good-bye! - I really will!"

She watched him run off the pavement and on to a moving bus. She thought how lucky he was with adventure before him - the sea – Africa - another world. Suddenly she remembered that he had touched her hand and put the other over the place. Just there it had been - well. She sighed and looked down the road. The bus had gone. "Oh, well," she murmured, smiling, "he'll come back again," and calling May she ran into the house.

When the rain had ceased, which it did quite early, Honor escorted her young charges to the pier. She tried to feel sorry for them because evidently their parents did not want them or were far away or dead, but as she had to keep reminding them not to hop with one foot in the gutter or tip the hats over the noses of the girls in front she became more sorry for herself. They chirruped and straggled along the promenade, attracting attention and grins from passers-by. On the pier she supplemented their pennies from a collection given her by Miss Cottingham and noticed that the largest contributions went in exchange for the spectacle of a murderer hanging at eight o'clock.

They fed the gulls from mysterious resources in their pockets - no wonder there had been no bread at lunch - while Honor watched the summer crowd: blistered, sweating and noisy, they seemed to be enjoying themselves, and she wished she were free to mingle with them instead of escorting the little girls. Once or twice she counted her charges anxiously, thinking it would be just her luck to have one of them fall into the sea. Placards besought her to have her photograph taken, her fortune told, her weight recorded, to take a ride in a racing car. She turned her back upon these delights and saw Mr. Walker on a low camp stool, gazing with distaste at the canvas in front of him. As she stared he looked up and hailed her, and rose as she approached.

"Miss Christow! Do come and tell me what's wrong with this horizon - or better still ignore it and talk to me instead."

"Won't I be interrupting you?"

"Far from it, I'd stopped out of sheer laziness and wanted a legitimate excuse."

As Honor peered at the blues and green and purples, he said: "No - don't - let's talk about something nice."

"But it's beautiful!"

"Do you really think so? I've had a dreadful afternoon!"

"So have I," said Honor, laughing, indicating the little girls. "Even now I feel I ought to be watching in case they tip over the rails."

"If they do I'll go in after them, though Heaven knows I don't swim very well."

He smiled at her kindly, thinking that she must have rather an awful time. At least he got away after school! He noticed that a slight tan had improved her sallow face.

"Don't you get away at half-term?"

"Not when Matron goes."

"Ah - Cinderella! What do you do with yourself?"

"Oh, there's plenty to do - all the girls who are left behind, you see. And mending - and tidying - and seeing that the little ones have baths - " And walking in the garden with her heart in her mouth and Albert's whistle in her ears, she might have added, but stopped and looked in silence at the sea.

"Is that all?"

"Isn't it enough?"

"It doesn't sound very satisfying. Don't you ever go out on your own?"

"Yes, of course, and with Celia - Miss Warrender - but she's away just now."

Mr. Walker disapproved so strongly of Miss Warrender's enlarged muscles and hearty deportment that he said nothing, but, "Don't do that!" to a little girl who was squeezing his paints.

"Are you happy in your work, then?" he asked, stooping to collect a paint rag from the boards.

Honor laughed. "No! I hate Matron and she despises me. But as a matter of fact," she added slowly, "this term hasn't been quite so bad."

"Oh?"

"Perhaps I'm getting used to it."

"Resignation," said Mr. Walker, who was forced to practise it, "is a most unlovely virtue, I think."

He looked again at the picture which Honor considered beautiful and thought that the school, which was a source of irritation to him, must be something worse for her. To be tied to those lovely, tiresome little wretches indefinitely without even an academic interest to ease her mind! Two of them at the moment, he noticed, were squabbling over a hat and started to pull each other's hair. "Behave yourselves at once!" he called loudly, before Honor had time to interfere, thus surprising them all, and himself, so much that the children stood still and stared.

Honor laughed and he saw grins break out on the cheerful faces he had rebuked. "Come and look at my picture," he said. They came, and gave him a great deal of unsolicited advice. When they were tired of this and he was left with Honor he suddenly made up his mind.

"What will you do when you take them back?"

"Supervise their tea, I suppose."

"Do you have to?"

"Not really, Miss Cottingham will be there."

"Then won't you come to tea with us? It isn't very far. My mother," he added truthfully, "will not be at all pleased to see you, but I should like it very much. She doesn't encourage visitors, so you see you would be doing me a good turn. If you don't mind being barked at now and again?"

"I should like it very much," said Honor, rather touched by his honesty and glad to get away from the school. "If I can put up with Matron I won't mind your mother," she added with more directness than tact.

Mr. Walker laughed and folded his easel and stool. He told the children to get themselves into some sort of order and not go dashing through the turnstile on to the road; it seemed easier to perform these tasks for Honor than to keep them in order for himself. They trailed up through the town behind the bobbing panama hats.

At the gates he said, "I'll just look into the studio while you deposit the girls. Then I can take you along."

When she appeared again she had powdered her nose and changed her dress. "I must be good for the girl's morale!" he thought, leading her away.

Mr. Walker's mother, as he had prophesied, did not even pretend to be pleased. She produced a quantity of weak and chilly tea and rock cakes which Honor felt had been well named.

Honor, taking in the neat, unlovely room with its comfortless chairs and brocade draped piano which she was sure was never played, wondered how Mr. Walker could stand such a place. I may not get home until the holidays, she thought, but at least I am happy when I do. As they listened to the old lady's complaints about her health and her neighbours they each felt that the other's lot was hard and exchanged little smiles over the harder cakes.

Mr. Walker suggested that Honor would like to see his pictures. "Really, I hardly think they would be very interesting," said the old lady, who hoped to get some information out of Honor about the school.

But Honor said, "Oh, yes, please!" and they escaped through the kitchen to the sun.

Here, stepping over uncut grass and daisies, a pleasant sense of conspiracy possessed them. The chaos in the garden reminded Honor of Albert's neat way with borders and lawns and she turned upon Mr. Walker a warm and friendly smile - poor fellow, what could he know about love!

He opened the rickety studio door for her and drew back a green blind. Stacks of canvases, broken, dusty chairs, an easel and cigarette ends filled the room. A pleasant smell of paint assailed her and she stumbled over an oil stove. "I have to keep them warm and dry in the winter," explained Mr. Walker, moving it out of the way.

He turned canvases away from the wall and held them up, and her rather uncertain judgment convinced her that he really was an artist. She had vaguely expected such people to be different, not like this mild, kind, mother-ridden man.

"Then there's my masterpiece," he said, smoothing the canvas lovingly as he turned the easel round. "It's Apollo. One can't judge one's own work, really, but to me - to me it's good." He turned it gently to the light and flung away an old sheet.

He had hoped, for the girl seemed sensible, for some at least discriminating praise. He had shown it to no one but Albert, and now stood for a moment himself, staring thoughtfully, for the picture had filled his mind for weeks. For the violence of Honor's reaction he was in no way prepared. She went scarlet and then white, and with a piteous little exclamation she put her hands over her face. For a moment the wild supposition that the appearance of a naked young man had upset her crossed his mind and was dismissed.

"My dear girl," he said, touching her shoulder, "are you all right? My dear girl!"

Honor looked up again at the perfect creature who had filled her dreams all the term. As God had made him - a term which was more apt than she had realised, for God, she felt, would be unlikely to drape such a being in khaki flannel - he started out of the canvas towards her, a look of baffled surprise on his face. "He'll never look like that for me!" she thought, and turning away from Mr. Walker she leaned her forehead against the window pane.

Something in the droop of her shoulders told Mr. Walker the truth. He put a hand rather awkwardly on her hair. "She loves that worthless fellow," he thought. "Well! what a to-do!"

Albert, beautiful, unconcerned, arrogant, gleamed above them, and suddenly, with a little exclamation of anger, Mr. Walker flung the sheet in his face. He pulled it over the easel and said to Honor, "Won't you sit down?"

She did so and said, without looking at him, "It was nothing, just - just surprise." She did not see how she could pretend it was not the picture which had surprised her and he was glad she did not try.

"I'll get you something," he offered, looking wildly round at two jam jars filled with turpentine and paint brushes and a can of paraffin for the stove. Then, wondering how to ward off his mother, he started towards the door.

"No, don't - really. I'm quite all right," and to prove it she looked up and smiled.

He took her into the garden and sat her down in the shade where she might attend or not, as she wished, while he told her about his work, himself, his mother - a recital which he hoped might ease her mind. She did not appear to be listening, but she looked more herself, he considered, by the time he decided to take her home.

As she smoothed her skirt and declared herself to be ready he wished that there was someone in whose care he might deposit her. He thought of Matron and the rather bleak atmosphere prevailing in every institution. He did not like the idea of her returning to the school with so much weight on her young heart.

Honor thanked the old lady for her more or less involuntary hospitality and allowed Mr. Walker to lead her away. As she parted from him at the cloakroom door she thought, "How kind he is!" and, turning in among a stream of girls, she immediately forgot about him and fell to dreaming of Albert again.

That evening she leaned her elbows on the window sill, staring over the garden and the town. She thought of Albert and wondered where he might be.

As it happened he was kissing Poppy across the bar.

CHAPTER XV

THE stove had sunk into a rusty stupor, cobwebs festooned the kitchen window, the cupboard door had jammed. Two mice, grown bold in solitude, watched Miss Meadows' losing struggle with prickers and oil. When a flare which hit the ceiling had singed her eyebrows and so surprised the mice that they retired until darkness fell, she went out and bought three dusty buns in the village and a bottle of lemonade. Letters, housework, mending, gardening, piled together, loomed like a trackless mountain at the back of her mind but she collected a deck-chair and the *Iliad* and sat down with her feet in the sun.

She had been faithful all her life to her first love but the service of the classics had been hard. It had not been remunerative either and the holidays she would like to have taken had remained for the most part in her dreams.

Now, while accumulating tasks waited, the sun crept up her legs and on to her thin ink-stained hands, and a bee, climbing over her shoulder, rose and fell with her breath. She dreamed of the Mediterranean and Asia Minor and wandered in Carthage and Troy.

Mrs. Prior also slept. She had kissed Jim in the doorway of the cottage and watched his departure down the dusty lane. When he returned she would hear his impression of Shirley's family; she had no doubt about what they would think of him. In the empty kitchen she opened the back door widely, for she liked the summer in the house. She pushed the dirty crockery to one side, straightened the plush tablecloth, finished the Guinness and ungummed the shoes from her distended feet. She smoked a battered Woodbine and when it was finished the lids drooped over her eyes. The ash that had fallen on to her bosom was blown, in little flakes, into her lap.

Jim wandered through a field of buttercups to delay himself on the way to the bus. For the first time he wished he had taken up some stationary occupation, like farming, so that he might keep Shirley with him all the time. It must be pleasant to stay on one piece of land with your wife beside you and the same sky overhead! Besides, if he left her for a long time she might forget him or get ill or die. Realising that he was lingering partly because he was afraid of the Briggs family he turned and ran down to the road.

He arrived at Shirley's door with pollen on the bell bottoms of his trousers and a feeling like palpitations round his heart.

A row of goggle-eyed little Briggses, newly washed and scrubbed, waited to inspect him round the parlour table, which blossomed with the pink china, kippers and cakes. The clean, staring faces of the little girls did not disturb him, for they all bore a family likeness to his love. He received Mr. Briggs' huge paw with a feeling of comfort and was aware that something - he did not know it was his blue eyes and his uniform - had made him acceptable to Mrs. Briggs.

Shirley poked vaguely at her kipper in a haze of

beatitude. She wondered if any girl had ever been so fortunate. Her family were united in each other and their approval of Jim, and one day in their turn she and Jim would watch their own children bring home husbands and wives and so it would go on, smoothly for ever, until they were both old people and she was too tired to do anything but sleep. She smiled round the table with an expression which made her mother, remembering but not regretting her own lost youth, kiss the top of Mr. Briggs' cranium as she passed behind his chair.

In the school garden the soft sounds of summer were uninterrupted by the noise of little girls. On this last afternoon of half-term Miss Cottingham had taken the remainder of the School House for a picnic and in a shady corner of the lawn Honor listened in peace to the faint drone of insects and the flutter of the leaves of her book. She found she had no idea of what she was reading so she let the book lie in her lap with her young, ungainly hands resting idly upon it and watched the rose and white hollyhocks glowing in the sun. In her mind she held an image of Albert so that when he appeared within her line of vision it was as if he had walked from her thoughts on to the grass in front of her.

She turned her unsurprised gaze upon him and gave him such an unthinking, radiant little smile that he thought, "Why, she's sweet! An' young - younger'n them girls, even!"

Upon some unexpected impulse he moved forward and, to be nearer, kneeled down beside her chair. He wore a puzzled, half enchanted expression which made Honor forget even to be thankful that trees and hollyhocks shaded them from the windows of the school. Albert took her hand and went on looking at her, forgetful, in this ever surprising magic, that the game was not new to him and that it would run its relentless course as it had always done; while Honor, with no experience to guide her, was only aware that she and Albert were in some strange, new fairyland of which the ways, though unfamiliar, were understood.

He leaned gently across the book and kissed her so that the deck-chair, the grass, even the earth itself seemed to dissolve and sink away. When he had finished kissing her he looked round him at the lawn and the hollyhocks and deciding that, what with one thing and another, the place was extremely inconvenient, he stood up and held out his hands.

Honor, upon her feet, made a little desperate movement towards the school but Albert said softly, "Don't go for to leave me!" and her hands, in his warm, not too clean brown ones, seemed so secure that it was impossible to draw them away. They went across the lawn towards the wood and behind the tool shed Albert stopped to kiss her again, with the kisses that had made Poppy leave the tap of a beer barrel running and Mrs. Munnings take on permanently what her mother described as "That there Good-Fer-Nothin'."

Albert moved the branches that reached towards her in the wood and Honor, stepping over moss and logs beneath the golden sunlight and the calls of birds, thought, "All the summer afternoons that I have known, even as a little girl, were the forerunners of this!" She turned her wide and trusting gaze on Albert with a look which momentarily so disconcerted him that he closed her eyes with a kiss.

They moved on among the trees and as she turned to smile at him and a bird sang out above the branches, Albert, smitten with some sudden, sweet poetic vision of the moment, touched and held her as if she were really the dear love that she supposed herself to be.

Honor had no idea of repulsing him; indeed, she knew so little about love that though she might have resisted it in a less attractive form, Albert's charm and efficiency were so unprecedented that she was dazed.

They stopped eventually and stood looking at each other. Honor, with her hands resting lightly in his, began slipping away from the familiar world.

Suddenly the birds seemed to have stopped singing for she could hear nothing but the beating of Albert's heart, and the leaves above her head were blotted out by his face, which wore a look so lost and helpless that she drew it towards her own.

Mr. Walker spent his last day of freedom in the world that he loved best. In a pair of paint-stained flannel trousers and an old overall of his mother's, he moved, absorbed, about his studio, refreshing himself occasionally from a thermos of cold tea. It was hot and stuffy in the shed, though the light was good, and sweat stained the overall as he stepped back to view a picture and thrust chrome yellow through his hair.

In the house his mother removed invisible specks of dust from the carpet and reminded herself to tell her son to wipe his feet. Suddenly she decided to move the piano and having turned it half-round and rucked up the carpet she waited to be found, martyred and helpless, left to struggle with such odds alone.

Her son, unaware of the time, had forgotten to go in to tea. He had started upon an impulse a charcoal drawing of a female figure, a little lost, a little ungainly, in a rather shapeless dress. The droop of the shoulders and surprised turn of the head, the uncertain gesture of the hands, expressed to his mind the vulnerability of youth equipped with nothing, not even beauty, with which to face the attacks of love. "I mustn't let her see it," he thought. "It's good! Yes! Heartless of me! Well! Poor girl!"

In the house, Mrs. Walker, despairing of an audience, squeezed two tears on to an antimacassar and pushed the piano back against the wall.

In the school drive Alice called a farewell to Mrs. Munnings and started to climb up the hill. She felt that the building, as she approached it, was held together by her affection which swept round the grey walls and over every object they contained. One or two heads, attached to pigtails, were thrust from windows and Alice smiled as she made for the back door. Half-term was a little quiet, she considered, with so many girls away. To-morrow would be better. She liked to feel that they were all safely returned.

In the late summer twilight Shirley and Jim wandered, without awareness of their surroundings, from the promenade to the dirty stones at the edge of the beach, round the deserted winkle stall, back to the bathing-huts now fastened for the night. Close to the sea they stopped beside a breakwater and stared in the last light at each other's faces as though they were searching for the answer to the puzzle which neither could explain. Jim moved Shirley's hair back from her forehead, then watched the soft wind blow it over her face. A gull, flying low beside them, gave its lonely call.

"Don't never change, my love," he said.

"No," said Shirley, moving her hands over his shoulders, "not never I won't."

Reassured, they moved off again on their aimless tour. Once they leaned so long against a breakwater that a little dog, who had come down to scavenge, scampered noisily over the stones when what he had taken to be a stanchion moved away.

Closely entwined, they made their way over the deep shadows in the streets towards the school. They climbed the scented silence of the drive to the back door and parted in a dark recess below the pantry window.

"Good night," whispered Shirley, disengaging herself, "Good night!" She released the tips of his fingers and turned towards the door.

"Oh, my dear young love," said Jim below his breath.

CHAPTER XVI

BENEATH her exercise book Jasmine fingered a piece of note-paper, then slid it gradually along the desk so that she could begin her letter.

"Dear Tom," she wrote in her clear, youthful hand, then stopped to wonder if, for his pleasure, she might have prefixed this with "My." While she wondered she turned her intent and candid gaze upon Miss Truscott, for all the world as though her life depended upon an understanding of the Napoleonic Wars.

Miss Truscott, for once deceived by Jasmine's thoughtful frown and apparently guileless scrutiny, directed a fire of questions elsewhere.

Sophie, who really was interested in Napoleon, drew a little tricorn hat upon her desk. She bent her round, flushed face over her pencil and smiled to herself as she remembered how Jasmine had asked her, "Why ever that old thing?" when she confessed to an affection for the Emperor. "Because I like his hat." "His hat? Well, for crying out loud, Soph," had muttered Jasmine, "you might just as well like Henry the Eighth." "But I do - I do, Jay. Don't you see? I never see a large flat tammy - especially with a feather - without a nice little sense of recognition. It's the same with Napoleon of course. I think all important historical figures," she had added gravely, "ought to wear funny or at least distinctive hats." Remembering this she placed an arm within a coat front beneath the tricorn and added a pair of high boots. Then she drew a round, flat hat and suspended from it the large face and stiff suiting of the knave of hearts which she connected with the historic sovereign.

Jasmine, from the corner of her eye, observed these artistic efforts then returned her attention to Tom. "I hope you had a good voyage and were not sick much. I am being continually interrupted by remarks about Napoleon but will try to write a sensible letter. Sophie likes him because of his hat. I meant to ask you if you wear a bush hat or a topee? Uncle Arthur says topees are old fashioned. Sophie and I made a brace of ducks in a match against the Upper Fourth yesterday - our services were only requested to fill up two vacancies at the last moment and we will not be asked again. However at tennis we have been doing rather well. Miss Bishop is torn between a desire to be modern and a dislike of seeing us in shorts; she and Matron have decided on a compromise which has resulted in a long and pleated variety which are more voluminous than skirts. Aunt May says she is going to play again these holidays which will be fun. And next summer holidays, just over a year from now, I won't be coming back. That looks so exciting, just to see it written, that I don't think I'll dwell on it, it might be bad luck. I half fear the outside world might have changed or gone away before I get to it. Sophie and I are quite happy here, of course, but bored, rather. The people we like best, respectively, are the gardener's baby and Mrs. Prior, who is the cook. She tells us wonderful stories about the places her son Jim, who is a sailor, has been to. He is very handsome and is engaged to Shirley who is second housemaid. I had better stop now because Miss Truscott is going to ask me a question. I envy you your palm trees and alligators while we have only the echoes of the battle of Waterloo. I hope you will have a lovely time there. Sophie sends her love and so do I.

JASMINE

Since it was impossible to inform Sophie, with Miss Truscott's eye upon them, that she was sending her love to her cousin, Jasmine grinned round at her and then, deciding to devote the rest of the lesson to her Form mistress, jotted down a few notes upon her remarks.

May put the last stitch in the turquoise chiffon and then went up to tidy Jasmine's room. She wished, as she put a small and shabby pair of black shoes at the back of the cupboard that she could cajole more money out of Arthur, or, to be exact, that he had more money to be cajoled. The few clothes, suspended from May's old coat-hangers, reminded her so acutely of their owner that she ran her fingers over the dresses before she shut the door. Every chair in the house, during term time, reproduced for May the way that Jasmine sat or sprawled, the stairs bore almost visible traces of her light and hurried steps, her voice echoed from floor to floor. The sudden, idiotic remarks which provoked May to instant laughter made Arthur's complete lack of entertainment value unimportant.

She straightened, upon the dressing-table, a wooden horse, a Victorian pin tray and a little box containing two glass bracelets and her own débutante pearls. These recalled her youth and the complaints of dowagers as they trailed endlessly to dances in pursuit of their tiring, faithful tasks. How willingly she would do what was necessary for Jasmine! Her only regret was that she would not have the money to do more. When Jasmine left school there would be a little while, perhaps, that she might spend at home. They would enjoy it! May looked forward to this as much as Jasmine, for she considered her niece the best company she knew.

In the empty hall she was overcome by a sudden feeling of depression and reaching for the telephone she dialled Sylvia's number. She was out and May, for once idle, sat sighing and dreaming in the hall until it was time to do the potatoes.

During lunch what was euphemistically termed the evening post arrived, containing a letter for May from Jasmine. She read it with half an ear on Arthur, answering his questions and smiling to herself behind the flowers. Jasmine explained why the letter was accompanied by another one for May to post to Tom - "You know what our Unity is," she had written. "Of course we wouldn't wish to *read* your letters, dear! Of course not!" May, remembering Miss Bishop, smiled.

"Any news of Jasmine?" asked Arthur.

"Nothing of interest, dear," May murmured, and popped the letters under cover with what she hoped was a quiet, feminine little gesture. It wouldn't do for Arthur to see a letter to Tom! As always, when she received from the school a communication which was no business of the

Reverend Arthur's she managed to convey by her expression that Jasmine was asking for another pair of knickers.

Later that afternoon she strolled round to the post office and the letter addressed in Jasmine's schoolgirl hand to Thomas Williams, Esquire, which May had sealed but had not thought of opening, started off on its long journey to the south.

When she returned she sat down and, upon a sudden impulse, indited an epistle to Miss Bishop. Between the grim forces of Miss Bishop and Arthur she saw Jasmine, a small, darting, yellow-tipped figure, moving warily, with herself, timid and clumsy, following in an attempt to keep those opposing walls apart. She assured Miss Bishop that there was no real need to worry about Jasmine, that she was, in any case, receiving just what she needed from the school. She tried to tell, without putting it in so many words, the lie that Arthur was also pleased with his niece and added a hint that no communications except those of a complimentary nature need actually be received by him. Which would mean, she reflected, that he would be unlikely to be addressed at all.

She wanted to suggest to Miss Bishop that Jasmine would prefer to be left alone, but remembering that the headmistress knew, or must be presumed to know, a good deal more about girls than herself, she abandoned the idea.

At the end of what she felt to be two rambling and altogether futile pages she signed herself, as ever, "May Tern."

A ridiculous name, she thought, reaching for one of Arthur's stamped envelopes. As if I were a worm. Only of course I never do.

The girls, released from Form rooms, scattered like spray among the grass and trees. Honor, as she subsided in the shade, wondered where they found so much energy to dart about. The untroubled state of their hearts, she supposed, closing two tears behind her eyelids, lightened their voices and their feet.

Sophie and Jasmine turned towards the little wood and lingered happily in the green silence which was not, for them, haunted by Mr. Walker's sad communings, Honor's departed virtue or Albert's graceless smile. Here, they hoped, since it was out of bounds, they would be uninterrupted, and might saunter and chatter as they pleased. The sunlight and the shadows of the leaves flickered over their young faces as they moved and laughed beneath the trees.

"We're going downhill now," said Sophie. "Towards the end of term I mean. It won't be so long."

"Yes - and exams before the end of it."

"We'll have to work a bit then. Oh, dear!" She heaved a tragic sigh at the prospect.

They made their way to a mossy clearing and Sophie sat down upon the log on which Mr. Walker had once rested to talk to Jasmine.

The summer, which had been young then, would soon be a little overblown. Jasmine, moving her foot in a patch of hot sunshine, sniffed heat and moss and heavy leaves.

"This time next year!" she said to Sophie.

"Yes - Sometimes I hardly believe it."

"Nor I."

After a moment Sophie said: "The Christow was trying not to cry."

"Was she? Whatever for?"

"Cherchez l'homme," murmured Sophie, smoothing the log with her hands.

"You haven't far to cherchez!"

"No."

"Poor little beast." Jasmine turned her flower face towards the sky. Suddenly the wood seemed a little desolate to Sophie. To love hopelessly, or to love and not be loved! Poor creature! And doubtless she had other troubles; for Matron could be wonderfully nasty and they themselves were aggravating most of the time.

She asked irrelevantly, "Is there nothing that you'll miss here when we go?"

"Nothing," said Jasmine, shaking her upturned head so that the flow of hair swung rhythmically across her shoulders. "You'll be pining for Geoffrey, I suppose?"

"Yes," said Sophie, "Yes, I will." In another year he would be running about the cottage and perhaps into the drive to meet her, and no doubt he would talk. And then, she supposed, when she and Jasmine came down on Speech Days he would have grown into some stumping, outlandish person with his babyishness prematurely disguised by cloth and boots. He would be unlikely to know her in any case. She leaned back over the log, just keeping her balance. "I'll go and see him before tea."

"Yes."

Jasmine's unusual preoccupation surprised Sophie, who stared with a little frown at her friend's face.

With the leaves which would soon be turning brown before her, with moss which would trample into next winter's mud beneath her feet, and Sophie mooning about the loss of that drooling child - a child who would grow old and ugly and draw his old age pension - she suddenly felt unsafe. Somewhere in the wood a cuckoo called and she remembered that in another month he would be gone. Her lost expression startled Sophie who asked softly: "What is it, Jay?"

"Time, transience, death," said Jasmine and turned away her head.

On the lawn below the tool shed they passed Honor standing forlornly with her hands behind her back. She turned such a desolate face towards them at Sophie's greeting that Jasmine took to her heels. "I'm going to run!" she called unnecessarily over her shoulder and from the devils of decay and other people's misery, her yellow hair streaming, she fled towards the school.

Honor turned her back upon Sophie and waited for her to go. Her eyes rested upon borders and roses and in agony she turned them away. There was not a sight or a sound within the school or garden, it appeared, which did not remind her that she had once seemed mysterious to Albert, who now thought her uninteresting and a fool. The day after her sojourn in the wood with him he had attempted, with success, to lead her there again, for feeling that she now belonged to him, it had seemed inevitable. This time there had been no wonder and no fairyland and as she watched him hurrying towards the cottage for his tea she had known that although at his rapid parting he had been kind, according to his lights, she no longer held any enchantment for him. His brown curls and the sweep of his lashes suddenly came before her so vividly that she unclasped her hands and held them up against her heart.

The little movement so touched and frightened Sophie that she moved from one foot to the other, holding her breath.

Honor, with her back to her, tried to fight away the vision of Albert which her mind had conjured up. How he would despise her, she imagined, for brooding on his beauty still! But there she was wrong, for had he known he would not have despised her; he was far too sensible of his attractions to blame any one for appreciating them.

She gave a small sound and Sophie, moving up to her, said: "Miss Christow, it's so hot here - won't you come and sit down?" Before she was quite aware of it she was on a green seat in the shade.

"It's just the heat," said Honor. "A headache. I shall be all right."

"Yes," said Sophie, standing in front of her.

It seemed to Honor a long time that they stayed thus and when she said, "You'd better go in now," it was half-heartedly, for she was grateful to this quiet young creature who waited gravely at her side.

Sophie looked wildly round and wondered what to do. Impossible to leave the poor thing with that haunted, gaunt, expression, marooned as it were in the middle of the lawn; impossible also to say, "Forget about him! Waste of time!" She leaned a little forward and half lifted a hand towards Honor's shoulder, then, deciding she might think this impertinent, she let it fall.

Beyond the trees came voices and laughter and the sound of footsteps on the drive. Sophie listened with relief. "They're coming in from games. I'll fetch Miss Warrender - if you aren't quite well - " She left her vague murmurings unfinished and dashed off across the grass.

Celia, following the Upper Third over the gravel, stopped and blew her whistle to halt them in their tracks. Their high voices and skippings ceased abruptly as they turned their bright faces to see what was going on.

"Put your things away quietly and go straight up to change down!"

"Yes, Miss Warrender!" piped the cheerful voices, and again the little figures started bobbing up the drive.

Celia listened to Sophie rather incredulously then pounded off towards the lawn.

"What's all this?" she asked kindly and briskly of Honor's despondent figure. "The vapours?"

Honor, grateful for this dull normality, smiled. "Something like that. I'll come in."

Celia, taking Honor's arm, said that she'd better go and lie down and if Matron wanted her she could sing for her. They went up towards the school.

In the dormitory Sophie slipped unnoticed past Charity's cubicle and into her own round which the curtains - tactful of Jasmine! - were already drawn. "One less unpunctuality report," she thought, dragging off her tunic.

As she combed the front of her hair without replaiting it she looked a question at her reflected face. What on earth had made Albert pursue that rather dull, pathetic creature? She settled the black velvet band between the brown waves, frowning thoughtfully. Life was very odd!

Albert, dispelling his irritation by taking it out of the new potatoes, was wondering the same thing.

CHAPTER XVII

THE sight of Honor's reddened eyes afforded Matron a good deal of quiet satisfaction; she saw Celia come out of her room and allowed herself to hope that they had quarrelled. Then she went through one of the dormitories with her confident tread and noted down the names of two girls to whom she would give reports for untidiness.

When she reached her room she took some bismuth tablets and put the kettle on for tea. She was not above gossiping with the maids and had learned from Doris that her subordinate had been seen with the drawing master in the town. This news had so upset her that it had spoiled her food. As the strong tea counteracted the effect of the bismuth and she remembered the traces of Honor's tears she began to take a more optimistic view. It was not likely that such a stupid, snivelling girl would attract an artistic gentleman; the thought that the girl she had nagged and bullied might acquire a man to protect her was almost more than she could bear. She finished the tea and decided that her fears were groundless.

All this was just as well for Honor who, having thanked Celia, rested upon her bed with eau-de-cologne on her brow, a twilight of drawn blinds upon her tired eyes and desolation in her heart. She had scarcely registered the fact that Matron's attacks of malice had increased during the last few days, or that their cause was not her inefficiency or a suspicion of her love for Albert.

The thought of Albert caused her to gasp and sob into

her pillow, and presently she washed down two aspirins with a glass of water left at her side by Celia and hoped she might make herself look respectable before she had to appear at tea.

After tea she passed the window of the school studio which framed Mr. Walker frowning at a drawing. He put it down when he saw her and asked her how she did. Her rather spiritless assurance that she was very well, thank you, was belied by her unhappy face and, somewhat stricken by it, he told her to wait and he would catch her up.

"Where are you going?" he asked as he joined her in the drive.

"Nowhere in particular."

"I mean are you going for a walk?"

"Yes, I suppose so."

"Mind if I come, too?"

Honor started to say that she supposed not, then, realising how ungracious it sounded, she said that she would like his company. They set off in vaguely embarrassed silence towards the town.

Sophie and Jasmine, on their way to the laboratory, passed them in the drive and Jasmine opened her golden eyes and murmured, without malice, "Well, still waters *do* run deep!" Sophie puckered her young brow and watched the two retreating figures. She hoped he would cheer the poor girl!

Honor and Mr. Walker went along the promenade to where the edge of the town straggled out towards the green cliffs. On a seat facing the sea they saw Mrs. Prior, whose afternoon out it was, accompanied by Jim and crowned with a hat like the Garden of Eden. Honor nodded sedately and Mr. Walker, recognising the face beneath the glory, waved his hand. He explained that he had encountered her on one of her rare sorties to the kitchen garden and had since cherished the hope that she might one day be persuaded to sit for her portrait.

Honor looked involuntarily over her shoulder to see what there could be remarkable in those enormous curves and creased and cheerful features; she was assailed by a gust of laughter evidently provoked by some sally of Jim's. She glanced back curiously at Mr. Walker and remembered how he had once assured her that there were more things in heaven and earth than were dreamed of by Celia. Were there perhaps more than she herself . . . ?

They had reached the top of the cliff before she remembered to be embarrassed by the fact that they had done so in silence and also that she had forgotten, for a few moments, to think of Albert.

Mr. Walker, noticing that the shut, drawn look had returned to his companion's countenance, attempted to entertain her as they walked. With what agonised raptures, he thought, would he have accompanied Jasmine over the windy turf and how awkward and foolish he would have felt. But with this gauche, unhappy girl it was easy to be helpful since she was more shy than he. He smiled and talked and sat her down beside a little patch of thrift, then leaned back and closed his eyes to the sun.

Honor, looking down upon Mr. Walker's pleasant but uninspiring features, thought how wasteful and ironical fate could be. A few months, even weeks, ago, she would have felt herself fortunate to be resting in this quiet intimacy upon the top of the cliffs with a man as nice as he. But now the face at her side was obscured by her mental vision of Albert's smile and curling mouth. What would Mr. Walker think, she wondered, if he knew she had given her love where only a few afternoons' possession had been wanted? As the tears started to gather again she wished that he would rouse himself and distract her.

He rolled over on his elbow and squinted at her against the glare. "I'm afraid I'm not very entertaining company."

"Oh, no - I was enjoying just sitting here," said Honor untruthfully.

He looked at the plain, young, unhappy face revealed in the strong sunlight and wondered if she felt as bad about the wretched Albert as he did about Jasmine: Jasmine whose golden youth would only challenge and reflect this glaring sun. And "Worse probably!" he answered his own questions, for to judge by Honor's woebegone face something more than the fact of unrequited love had happened to distress her.

"See those gulls!" he said, pointing where they swooped at the edge of the cliff before them, then disappeared suddenly in a dive to the invisible surf. "Both worlds at once!"

"Ye-es," said Honor slowly, thinking of the edges of the rocks below.

"Ever do any drawing?" he asked her suddenly.

"I do a little sketching at home."

"Ah," he said deeply, thinking just how bad she must be.

The sea wind blew Honor's summer dress around her not particularly shapely limbs. Silhouetted between the cliffs and sky she looked small and helpless and Mr. Walker thought suddenly: "She's sweeter than I knew! I'd like to kiss her. Better not!" and glancing sideways at her face he wondered how surprised she would be if she knew what he was thinking. "Very!" he answered himself, aloud.

"Very what?" asked Honor, looking puzzled.

"Nothing!" he assured her, shaking his head. "These expanses make me talk to myself. There's a lark above you!" And leaning back they listened and watched the tiny black speck which might have been the lark.

Below the cliff Jim escorted his mother's luxuriant hat across the beach. He took her arm when she lurched too heavily and she, recalled to the present and then the future, by this firm support, glanced sideways at the bronzed, sweet face that soon she would not see for the Lord knew how many months. The brow, puckered in a frown, was indicative, she supposed, of brooding thoughts of Shirley. She sighed gustily and Jim, his face clearing, told her a dirty story about the bos'n in Shanghai. Their laughter was blown quickly out to sea.

In a quiet corner beyond the potato patch Margery settled herself on the ground. She crossed her legs and spread her gear around her: an Algebra text-book, a pencil pock-marked by her teeth, half a bar of chocolate which had become glued to its wrappings by the sun, a grimy note-book and a torn handkerchief with a penknife, for she was in the process of cutting it down for Augustus. She decided it would make him three at least. She arranged the little squares neatly on the grass and licked the chocolate. Her eyes slid reluctantly towards the textbook and then away to where she could see Albert enjoying some relaxation in the sun; he mopped his brow, sat down on a flowerpot and turned up his face. How lucky and carefree he was, she thought enviably, sunning himself between heaven and earth where the difference between Y cubed and Z squared mattered not at all. She scribbled frantically in the notebook, found her answers were wrong, scribbled again and found them worse than ever. Her thin little bosom started to heave convulsively and, not wishing to soil Augustus' linen, she seized the torn hem and wailed into the scraggy ends.

When Albert finally roused himself and passed round the top of the potato patch a few scattered sobs reached him and he hunched his shoulders up to his ears. Women, he felt, could be very trying and he thought that the Creator had slipped up badly over one or two points in the manufacture of Eve. There were, in his opinion, several ways in which she might have been made into a considerably more restful helpmeet for man.

As he passed the main building he glanced involuntarily at a window from which he had once seen Honor lean, then went on down to the cottage to see what his wife had got for tea.

While Albert consumed tinned salmon, Mrs. Prior and Jim ordered an expensive feast of port and sandwiches in the pub near the beach; Margery sucked the chocolate wrapping and Mr. Walker, remembering his mother, said he supposed they had better go back.

As they went Honor turned to look behind her at the windy expanse, where, remote from the school and town, she had seemed almost free from her distress. Reassuringly, Mr. Walker took her arm and guided her down the narrow path at the edge of the cliff. "I suppose I'll get over it," she thought hopelessly, watching stones and little tufts of grass disappear under her feet, "people do."

Shirley turned the ring on her finger beneath the shelter of the table-cloth then raised a hand to take her plate from Maud. When her eyes had finally focused upon the plate before her she passed it back and asked for a smaller helping.

Doris, waylaying Shirley's supper, explained to the others, "It's only love, pore girl. Just the same I was with my George. Couldn't eat fer thinkin' of 'im. Up to me 'eart me stomach was." She tipped most of the food from the plate on to her own, proving that George's day was done.

Shirley picked at the edge of the potato with her fork. "I'll feed Timoshenko after supper," she thought, "as Mrs. Prior's out, and if there's no one in the kitchen I'll have another look at that picture of Jim." The hand with the fork in it went up to her chin and she gazed across the cloth into space.

Upstairs, Miss Bishop poured coffee and milk into two little cups and handed one across the desk to Miss

Meadows. In the evening sun the tired lines on Miss Meadows' face showed clearly and her shoulders seemed to droop over the cup.

"Then you think," said Miss Bishop, "that there really is something worth while in the girl?"

Miss Meadows put down her spoon and nodded her head.

"I know she's clever," Miss Bishop murmured, "but she's laziness itself. And Matron - !" She left the sentence unfinished and sighed.

"Miss Cottingham approves of her."

"Miss Cottingham is too soft-hearted for unbiased judgment."

"Then, my dear Unity," said Miss Meadows briskly, "you need fear no such bias from me! Jasmine Tern," she added, frowning at her junior and superior, "is neither dishonest nor a fool."

"She's spoilt." Miss Bishop stared at the dregs in her cup.

"Perhaps," said Miss Meadows.

"But," continued Miss Bishop honestly, "that is hardly her fault."

The beauty for which Jasmine was not responsible seemed to hang like a bright curtain in the room. Into the mind which Miss Meadows had declared to be unbiased came the memory of her golden smile and hair. "How hard for Unity," she thought, watching her smooth, high brow, "to be just to all her girls! And how hard she tries!" She leaned back and smiled.

Miss Bishop said aloud, "I will be guided by your opinion." Of herself she asked: "How many more terms will she be able to stay and help me? One perhaps or two? Already, these last weeks she looks years older. I mustn't worry her too much!"

She refilled the little cups with coffee and they talked of the New Look, and then of Sappho, for a rest.

CHAPTER XVIII

Tom had written to Jasmine:

DEAR JASMINE,

It was good to get your letter - cricket and tennis in England, on the conventional grass, have a lot to be said for them. Of course we play cricket here, but on a strip of scorched earth. They advise us to take our leave in the winter to pep up the red cells, but I shall try to wait until April or I should feel I had been swindled. By the way, talking of games, you should see the Africans playing soccer with bare feet. And very good they are, too.

My house is high up over the harbour. I can see the smoke of the mail ships appearing over the horizon. At least, one always hopes they are the mail! It's a five-roomed house with a veranda, on which one lives and eats and usually sleeps, and the whole affair's on stilts, with a store-room underneath. The kitchen's across the yard and in front of it to-night's dinner and to-morrow's lunch are pecking around the dustbins - everything has to be kept alive until the last moment. There's an orange tree outside the bathroom, a very sensible arrangement, since oranges can be picked through the window and eaten conveniently in the bath. There are a lime and frangipanni tree in front of the veranda and my Small Boy, when he's tired of banging my clothes to pieces against the side of the bath (he calls this process "brooking" and, in fact, in all the streams you can see them pounding their own garments against the stones), picks the frangipanni and brings it indoors so that whoever goes near it is bitten by white ants. This may sound a bit unpleasant but it's not a bad place really and I have grown attached to it.

In the mountais behind the town we can climb and walk for miles, there are small monkeys in the trees and sometimes, in the dry season, a leopard comes down as far as the garden, looking for water. They are a small variety and not, I think, very ferocious.

There are usually some Naval types stuck in the town and we do a good deal of fishing and sightseeing in launches. Midnight - with a moon - is a good time for a picnic and the Africans from the village nearby come out and sit round us and laugh while we cook our supper on the beach. The bathing here will make me for ever frightened of the cold water at home.

This last leave was a very good one. By the next you may have left - or soon be leaving - school? I must come and stay with Sylvia, and you and Sophie must help me catch up with London.

I hope you'll manage comfortably in your exams and things. Now I've seen Miss Bishop I wonder you aren't terrified of her - I would be.

Remember me kindly to Mrs. Tern and give Sophie - and yourself - my love.

TOM

PS. Please write again.

In Greenock the Commanding Officer of H.M.S. *Indestructible* received a cable ordering him to transfer to tropical waters and to start at once. All over England and Scotland telegraph wires hummed recalling sailors on leave.

Poppy brought the telegram up to Jim's room at the Silver Herring and leaned on the bedrail, ogling him, as he stood in his vest and trousers, reading it over. When he had read it for the third time he raised his blue eyes and focused them on Poppy.

"Bad news?" she asked.

"No," said Jim. "Well, that is - Yes." He went on standing in the middle of the room.

"Goin' out s'evenin'?" said Poppy.

"Yes." He reached for his jacket. "Now." At the door he said, "I'll be goin' in the morning. They pinched a week off my leave. You bin good to me, Poppy," and went downstairs. As the door swung from the bar into the street Poppy crossed to the window to watch him go.

At the back door of the school he was admitted by Maude and escorted to the kitchen and his mother.

"Well?" she asked.

"Recalled to-morrow," he said, putting the wire on the table.

"I knew it," said Mrs. Prior.

"You couldn't 'a' known this."

"I did an' all." She sat down suddenly as though her legs failed her and Timoshenko gave a frightened squeal as he escaped.

"Soon be back, Mum." said Jim, crossing beneath his

smiling portrait to her side. "Where's Shirley?" he asked, stroking her cheek.

"She's 'ere."

"Could she - ?"

"Yes, she c'n get out - I'll see to it."

"Thanks a lot," he said, leaning down to give her a kiss.

In the summer darkness, at the side of a breakwater, Jim lay with his head on Shirley's heart. From behind them came the gentle wash of the sea and to Shirley it was the sound of an enemy which would soon be stretching between herself and Jim. She lifted his head so that she could move her lips along his warm, smooth skin.

"Maybe the ship'll come 'ome soon, darlin'."

"Maybe," said Jim.

Shirley closed her eyes upon the thought of all the dreary months ahead. Unconsciously she held Jim more closely and felt him stiffen. "Better get a move on," he said.

They ploughed along the beach with difficulty, with their arms round each other, and stopped beneath the shadow of the cliffs.

Helplessly, with the stones pressing their feet, the sea in their ears, they kissed, leaning against the cliff. The moon moved out from behind a cloud and Shirley wondered if it were the strange light that made the face above her own look green. "Darlin'," she sighed, "take care o' yourself."

Jim, who had not heard her, said, "Shirley! Shirley - please."

Panic seized her and she held him gently as though he

might be ill. "No," she said. "No, Jim."

"Oh, Shirley - Shirley!" he said.

Shirley opened her lips to say what she could not explain. No sound came and through her mind there went a picture of her family and the expressions on their faces if she disgraced them. And beyond her family she saw herself coming out of church in a white dress in the sunshine and Jim holding her hand; beyond that she saw peace and time and solitude and some place where she would still be there to comfort him when he woke. "No," she said firmly and distinctly. "Oh, darlin', darlin' Jim, not now."

Jim laid his ravaged face quietly on her shoulder, accepting her decision, she supposed, as he accepted the piece of paper from an unknown hand which summoned him back to duty on H.M.S. *Indestructible* a week before his leave should end.

The news of Jim's return seeped through the servants' hall and, mysteriously, reached the ranks of the Upper Fifth. Sophie heard it on her way in to prayers and conveyed the information to Jasmine when they knelt to pray. Whatever reflection of this disaster their faces bore behind their devoutly protecting hands they were expressionless as they stood up for the hymn.

"Kitchen – now!" fluted Jasmine as the school intoned the "Amen."

"So be it," whispered Sophie under cover of the scraping chairs as they sat down.

As the Upper Fifth filed on their way to their Form

room Sophie and Jasmine slipped from the line and, turning two corners, dodged out of the side door.

"Safe!" gasped Jasmine and they ducked round the building to the kitchen windows. "Any one there?" she asked of Sophie, who was peering in.

"Only them - come on!"

They burst into the kitchen and slammed the door with such vigour that Mrs. Prior said: "Lawks a mussy!" and Jim and Shirley, who were holding hands, moved apart.

"We've come to say good-bye," said Sophie, leaning on the door to get her breath.

"Thought you'd come from a rocket," said Mrs. Prior, but she beamed upon them, for it was no crime in her eyes to admire her son.

"Good-bye," sighed Jasmine, holding out her hand, "I hope you'll have a good voyage!"

"It's been wonderful meeting you," said Sophie, adding hers.

Jim took each of the extended hands in one of his. As he looked from one to the other of the eager faces, "Mum must 'a' been stuffin' em up, not 'arf!" he thought. He gave the two soft hands a squeeze and said: "I bin that glad to know you. N'I'll be thinkin' of you while I'm away. N'I won't forget the postcards neither. God bless," he added, smiling down at them.

"Good-bye - God bless!" they stammered. "Priory, we must run!"

They did so, banging the door. They presented themselves at Miss Stebbing's lesson and said that they had been excused.

Miss Stebbing, who was discussing Molière, told them to hurry up and get out their books. She did not believe them, but it was a point upon which she felt unqualified to argue so she left it at that.

In the kitchen Mrs. Prior cut Jim a round of sandwiches from the school rations and, waving the meat knife at Shirley and her son, told them to go and leave her room to move. When Jim had closed the door her bosom heaved and two tears rolled down on to the bread.

Arm in arm Shirley and Jim skirted the vegetables and made for the wicket gate and the privacy of the kitchen garden. They saw Albert and Jim called a greeting over Shirley's head. Albert looked a little sadly after them as they disappeared; that was a proper dish now! Oh, well! He lowered his lashes as Shirley went out of sight, sighed and ran his fingers through his curls.

"Tell your Mum," said Jim behind the bushes, "to be ready for a weddin' my next leave. God only knows when it'll be. N'it'll always be like this - comin' and goin'. Sure you won't mind?"

Shirley's grey eyes reassured him as much as her murmured: "No one else'd do."

He twisted the ring on her finger that he had given her and they stood in desolate silence. "Afterwards," Shirley was thinking, "there will be all the things that we had meant to say and we'll wonder why we didn't say them now."

Jim said, "We'll say good-bye here."

When he came into the kitchen Mrs. Prior had dried her eyes and Timoshenko was licking a plate.

" 'T won't be long afore yer back," she said defiantly, shuffling from the table to the sink. The stone floor seemed to shake beneath her tread.

"That's right, Mum," said Jim. He picked up the sandwiches. "Comin' to see me off?"

"Just to the door I'll come. Where's Shirley?"

"Upstairs," said Jim, who pictured her, correctly, crying upon her bed.

"I bin thinkin' - the 'ouse," Mrs. Prior muttered, who had been picturing the little cottage waiting for her solitary return. "I'll get some paint an' that - you an' Shirley – " It would be something to concentrate upon when she was alone.

"Thanks, Mum. See you gets a nice dress for the bridegroom's mother!"

She laughed, holding his arm. "Ah! That'll be the day!"

At the back door she held up her huge crumpled face to be kissed.

Jim disengaged himself and slapped the round hat on sideways, over one of his blue eyes. "Keep smilin', old girl. See you soon!"

She watched, blinking in the sunshine, while he went down the drive and turned to wave at the gate.

Doris opened the attic door and did not like what she heard. She sat morosely on her bed looking at Shirley's crushed cap and apron where she had flung herself upon the other counterpane, and listening to her sobs.

"Cheer up, Shirl," she admonished her, "you'll be worse afore you're better." She kicked off her shoes and regarded her toes. "An' there's plenty more fish in the sea." She received no answer. "Lawd, me feet do swell," she said.

In the train Jim swung his kitbag up on the rack, wondering where he would be next week. And in his cabin in H.M.S. *Indestructible* the Commanding Officer took his pipe out of his mouth and said to the Navigating Officer: "Well, here's a nice how d'y'do. I hope you'll like the White Man's Grave, John."

CHAPTER XIX

THE girls ran out of the studio in a noisy stream. Mr. Walker hoped that none of the senior mistresses would pass and see that this was the way the Upper Fifth behaved when in his charge. He knew that in their Form rooms decorous deportment in front of the staff was required - and obtained. He wondered if they would return and walk out slowly if he dropped a pile of boards and shouted into the silence which would ensue. On the whole he thought not and in any case he was never likely to make the experiment; it was, he reflected wryly, turning away from them, just an idle dream.

He found Sophie at his elbow and saw that Jasmine, while she waited, was filling in her time by giving a tolerably good imitation of a bored young lady at an exhibition. "Oh, my dear," she sighed, drooping languidly in front of a picture of the 'Sports Day' by a member of the Sixth. "Don't you think that's too, too - ?" she broke off and smiled cheerfully at Sophie and Mr. Walker, who tried to look resentful and failed.

"Yes, Sophie, what is it?" he asked.

"You've hung my 'Summer Meadows' on the line!" Sophie moved from one foot to the other. "Then you really think - ?"

"If I didn't," he said gravely, "it wouldn't be there."

"No, the point is - it was an experiment - and it's come off?"

"Yes, I think it has." He looked from her anxious face to

the unexpected blues and purples which reproduced, he felt, so accurately, clover and an evening sky. "Just go on - don't worry - you'll be all right."

Her eyes widened with excitement and Jasmine's voice, which had changed to the caretaker's, intoned cheerfully: "This 'ere prorblem picture in mauves and blues, ladies an' gen'lemen, is entitled 'Arf Seas Hover,' the prorblem bein' as to which 'arf - "

Sophie giggled and interrupted her: "But as hall the Sophie Berwick pictures his sold himmediate – "

"Go away, both of you," said Mr. Walker and laughed.

They skipped off in the wake of their Form and Mr. Walker went up to Sophie's picture again. After all, he thought, looking at it, one doesn't entirely waste one's time.

Upon consulting their time-tables Sophie and Jasmine discovered that they were both down for piano practice and, owing, obviously, to an oversight on the part of Miss Cottingham, in adjacent rooms. As they entered the music corridor there came faintly, from behind the row of double doors, varying streams of a peasant mazurka, Chopin and "The Minstrel Boy." They slipped into the same room. Sophie raised her eyebrows and Jasmine, nodding, murmured, "What indeed, are one or two among so many? They'll never miss the little noise we'd make."

When they decided that all the other musicians had had time to get under way, they slipped between the baize and mahogany doors, tip-toed over the parquet and made their way with extreme caution and one bad fright to the attic. The fright occurred in the main hall where they had just come into the open and heard footsteps approaching from the other end. But they turned out to belong to Alice, who, although she observed that both girls looked far too virtuous to be upon their lawful occasions, felt that it was none of her business and wished them a very good day. When they reached the top landing they paused for a moment to lean over and wave to Alice's foreshortened little figure in the hall. She waved her duster in return.

Once within the sanctuary of the attic they subsided upon the floor. Then Sophie opened the windows and leaned out. Far below on the terrace, Miss Bishop paraded, lost in thought. In the playing-field over the road she could see Albert enthroned upon a motor mower and beyond the uneven roofs of the town the sea glistened, silvery blue.

"What price our ivory tower?" she said, turning round, and Jasmine laughed.

"I don't really want to get away from the world," she answered her. "Quite the contrary, it's only - so much organisation gets one down."

"I know. Golly, the dust settles up here." She wiped her grimy hands on the backs of her stockings and then her skirt.

"D'you think any one else will ever discover this when we're gone?"

"I shouldn't think so. Anyway, we won't tell them. Even when we leave."

"Just leave it as it is?"

"Yes. As a sort of perpetual memorial."

"To what?"

"To our peace of mind!"

Jasmine made herself more comfortable upon Sir Roger's coat and took a letter from the pocket in the pleats of her tunic. When she had reread it she passed it to Sophie. "There you are," she said, "Tom!"

Sophie perused it and handed it back to her. "Well, I call that very civil of him," she said.

Jasmine put her hands behind her head. "Yes, it sounds a lovely place."

"It isn't really lovely. It's like hell."

"I suppose it is - all the same - " She rolled over on to her stomach. "Lucky, lucky Tom!"

Sophie, regarding Jasmine's indolent beauty and the casual way she held the letter, wondered if he were so lucky after all. She looked out at the sea again and imagined that perhaps, on the other side of that blue horizon, his ears might be burning. She wondered if he thought of Jasmine and thought it probable that he did. "That's the first real love letter," she murmured, looking at the neat collection on the floor.

"You could hardly call it that," sighed Jasmine, thinking of Tom's carefully worded phrases of information and goodwill.

"It's the best he can do I dare say," said Sophie, "he never was the romantic type."

But Jasmine shook her head thoughtfully. He was not to be dismissed so easily! She remembered his expression at the vicarage and felt that Sophie was wrong.

At the end of the drive the door of the gardener's cottage opened and Mrs. Munnings carried Geoffrey into the sun. Sophie hung dangerously out into the sky. It would be so easy to wave and shout to them - Mrs. Munnings would hear if he did not - but the sight of her headmistress's smooth cranium gleaming below her caused her to wriggle back.

"What is it next, Jay?" she asked.

"Old Testament."

"Oh, well, that'll be all right. I didn't do my prep, I think, but you can answer if she looks at me."

"Thanks to Uncle Arthur," said Jasmine, yawning and stretching, "I can." She fingered Tom's letter again. All those miles it had come, from what Tom described as steamy sunshine and bursts of tropical rain. She put it back in the envelope and added it to the Strictly Private pile. Sophie, she saw, had tied them all together with a blue ribbon.

"Why have you done that?" she asked.

"Because if one of us dies young it's how they should be found."

"Will you never grow up?" asked Jasmine in Miss Cottingham's voice. And added in her own, "But I expect we'll all live to be ninety. And by then there will be four. Who will you have for your young man, Sophie?"

"No one," Sophie assured her, for already she despaired of finding Mr. Knightley's equal.

She stayed on at the window with her chin in her hands, brooding upon Geoffrey and Miss Bishop and the sea, while Jasmine dreamed of Tom.

Electric bells all over the school disturbed them. Sophie blew a kiss in the direction of the cottage and, quickly and quietly, they joined the streams of girls changing from rooms in careful silence and not quite at a run.

Miss Meadows, coming against the tide, watched the hurrying girls pull up at sight of her and stand politely aside for her to pass. When she came to the front stairs she mounted them very slowly with her eyes upon the green carpet, holding the slippery rail. She hadn't been sure, passing all those girls, if she saw them at all: eyes and cheeks and pigtails swam together in an alarming way. "I'm old," she thought, opening her door. "Very old." She sat down in a chair by the window and folded her hands in her lap.

The memory of her quiet cottage was almost painful, she felt so tired. She was still thinking of it when she fell asleep. When she woke the next set of bells was ringing and she reached automatically for the Latin verse for the Upper Sixth. She sat for a moment holding the sheaf of papers, then remembered how among the sea of faces in the passage she had distinguished Jasmine's nod and smile. She got slowly to her feet.

In the studious quiet of the Upper Sixth Form room she regarded the smooth heads bent over their desks. As she raised her own spectacles she caught an answering gleam from Charity's, which reflected the light. Such serious faces the girls had! I do hope, she thought, we are altogether wise. And upon a sudden impulse she recited to them a little poem of lost love by Housman, and, writing it upon the blackboard, instructed them to put it into Latin verse. That would serve the double end of occupying the girls to good purpose and of giving her a rest.

She sat down at her desk and watched the rounded shoulders and bent heads.

After all, one mustn't be too one-sided, they're really grown up, she thought. But as she observed the frowns of concentration she wondered how many were thinking of datives and ablatives and how few of what the poem meant.

Her head nodded ever so slightly and Charity, observing this, gave up the task as hopeless and drew a treble clef at the top of the page. The words of lost love seemed fatuous but the music went swinging through her head. She blinked through her thick glasses and Miss Meadows and the Form room disappeared.

Miss Bishop came in from the terrace and nodded to Alice in the hall. For the first time for many years she remembered the original occasion upon which she had crossed that threshold and had seen Alice, a much younger Alice, against a background of fumed oak and autumn leaves. The sudden appearance of a little girl with tear stains on her cheeks caused Miss Bishop momentarily to wonder if she had seen a ghost. The little girl, looking equally startled at the sight of her headmistress, scurried off down one of the long corridors as fast as she could go.

Miss Bishop went thoughtfully up the stairs. On the first floor she encountered Charity with a piece of paper in her hand and a bemused enchanted expression on her face. Charity offered her no greeting and went by as though Miss Bishop were invisible, as indeed she felt that, temporarily, she was.

Quickened by this encounter Miss Bishop went into her

study and addressed two envelopes, one to Charity's father and one to a musician of her acquaintance. Then she put down her pen and looked through the window at the sea.

I ought not to forget too easily, she thought, trying to remember her youth. She, too, she recollected dimly, had once shed tears in the hall; she too, years later, had reached that strange, creative period which apparently engrossed Charity now. The scent of flowers and the note of a bird floated in from the terrace, and, unbidden, she remembered another girl. She could not feel that she, like Jasmine, had ever been in danger from her beauty, but she also had been sixteen and it flashed through her mind suddenly that pretty girls might feel disheartened too. She remembered what Miss Meadows had said of Jasmine and, picking up her pen again, she drew another envelope towards her and addressed it in her round generous handwriting to the Reverend Arthur Tern.

CHAPTER XX

ALBERT gave a perfunctory kiss to his wife's cheek, removed his child's sticky fingers from his trousers and sat down to his tea. He felt bored to tears. There were no more half-crowns forthcoming from Mr. Walker and the excitement of his pursuit of Honor was gone. The thought of his naked person hanging in what Mr. Walker had called a gallery provoked him to a puzzled frown. It was odd and rather impertinent for those visitors to leer and goggle at him, even if they did pay a shilling a time. He hoped no one would recognise him there! Well, none of his acquaintances was likely to waste their money in such tomfoolery. He remembered Honor's sad face and hurried greetings when she passed him in the garden and scowled as he tipped the sugar in his tea.

His son clawed himself upright at the edge of the table and Albert handed him a piece of cake.

"Give over lettin' that child drag the cloth, do," said Mrs. Munnings. "E'll 'ave the lot on the floor."

Albert moved the teapot and lifted Geoffrey on to his lap.

The fair rather colourless little head bobbed below Albert's chin. "Git yer 'and out o' me plate, duck," he said. With his son's roving fist in his he felt suddenly uncomfortable and sad. That was all it came to! Well! And this poor little beggar on his lap would go on growing and reaching out for things he wanted - and when he got them, what the hell! He touched the child's pasty cheek with his own brown one and put some jam on his cake.

"You goin' out to-night?" asked Mrs. Munnings.

"Yep."

"Then you might bring me back a pint."

"O.K., old girl, I will that," he said quickly, feeling that indeed he might. He wished he'd thought of it himself.

He sat in a corner of the Silver Herring drinking in solitude. Young Prior was gone and no doubt his mother was in mourning so there was no chance of company. When Poppy asked him if he was lonely he replied coldly that he was not. He took all the coins out of his pocket and decided that he would stay there until he was drunk.

When he was satisfied with his condition he swayed down to the beach. He slept solidly beside a breakwater and when he woke he found that Mrs. Munnings' bottle of beer, which he had mercifully remembered, was making a bruise in his side.

The kitchen clock ticked with hideous concentration, a tap dripped forlornly, the kettle boiled over, the cakes ran down the sides of the tins. Mrs. Prior rose slowly to attend to the kettle and the oven then sank into the creaking fastness of her chair.

Her hands lay idly in her vast black lap and through her mind there passed a succession of storms, earthquakes, waterspouts, octopuses and sharks. When the clock struck ten she dragged her spirit from the centre of a cyclone and her body to its feet. Jim smiled serenely from the mantelpiece and she gave him a cheery grin. "Bloody old fool I am!" she admonished herself and let out a bellow for Maude.

Maude, justly incensed at being called upon to remove hot cakes at such an hour, assisted with a heavy hand. "All right - git to bed, now," said Mrs. Prior when all the tins were out. And she added, half to herself, "I likes to 'ave summat on 'and." But when Maud had gone she sat down again and watched the summer evening growing dark.

She thought of Jim as she had first known him and that sweet blue smile of his which had seemed to her like no other little boy's. She remembered him, a little larger, on Sundays, stumbling round the untidy garden, clad prophetically in a clean sailor suit. Roaming easily across the years of his short life she could remember no moment when she had considered him anything but an unqualified success. "I'd orter be thankful an' not mope," she thought, getting up to rake out the fire.

Celia's patient footsteps dogged her friend across the garden in the dusk. Honor, after requesting her company, seemed little disposed to listen to her conversation, and having said, "Buck up, my dear!" twice she confined her pronouncements to the rendering of a song.

When the song began again Honor suggested that they should go down to the sea. The quiet garden reminded her unbearably of Albert and still less did she like the prospect of beginning her fruitless efforts to sleep.

"Good idea!" said Celia to whom a sharp walk until midnight seemed as satisfactory a form of exercise as might be obtainable. She thought that Honor's passing phase of depression might be due to Matron and a lack of fresh air.

Matron herself, raising her third cup of tea to her lips as she sat at her window, observed their dusky forms with irritation for she felt that Honor should have something better to do. She put down her cup and set off on a tour of the dormitories to make certain that no girls were amusing themselves instead of going to sleep. Margery, seeing her approach, pushed Augustus gently down so that his ears might not be observed above the sheet. She lay quietly in the twilight when Matron's steps had gone, thinking that she would never have believed she could have survived until so near the end of term. She wondered when she had last cried before she slept but could not remember and, seeing the summer holidays stretch sweetly, like a green oasis, she began to breathe regularly, with her hand on Augustus' head.

Matron observed Jasmine's yellow hair spilled over the pillow and Sophie's night plaits resting demurely upon the sheet. When she had gone they opened their eyes and grinned. A bar of chocolate passed between the beds and they chewed in contented silence, waiting for the dark.

On the promenade the summer trippers lingered. Honor walked sadly along beside Celia where the coloured lights glimmered, music sounded from the pier and below her, had she known it, Albert slept with his head upon the stones.

All day she dragged herself sorrowfully from linen cupboards to dormitories, from bathrooms to basement, and wherever she went she was haunted by the memory of Albert and her own despair. To have loved misguidedly and in vain, to have made, she felt, in Albert's eyes a complete and utter fool of herself - though there, as it happened, she was wrong - seemed to her like the end of the world. As she had only survived twenty-three of the years allotted to her she saw the remainder stretching endlessly and emptily, and turned with a sudden jerky movement from the void to find herself staring into Celia's concerned and kindly face.

"I suppose it's been a fairly awful term," she suggested, "but never say die, you know! One day dear Matron may take a cup of tea too many and die of indigestion - one day you may marry a nice young man and snap your fingers in her face!" This idea so appealed to Celia that she leaned on the promenade railings and laughed.

Honor, grateful for her misguided kindness, remembered that she had once intended to ask Celia to stay with her during the summer.

"Will you come?" she asked, returning with an effort from the depths in which her mind wandered.

"Come? Where?" asked Celia, puzzled.

"To stay, perhaps, in the holidays. For a week - or more - if you could? We might – " Her mind went back to the girl who had found the prospects of home, the companionship of Celia and the exertion of physical jerks enchanting, and she stopped to ponder in amazement upon her innocent, careless, two months' younger self.

"I'd love it," said Celia, "you've no idea how I long for the country in London - flowers and walks and tennis - She smiled down at Honor. "And I can eat anything," she added generously, "for I don't suppose you're much of a cook!"

215

"That will be lovely," said Honor, and to Celia's amazement burst into tears.

Mrs. Walker took a secret reticule from under her pillow and placed two pound notes within the depths. Thus, month by month and week by week she hoarded a store for a possible and still older old age, serving the double purpose of ensuring that, while housekeeping was apparently so expensive, her son would be unlikely to be able to afford to marry, for she would find herself, she considered, much put out if he did.

When she had hidden it away she went round the house straightening lace curtains and looking for crumbs.

Her son lingered in unwonted inactivity in the twilit studio. A star showed in the deepening blue beyond the window and sitting upon a dusty stool he stared idly at the dim outlines of his hands. The patient routine of locking up the house, attending to his mother's bedtime drink and then listening to the silence as it fell appeared increasingly forlorn. He looked up at the star and felt that it was no farther from his reach than Jasmine, then fell to wondering if his picture of Albert would sell for much and felt it would not greatly benefit him if it did.

The boards creaked in the dormitory as Charity, who was suffering from insomnia, crept down them in her dressing-gown. When she reached the bathroom she drew a piece of paper from her pocket and hummed to herself gently the notes she wrote upon it by the light of a torch.

In the attic, which smelt of mothballs and Doris, Shirley moved her fingers softly where Jim's head ought to be and cried into her pillow.

Honor also wept and the star which Mr. Walker had observed looked palely in upon her shaking form.

Albert lurched unsteadily up his narrow stairs, burst into the bedroom, said: "Where the 'ell - " and was sick on the floor.

Mrs. Munnings said patiently, "There you goes again, Albert - Gawd 'elp me lino," and scrambled out to see if Geoffrey was wet.

As he opened his window Mr. Walker wondered suddenly if Honor were asleep. The star which had reminded him of Jasmine retreated behind a cloud and as he turned back into the room he thought with surprise how companionable Honor's presence would be.

Mrs. Walker, mercifully unaware of these reflections, slept without a flicker upon her bland expressionless face.

In Freetown Harbour, on the deck of H.M.S. *Indestructible*, Jim Prior wiped the sweat from his chest for the ninth time, cursed freely, flung a towel out of the hammock and turned his golden limbs to the moon.

CHAPTER XXI

ON Speech Day, May and Sylvia forgathered at the station and made their way happily among the crowd, some of the smaller of whom were armed with spades and buckets, and also appeared to be going to the sea.

"I knew it!" said Sylvia when May produced a green ticket and went off to change it for a white one and procure her own.

They settled themselves gaily against the green cushions in the comfort and seclusion which Sylvia considered due to them. May took off her three-year-old hat, which sported bunches of rather ill assorted ribbons where the straw had faded, and leant her head against the Southern Railway's antimacassar to enjoy a view of Sylvia's perfectly tinted face and frivolous hat, which appeared to consist mainly of voile and flowers.

The sun-washed woods and downs swept past the window and the bright moving light swung in and out of the carriage to warm them through their summer dresses as the train twisted. Sylvia uncrossed her slim ankles and produced a box of chocolates.

"How on earth - " began May, and, "Hadn't we better -?" as she remembered the girls.

"I've got another. Tom left me some and Roger and Algy never take them you know. I'm afraid they've forgotten what they taste like," she added contritely and May laughed.

"This *is* fun," she murmured, turning Sylvia's magazines.

They stepped out of their taxi on to the lowest terrace and climbed Albert's tiers of flowers to the front door and the view of the sea.

Alice answered their ring and greeted them with her wide smile. She said, "Miss May, now! And Miss Sylvia!" as though they had not grown up and married at all. She led them through a swarm of visitors, of whom May noted with satisfaction that there was no one as lovely as Sylvia, and up to Miss Cottingham.

"Changeless as God," murmured Sylvia, as they wandered away.

But Miss Cottingham did not feel changeless or at all like the Deity where, rather hot and weary, she continued to appear cool and knowledgeable to the parents and governors who came her way. She hoped, as she watched Sylvia's gracefully retreating back and May's plump one, that she had done rightly in telling them that she was pleased with both Sophie and Jasmine and she would be sorry to lose them in the house when they left. Much more sorry, she felt a little guiltily, than she would be about the gap which Charity would leave at the end of term, and she greeted the girl's gloomy father with more warmth than she felt and added, with truth, that his daughter had been a great help in the school. She saw Charity's plain face flush suddenly as her father repeated the praise, and turned, satisfied, to the oldest governor with a smile which belied the swelling of her feet.

May and Sylvia heard a commotion behind them and found the girls' arms around their necks.

They both murmured "Darling!" and Sophie, stepping

back from Sylvia's elegant form said, "Well, sweet, you do look absurd - and lovely!" and linked her arm in hers.

Jasmine slipped her hand over May's soft shoulders and down to her waist. She gave her unfashionable dress a squeeze. "I'm so glad you're here, duckie! So glad!"

They went, laughing and chattering, through the side door and on to the lawn.

"I'm sure we ought to be doing all sorts of things," said Sylvia, relaxing gracefully in the sun. "Such as finding out your batting average from the games mistress and asking Miss Bishop why you haven't any prizes - you haven't, either of you, I suppose?"

They reassured her, shaking their heads and laughing as they sat down.

"The man who gives away the prizes always explains carefully that prizes are not everything - in fact are not anything at all, so that no one need feel disheartened, which of course nobody does." May twisted a daisy between her fingers and smiled. "But it does always make one wonder why, in that case, they don't do the whole thing so much more cheaply without buying prizes at all."

"But they're only special ones to-day," pointed out Jasmine, "and very few of those."

"Yes, I know, darling, but the principle's the same."

Albert, looking extremely smart for the occasion, crossed the grass and hammered quite unnecessarily at one of the pegs of the marquee. He thought that all the girls in their white dresses looked like flowers scattered on the lawn, and Sylvia's gay hat and laughter earned her an appreciative stare. He went on to one of the other pegs which afforded him a better view of Jasmine lolling at May's feet. She leaned back on her arms with her face tilted upwards and a yellow sweep of hair falling past her shoulders to the grass. "That's somethink like!" he thought.

"When's Daddy coming?" asked Sophie, looking up. "In time for tea - he has to work, darling," Sylvia reminded her, feeling glad that she did not.

Sophie laughed and a little smile stayed round her mouth. She thought how Sir Roger would come bustling up to the school, anxious to do her credit and so certain that everything she did was right. "I'll be at the gate to meet him," she said.

The visitors lunched with the governors and the staff in the School House dining-room while the girls, under the eye of the prefects, wandered round the large recreation-room and, standing about in their white frocks, consumed what Jasmine remarked would be hardly Bertie Wooster's idea of a cold collation.

Miss Bishop, who believed that there was a use for everything, and sometimes dropped remarks about tides taken at the flood, placed Sylvia next to a cross and deaf old governor, which far-sighted action resulted in a gift of ice-cream to the school every Sunday, since the old gentleman, seeing Sylvia's sigh of rapture when these appeared before them, and gazing into her limpid eyes as she consumed his own, forgot, temporarily, that she would not be there to enjoy his generosity.

Sylvia turned her flowery hat and waved her spoon in a little salute to May who was smiling between Miss

Truscott and the curate. The governor retrieved her attention by asking if she thought he might fetch her another ice and Sylvia, looking round at Shirley's neat figure moving behind the chairs, said she thought not, but perhaps later, in the garden - and made a silent resolution to enjoy herself elsewhere with the girls.

After lunch Sylvia, who had been relieved of the governor by Miss Cottingham, joined May and Miss Truscott and the curate upon the terrace, where they chatted and drank the little cups of coffee which Alice served in the hall. The sea sparkled, the flowers glowed, and the young man was so charmed by Sylvia's lovely face that when Sophie called "Mo-ther!" from the drive he thought there must be some mistake.

Miss Truscott leaned from the terrace and said: "Go away, dear!" in a voice which made May exclaim: "So easy!" She laughed, but wondered a little uneasily if, after all, her young man would quite recognise her in these surroundings, and thought perhaps she had better marry him quickly before she became the managing type, then, catching sight of the curate's amused expression and Miss Cottingham's motherly form issuing from the common-room window she decided not to worry herself.

Miss Cottingham said she thought it was time they went to the main school hall, and, indeed, bells pealed suddenly round the building, startling all the guests.

Sylvia settled herself beside May and slipped her feet comfortably on to the rung of the chair in front. The view of the lady behind her being quite obscured by her hat she removed it graciously and took the opportunity to turn round and look for the girls. When she located them, standing in a sea of white at the back of the hall, she waved gaily and received guarded nods and smiles.

The special prizes were delivered by an elderly and titled prelate imported for the occasion by Miss Bishop, and during his oration Sylvia absently took her cigarette-case from her bag, only to find May's grey gloved hand gently pressing hers. She sighed, remembering where she was, and put it away again.

Miss Bishop made a brief speech which was chiefly a résumé of the progress of the school and this was followed by a somewhat longer one by the head girl. When this was capped by excerpts from Racine, without costume or scenery, Sylvia wriggled sadly in her chair and rearranged her feet. Even May sighed as a plain girl with a pigtail which reminded her unaccountably of a Chinaman stepped to the piano on the platform with some music in her hand.

Miss Cottingham sat back with quiet satisfaction and after a minute the school was still. Even the little girls stopped jostling each other and stared at Charity and used their ears; Sylvia's old governor propped a hand behind each of his and heard enough to imagine himself young again, in a green field with Sylvia at his side. Mr. Walker watched Jasmine in her white dress, so that his eyes and ears were one. Honor gripped the seat of her chair in her obscure corner, praying for the music to stop.

When it did, Charity, blinking through her thick lenses, found her way down from the platform and round the hall to where her father, as Miss Bishop had intended, was thinking that they must be right about the girl.

May came back from fields of asphodel and smiled at Sylvia who, dabbing her eyes and looking like a rainbow, whispered, "Well, who would have thought that hideous girl – "

May said, "Ssh!" and turned away.

When they were released they flocked round the gardens, where the school band entertained them upon the lawn, and Matron gathered Honor and Alice to assist her behind the trestle table in the marquee. Sophie slipped the best of the cakes she was supposed to be handing round to guests into Sylvia's handbag and ran off and down the empty drive.

Geoffrey crawled in solitude upon a rug beneath Mrs. Munnings' front window and Sophie, having called through for permission, sat beside him and opened the bag. She stopped a moment to wipe his earthy fingers vaguely on her handkerchief and give his cheek a kiss. His eyes opened widely as Sophie detached her mother's engagement book from the cream. She spread the repast on the rug. The little fingers closed over the cakes and then sank into them.

"Isn't Speech Day fun," she murmured, smoothing his hair.

Upon this scene Sir Roger arrived, glancing from his taxi window, and called upon the man to stop. His daughter ran out into the drive and held up her face to be kissed.

"Who on earth - " he began.

"That's Geoffrey, I told you about him - isn't he lovely?"

"Lovely!" echoed Sir Roger, looking down at her

224

upturned face.

Sophie slipped her arm in his and led him up the drive. "Dear," she murmured, "I am glad you're here! Come and get some tea and see all the merrymaking on the lawn. Mother looks prettier than any one there."

"Ah!" said Sir Roger deeply, remembering no gathering at which Sylvia had done anything else.

She patted the grass beside her chair when he appeared and said: "Dearest, you have been sensible. You've missed all those dreary speeches and now you can just relax."

He greeted May, accepted his tea from Jasmine and looked round the lawn. The girls' white dresses, the flowers, the grass, the striped marquee and the chattering visitors made a picture he considered very pleasant. He saw Miss Bishop's dignified passage through the guests and moved a little closer to Sylvia's chair.

"Don't worry, dear," she said, "we've done all that."

"I was afraid I ought to ask if Sophie's been behaving herself."

"She has," his daughter assured him, "Miss Cottingham says we've improved."

He looked up at her grave young face feeling vaguely puzzled and indignant that any one should consider there was room for improvement there. How satisfactory daughters were! He remembered vaguely his own school and the times they had visited Algy's: more formal arrangements, not as nice as this. He caught sight of Matron's starched apparel as she crossed the lawn, head bent slightly sideways, having what Angela's mother described as a nice, quiet little chat, which turned out to be about the loss of Angela's handkerchiefs, and, reminded by her suggestive white cap of his lumbago he said he would like a chair. He found one and crossed his legs in it while the school band, enheartened by fizzy lemonade, regaled them with selections from the *Mikado*.

"Happy, darling?" he asked his daughter, squinting round at her beside his chair.

"To-day - yes!"

"Only to-day?" he asked, alarmed. "Do they - ?"

Sophie laughed. "Oh, no, of course not! It's just - one feels shut up."

"But it's all very free and easy?"

"Yes," said Sophie doubtfully, looking at her toes.

"You want more gaiety?"

"Perhaps that's it."

But she did not look restless, only expectant, as she turned her wide gaze from him to the trees. He watched her anxiously, seeing in his mind's eye her plait rolled up or twisted, her skirts longer, her lips reddened a little - she would be unique!

Sylvia said distastefully, turning to May, "I've just seen three girls with spots - quite a lot of spots each. And one, being introduced, apparently, to someone else's father, rubbing her shoe on a stocking and moving her shoulders as if she wore a hair shirt. I'd thought there was much less of that than in our day?"

"There is," said May comfortably, "much."

"Then why - " she began, dissatisfied, but forgetting this display of gaucherie inquired of Jasmine: "Do people still get passions for the mistresses, or for each other, and go scarlet if they speak to them, and cry in chapel - and read Oscar Wilde?" She stopped.

Jasmine, feeling there was more to come, said, "Go on!"

She continued dreamily, "I once had what one might call a quite involuntary love affair. In those days the Upper Sixth sometimes kissed the Upper Third in music rooms - "

"Do they still?" asked Sir Roger, turning round.

"It has been done," Jasmine murmured. He looked at her downcast golden eyes and little smile with slight misgivings; ought one to be detached and critical, so young? but when she raised her eyes and smiled at him he decided that whatever she was must be correct.

"I was practising the 'Merry Peasant'," continued Sylvia.

"How dreadful!" said Sophie.

"Yes, it was. It was all I ever learnt, as far as I remember, and no doubt that was why I was indignant because the girl next door stood permanently on the loud pedal, so that I could hardly hear my one piece. So I dashed out and into the next music-room and when I got in and saw a Sixth Form girl sitting there - I was only Lower Fourth - I just stood silently inside the baize door, not knowing what to say, and I suppose she mistook my expression because she kissed me and told me to run away." Sylvia spread her hands and shrugged her pretty shoulders. "Well, I ran. And then, you know what's expected under the circumstances - I didn't want to disappoint her so I gave her flowers out of my garden for the rest of the term. And my garden grew so little - it quite wore me out. I was so glad when she left."

At this alarming story Sir Roger looked round at the grey building wondering if he ought to suggest that they demanded the girls' trunks at once. His anxious eye encountered Miss Meadows chatting to the vicar, and somewhat reassured, he allowed Sophie to tell him that she thought she fancied herself as an artist. That sounded a nice outlet, and the drawing lessons, he was rather relieved to hear, were given by a man.

The band had deserted the *Mikado* for the *Yeomen* and as they climbed the terrace to the school Sir Roger was pleasantly reminded that someone or other had died for the love of a lady. He murmured, "Very nice," to Sophie and hummed softly to himself, patting the well pumice-stoned hand upon his sleeve.

They inspected the Form rooms and wandered round to the dormitories, Sir Roger remaining delicately in the corridor. Outside Miss Cottingham's room he caught Miss Nightingale's eye and winced.

Sylvia, seeing the straight rows of beds and remembering the morning bells she had been so thankful to forget, looked at her daughter with gentle respect. "I'm so sorry, darling," she said with sincerity, "there were two boxes of chocolates really - we ate one in the train."

"It's all right, don't bother," said Sophie, smiling, and asked if she wouldn't like to tidy up at the mirror by her bed.

"Why, do I look a mess?" said Sylvia, startled.

Sophie shook her head and steered her towards it, where Sylvia automatically opened her bag. She did not explain that the dust of Sylvia's powder and its lingering fragrance were a grace she liked to have shed upon her grim cubicle. Jasmine, a little behind with May, mentioned, as they passed the attic stairs, that she had heard from Tom.

May looked a query.

"Yes - such a nice letter. Kind and informative!"

May opened her mouth to tell her not to laugh, then changed her mind. Her niece's face tilted thoughtfully beneath the yellow hair, which fell to her white dress, was vaguely puzzled and she regarded her hands with a little frown, as if Tom's grave restraint seemed odd. It wouldn't seem so odd if she could see herself as May saw her, thought her aunt - rose and white and yellow, against the dark panelling of the stairs.

Jasmine looked up and smiled. "It's in a quite inaccessible place - tied with blue ribbon by Sophie - or I'd get it for you."

"I didn't mean - " began May.

"But of course, love!" said Jasmine. She laughed and squeezed her arm.

In the dormitory they passed Margery. She was smoothing a bumpy object beneath her pillow and her lips moved. "Never mind, dear," she was saying soundlessly to Augustus, "it was very disappointing that Nannie couldn't come, but there are the boys, you know, and Daddy enjoyed himself. I had three ices. And you heard the band through the window, didn't you, dear?"

The girls waved energetically at the last glimpses of May, Sylvia and Sir Roger as the taxi carried them out of sight. They went in to change their white dresses for working garments and filed in to prep. Sophie ran up to the attic and ticked off one more landmark on Mr. Pickwick's calendar. "Now the end really is in sight," she murmured to Ronnie, straightening his photograph, and whisked downstairs.

Matron told Honor to take all the Junior School temperatures after prayers because one never knew. One never knew, her darkling brow implied, what might have been picked up with parents all over the school.

Albert whistled as he dragged the trestle tables from the marquee and Shirley, carrying cups indoors, moved one hand from the tray to touch a letter from Jim in the bib of her frilled apron. It crackled satisfactorily against her heart.

Sir Roger leaned back between May and Sylvia and closed his eyes. Against the dark lids he saw his daughter standing in the drive.

Miss Bishop said to Miss Meadows, "I think we ought to start a summer school for parents."

Miss Meadows, who was tired, said with unusual asperity, "Yes, Unity, it would fill a long felt want."

Miss Cottingham shut her door, took off her shoes and read thankfully: "Both bodies had begun decomposing. The young earl took out his magnifying glass."

In the gardener's cottage Geoffrey was sick.

CHAPTER XXII

THE end of term, after Speech Day, suddenly stopped being a vague possibility and became a dependable fact. Miss Meadows wrote out a list for Foyles of all that she hoped to read in two months. Miss Cottingham sent for a list of summer tours and received, unaccountably, a map of Scotland which she hung on the common-room wall. Mrs. Prior started saving rationed foods in one of the grocery boxes, which she intended to take away with her. Doris told The Fish that she would be glad to make a date with him again because she foresaw the whole of August with no one to take her on the pier. Margery hoarded her purchases from the tuck shop as a present for Nannie and the boys.

All over the school fiction flowed back into the libraries and in view of the impending examinations, text-books were taken out of doors. Even Jasmine lay on the grass with mathematical problems and answers before her and asked Sophie for heaven's sake to show her how the working was done.

In London, May forbore to look surprised when her husband showed her a letter from Miss Bishop saying Jasmine had improved. She considered it a propitious moment to suggest new curtains for her room.

Shirley divided her last month's salary into three little heaps in her drawer. One was for her mother, one for holiday expenses and with the third she sallied out to the Co-operative, thinking of her trousseau, and bought four yards of tea rose nylon.

The proprietor of the bathing-huts on the promenade shook the mothballs out of the striped cotton drawers in preparation for the holiday rush; the heat shimmered and danced at the edge of the beach. Miss Truscott bought a bottle of sun-tan lotion. Albert dug up tulips and iris roots and planted autumn crocuses below the lawn.

The children's wild rose faces were a little darkened by the sun. Their voices, calling across the garden, which at the beginning of the term had hung distinctly in the clear spring air, now seemed caught, a little muffled, and disappeared among the leaves. At recreation their thin brown legs flashed over the dried lawn and damp hair clung stickily to their brows when they flung themselves down in the shade.

Matron started fussing about buttons and name tapes and turning out the more inaccessible shelves in the basement. Celia went over the playing-fields and consulted Albert about the cuts in the now hay-coloured pitch.

Honor went out alone in the evenings and, dragging her leaden feet to the turf where she had rested with Mr. Walker, stood looking down at the sea and the rocks below the cliff.

CHAPTER XXIII

THE tropical rain, which had fallen for four days upon the ships in the harbour, the town and the hills, ceased abruptly and the decks of the *Indestructible* began to steam.

In Tom's dilapidated garden his servant hung out the washing; he shook, in passing, the water from the petals of the camellias and watched the white ants move out from the shelter of the hibiscus into the sun. The white people in the town went on to the verandas and shaded their eyes to look at the ships. Through their field-glasses they saw the white figures of sailors pouring on to a launch. Poor devils, they thought, looking at the soaking grass below them, they've come at a nice time!

The launch, manned by black sailors whose smooth skin glowed like polished marble above their white tropical drill, made its way towards the landing-stage. Jim, who found the glare exhausting, slipped down upon a coil of rope.

"You got fever, mate?" asked the man beside him.

"I dunno," said Jim. "Perhaps."

On shore he watched the sailors who climbed joyfully the old stone steps to the town; sweat running into their eyes. Beside him cranes and derricks creaked and clattered; he turned away from the glare, the smell of melting tar, the Africans carrying packing-cases on their heads, one of whom, he noted, wore a girl's sun-bonnet and striped pyjama trousers. He followed the man beside him into the waiting lorry, for on the beach, he hoped, there would be palm trees and shade; as it made its way through the town in the streets and doorways people interrupted their dawdling and chattering and turned to wave. Until the lorry turned a corner they stood, staring and laughing, as though time were all their own.

The lorry bumped out of the town past the cemetery whose huge marble monuments contrasted oddly with the rickety dwelling shacks, as though, thought Jim, the inhabitants realised they were a long time dead. It headed down the straight dirty road between palm and mango trees, where hens and dogs raised their heads from the ditch as they went by. Jim closed his eyes against the sun.

On the beach he sat down in the shade of a giant cotton tree, hearing the voices of his companions in the water and the calling and laughing of Africans on the sand; he heard them faintly, from beyond a preoccupation with a violent headache and the aching in his limbs.

In front of him the sea stretched, warm and dazzling, to the horizon, to England, to Shirley. Behind him small, pale blue birds darted between the trees where the thatched African huts huddled from the sun. Children rolled and scrambled on the ground and beyond the huts the damp bush steamed.

"Come on in an' give them sharks a run?" asked a sailor at his side.

Jim opened his eyes, shook his head and, scratching the bites upon his legs, lay down again.

Behind his closed lids he tried to visualise Shirley, the cottage, his mother, the school drive. At one moment they appeared quite closely, the next they retreated beyond immeasurable distances of discomfort and heat. He put a hand over his eyes and shaded them to watch two African girls fetch bottles of water from the sea to wash the sailors' feet. They performed this service with grace and care, laughing and chatting to each other, and when they were satisfied that no sand remained between their patrons' toes called for towels and dried them carefully before putting on their shoes.

"Be tired, sah?" said a soft little voice at his side.

Jim rolled over and opened his eyes. The girl who smiled at him from beneath her black curling lashes he judged to be about fifteen. She wore a garment of bright cotton which hung from her hips to her knees, and red bracelets and anklets. The rest of her ebony person glowed in the sun.

"B'linda wash you feet, sah?"

"No, thank you," said Jim, who had not taken off his shoes.

"You sick, sah?"

"Yes - I mean no," he said, closing his eyes.

"B'linda plenty sad for you." She slipped down at his side.

"Are you?" He smiled up at her with grateful surprise.

She slid her hand into his. "Small B'linda plenty sweet," she said.

Her soft little fingers in his, peeping coyly down at him, she was indeed all that she said. Suddenly he groaned and closed his eyes. "My head," he said, "my head," and tightened his grip on her hand.

She smoothed back his hair and lightly, like cool black feathers, her fingers stroked his young brow.

"You come with me, sah? Cool in house," she nodded towards the huts.

Jim's eyes focused carefully and his brow creased in a frown. The shouts at the edge of the water came from very far away, his limbs were growing heavier and his head, which ached infernally, could rest in comfort, he thought, upon that black and perfect bosom.

"Yes," he said, "don't leave me," and allowed her to pull him to his feet.

He followed her under the palm trees and through the village, nodding vaguely at small Belinda's friends who hailed them as they went by. Before her house they came upon her father, sunning himself, cross-legged, upon his patch of ground-nuts. He greeted them hospitably and aimed a friendly slap at Belinda's behind as they passed. When they entered the house he continued to nod and smile at them until Belinda shut the door in his face. He sat on in his garden scratching himself luxuriously, his broad face lifted to the sun, until his portly sister, making her way around the bougainvillæa, offered to remove the fleas from his head.

They settled themselves comfortably, the sister seated behind him upon an upturned box, and enlivened the operation with a good deal of hilarious noise.

But Jim did not hear them where he slept with a little smile on his mouth, his dreams of flowery fields, while small Belinda went through his pockets.

The sea wind blew gaily through the attic window and fluttered the correspondence on the floor. Jasmine turned Jim's cards over in her hands; a view of Gibraltar addressed to Sophie and a portrait of a Spanish matador for herself. She touched them gently as she put them away. Bells rang in the building below her and the business-like stampede between Form rooms began, but Jasmine did not hear them for, kneeling beside these treasures, her fair head on one side, her knees in the dust, she felt that Tom's letter and Jim's bright cards were like threads stretching from her fingers to the world itself.

She turned her head and looking through Mr. Pickwick and the grey walls which would not enclose her for ever, she imagined merchants bargaining in far cities, elephants moving slowly beneath brassy skies, strange languages carried by the wind, untrodden mountains rising to the clouds; all waiting for her eyes and ears to bring them to life.

The Surgeon-Lieutenant entered the sick bay in the *Indestructible* and blinked at the dancing circular patches on the ceiling which were reflections of the water beyond the portholes.

The ship lay scorching in comparative silence in her afternoon siesta, and he listened to the sirens of other ships in the harbour and the whirring of the fan beside the sailor's cot.

"Well, old man?" he said.

Jim shivered and opened his eyes. "I'm that cold, sir." The cot began to shake.

The surgeon, whose clothes were glued to him with sweat, pulled up another blanket and turned off the fan. He breathed the cabin's stifling air.

"What is it, sir?" asked Jim.

"A nice dose of malaria."

"How - how long?" he asked between his chattering teeth.

The surgeon let go of his wrist. "It'll take you a week, my lad, before you're up. With no relapse."

But it took him longer than that for next day he developed a cerebral infection and was dead.

Sophie peeped into the kitchen and saw Mrs. Prior and Shirley at the table with folds of nylon in their hands.

"Just 'averlook at this!" said Mrs. Prior.

Timoshenko walked disdainfully around the edge of the pink sea, sniffed at it and turned away his head. Sophie lifted him up. "It's wonderful" she said.

"Feels like a cold fish to me." Mrs. Prior handed her a piece of cake.

Sophie accepted it and smiling at Shirley shook her head. "It's just right."

She forgot to put the cake in her mouth and her brow contracted slightly, for she was thinking that, having missed both Jim and Mr. Knightley, she would very likely be an old maid.

When the white people in Freetown heard a salute fired in the distance they said: "There goes another poor bastard," and imagining the flag being retrieved and folded for future use, went down and complained to the cooks about the lunch.

Then they sank on to chairs in their solitary sitting-rooms and from the street the noise of dogs, black men, and engines changing gear assailed them. The sun pressed viciously against the jalousies while the familiar smell of baked dirt, sweat, cooking and manure rose up to meet the pressure.

Downstairs the cooks wondered if the lunch, which was much like other lunches, would do again at night. They took up forks and scratched their woolly heads.

That night Mrs. Prior called for a greasy pack of cards and refreshment and told the fortunes of Shirley, Nora and Maude. In the dormitory Sophie dreamed of Geoffrey and in London Nannie and May sat up after their households were quiet and stitched at holiday clothes. In his house above the harbour Tom cried out to Jasmine in his sleep and under the cotton tree on the beach Belinda's father gave a party and got drunk.

CHAPTER XXIV

SHIRLEY moved Miss Bishop's furniture very gently across the room. She turned up the counterpane and put a chair on the bed. As she dusted she was careful not to bump against anything for she felt that any sudden noise or contact might be more painful than she could bear. She was so careful to preserve herself from further shock that she walked slowly along the centre of the corridors and if she saw any of the girls hurrying she stood aside until they had passed. When people spoke to her she said, "Yes, please" and "No, thank you," softly, and gave her grave, polite smile. As she followed the vacuum cleaner across the carpet she felt so light and unreal that it seemed as if she hardly touched the ground.

Miss Bishop came in to get a handkerchief and the sight of Shirley's small, expressionless face as she returned her greeting worried her all the afternoon.

Later she said to Miss Meadows: "That child looks dreadful, I must speak to Matron. Do you think a tonic?"

"No," said Miss Meadows, "I don't."

They sat in silence, stirring their coffee and looking, not at each other, but between the rose-coloured curtains at the sea.

When Miss Meadows went to her room she sat for a long time with her hands folded in her lap. She thought of Shirley as she went softly and automatically about her work and felt there must be something she could do. She was not going to have the girl's mind, which she had weaned from twopenny dreadfuls to literature in the shape of Miss Alcott, cast into the abyss by death.

She glanced around her with decision.

She moved towards the bell beside her bed but remembering that no one was likely to answer it she looked out into the passage. Sophie and Jasmine, carrying a horrid tangle of wool and needles, were on their way to the Wednesday evening gathering which Miss Cottingham, presiding over a variety of deformed garments, had so aptly called Knitting For Our Brave Boys. The woollen flood which had once during the war years descended upon the Services, had since been diverted, and now added, presumably, to the depression of Europe. Miss Meadows stopped them. Would Sophie run a message for her?

Of course she would. Sophie thrust her confused bundle into Jasmine's arms and ran downstairs while Miss Meadows helped to collect rolling balls and pins.

The kitchen door was open and at first Sophie thought that it was empty, but there sat Mrs. Prior before the cooling grate doing, astonishingly, nothing. The quiet startled Sophie; no rattle of tea-cups, no heavy footsteps, no cheerful abuse. Even Timoshenko barely lifted an eyelid before closing it to dismiss the intruder instead of rubbing round her ankles. On the mantelpiece Jim looked out at them with the same half smile.

"Do you – "

"Yes, dear?" Mrs. Prior turned her head slowly upon its layers of chin.

"I was looking for Shirley. Miss Meadows wants her - I

thought perhaps – "

"She'll be in the 'all, my duck."

"Yes - thank you. I - I'll find her."

Sophie hesitated, then meeting Jim's sweet stare she approached Mrs. Prior's back, put her arms childishly round her enormous neck, said "Good night, dear Priory," and went quickly out. She knocked at the door of the servants' hall.

"Come in," called the voices of Noranmaude as one, a little thickened by mastication.

There were tea-cups everywhere, two teapots, two basketwork occasional tables supporting aspidistras, magazines spilled over on to the floor, a wireless asking in a high soprano "Why-y - did I let you go?" and Michael Wilding, Bing Crosby, Mr. Churchill and the Duke of Edinburgh surveying the scene from between pieces of stamp paper on the wall. How much more convivial, thought Sophie, than our Form room!

"Is Shirley here?" she said.

Shirley came down from where she had been standing by the window and said gravely, with a faint polite smile, "Yes, Miss Sophie?" and followed her up the stairs. It was dreadful, thought Sophie, like accompanying a very gentle ghost.

Miss Meadows said, looking at her hands and away from Shirley's politely waiting form, "Come in, Shirley, and shut the door."

Shirley did so and stood islanded in the middle of the carpet as though she had no business with anything beyond herself. Indeed, she felt that she had not. People came and went about the school, Miss Meadows sat with her hands folded, furniture waited to be dusted and moved; but Jim, to whom she had refused even the love that he asked, had died where she could not reach him, leaving her without connection in the world in which she found she still remained.

"Yes, madam?" she said.

Miss Meadows looked up from her hands. "I want you to help me, Shirley. I don't quite know who else I could ask. It would have to be in your free time, I am afraid?"

"Yes, madam," said Shirley. "Of course." She gave the impression that she would have acquiesced gently if Miss Meadows had asked her to fly to the moon.

"A young friend of mine is going to Germany. I thought I would like to give a tea party. There are five of them as a matter of fact. I don't think I can ask five young men up to the school."

"No, madam," said Shirley agreeably, not hearing what she said.

"So I thought I would arrange - a tea – in - in their rooms - they are soldiers - before he goes? I don't feel I can quite manage it myself." She waited and said, "Well?"

"Would you want me to be wearing uniform, madam?" asked Shirley, who had a vague picture of herself drifting on and on, as if towards mirrors, with soldiers and tables reflected indefinitely beyond her moving cap.

"No," said Miss Meadows emphatically, "I would not. You had better wear a summer dress to help me with the shopping first and ask if you may have your free afternoon on - Thursday, I think?"

"Yes, madam. Is that all, madam?"

Madam said it was and after Shirley had picked her way carefully to the door and shut it very softly she sat on in her room staring at the carpet and made no move towards her books.

When Sophie joined the rest of the House in the recreation-room she said: "Excuse me!" softly, as she slipped past Miss Cottingham and sank into a chair. Jasmine knitted furiously at something which might have been a scarf or a dish-cloth.

To Sophie's whispered, "I say!" she muttered, "Can't you see I'm busy?" and stared at the work in her hands. She shut her mind against the thought of Mrs. Prior and Jim and listened intently to the comforting horrors which Miss Cottingham, who read aloud for their encouragement, expounded in her gentle voice, "The drip, drip, drip of blood assailed his ears in the darkness . . ." Her fair head bent over her flying fingers, she knitted so industriously that the dish-cloth lengthened definitely into a scarf. "I'll ask if I can keep it for Uncle Arthur," she said, holding up the grey length.

They passed Shirley on their way to bed and Jasmine said, "I think I'd like to run."

She lay awake that night seeing her golden world disintegrate before she got to it.

In the kitchen Jim looked out into the firelight and Mrs. Prior's chair creaked as she moved.

Timoshenko, left to his own devices, pushed open the larder door and dragged a haddock under the sink.

CHAPTER XXV

MISS COTTINGHAM turned the last page of the report, wrote ambiguously, "Elizabeth may have been working more industriously this term but her ear for music does not appear to have improved," added what she felt to be a generous estimate of her character in the space allotted to her House mistress and passed it on to Miss Stebbing. She took up the next.

Miss Stebbing said, "Honesty compels me to confess only that Elizabeth is lazy, indifferent and a fool. Yet here is this blank space which if not filled in will cause her parents to think that their money has been misspent. As indeed it has. What am I to do?"

"Say that her French leaves much room for improvement."

" 'Much' is too generous," said Miss Stebbing, writing it down.

"As her Form mistress," said Miss Truscott, "I am in worse case." She moved her pen against her cheek and stared out at the terraces beneath the driving rain. Would her young man, she wondered, stand forlornly at the bottom of the drive, with the water running off his hat, or would he brave the crowded common-room when he arrived? Perhaps he would take shelter with Albert. She smiled and picked up another report, then wrote "Jasmine - " and putting down her pen again frowned thoughtfully at the glass.

"No," sighed Miss Cottingham, gently, reaching for the

school note-paper, "it is worse for me. I am informing her mother that I shall be glad to welcome her sister in the House next term, whereas nothing - nothing," she repeated, pushing the paper away again, "could distress me more. A schoolmistress's life is a very dishonourable one."

"Even parents in their dim way must realise that some allowance should be made for tact."

"I think not," said Miss Cottingham. She flicked the pile of reports, thinking how variously they would be received. Charity's father, doubtless, would say bitterly: "I had cherished the illusion that to be a 'born musician' - as I see your instructress fondly claims - might be a lucrative achievement, rather than one which is gradually reducing me to penury"; some would say indignantly: "Never mind, dear, what nonsense!" and others, like Sylvia, would murmur, "Well, darling, you *are* clever!" and put it in the fire. We do waste time, she thought.

Mr. Walker opened the door and looked round him a little shyly. Miss Cottingham made room for him beside her. He sat down and wrote what she knew were overgenerous accounts of various girls in the Upper Fifth. When he came to Jasmine's report he put down his pen and stared unseeingly past the head of the lady opposite, over the terraces, the town and the sea. Then instead of writing his opinion of Jasmine's progress he started to doodle upon the notepaper at his elbow. Miss Cottingham sighed and took another piece.

The sight of an eager tilted face and sweep of hair upon the paper startled him so that he hastily screwed it into a ball and threw it away. He sat with his eyes on the untidy table, seeing the way that Jasmine moved and smiled. This time next year, he thought, I shall know that I won't see her again. What a fool he had been! Yet it was impossible, he considered, to watch such beauty and not be moved by it. What a waste! He thought of Honor wasting her affection upon Albert. Could I ever - ? he wondered, and shook his head - he didn't know! Miss Cottingham interrupted his musings to pass him a cup of tea and he looked up to see Shirley, expressionless, standing behind a tray. There's beauty! he thought. Why don't I fall in love with it? God knows! And feeling that it was the last, perhaps the only thing that he might do for her that term he wrote such a kindly account of the time Jasmine had wasted in the studio that she later had difficulty in disguising her surprise from her uncle.

He despatched the rest of the Upper Fifth and walked round the garden on his way home. The rain had ceased and girls coming in from runs filtered past him in the drive. Some were still swinging along easily and one enthusiast, he noticed, stopped to bowl uphill; he stepped rather disgustedly out of the course of the stone on the gravel. Some, arms round each other's waists, heads lowered confidentially, saw nothing as they passed. What on earth do they talk about, he wondered? he frowned in puzzled concentration as the brown legs and short tunics disappeared.

As he turned off below the terraces he saw Jasmine coming through the gates. She was alone and evidently her thoughts were pleasant, for she changed step with a little skip as she walked, her head, which turned towards

Albert's patch of garden, glinting in the watery sun. She wore a sweater over her tunic - much running she's been doing! he thought - and he wondered why clothes, which looked what they were on other people, suddenly assumed shape and grace on her. She stopped and smiled when she saw him and for a moment he forgot to acknowledge her, so intent was he upon the bright picture she made surrounded by the dull sky, heavy trees and sodden flowers.

He said, "Good afternoon, Jasmine!" politely, as though she were no more to him than the rest of the scenery, and she continued her light progress to the school, perfectly aware of his admiration and guessing, without turning her head, that he watched her out of sight.

When she had disappeared into the dark cavern of the cloakroom door he went past the zinnias to the untidy mass of children's gardens round the lawn. Here, in one corner, Albert was cutting down the buddleia. Mr. Walker watched him with his hands in his pockets and a frown on his face. No wonder! he thought, remembering Honor. But the fellow needed - what? A thrashing? A little surprised at his primitive instincts he poked a patch of groundsel with his foot. A hundred years ago, I suppose, he brooded, I would have wanted to call him out or something. But all the same he rather liked the fellow! And in any case, he reminded himself, he would have made short work of me!

Albert turned, waved the shears in greeting, passed a hand across his brow. "Proper damp, sir!"

"Yes."

The sun which had escaped from the clouds shone on Albert's brown arms and hair. Well, it's not his fault. thought Mr. Walker. One could blame him for his appearance no more than Jasmine.

Albert inquired after Mr. Walker's mother, rather too solicitously, Mr. Walker thought, in the tone of one who asks the progress of a disease. He said, "She's well - thank you," and, staring in front of him, saw, not Albert's beauty, but a little figure in a sweater with a sweep of yellow hair. I must forget about her, he decided and, scowling at her memory and at Albert, thought: the damage they do!

Albert, who would not ordinarily have chosen to tidy buddleia when it was soaking wet, lingered on the deserted lawn after Mr. Walker's departure, wondering if Honor would come out. Her face, in the rare glimpses he had had of it lately, had looked so drawn and listless that in spite of himself he was anxious about her. Not so had his other conquests avoided him! Vague stirrings, not quietened by the memory of the only literature he ever indulged in, the Sunday newspapers, increased within him. He hoped she was all right!

Matron passed him on her way to the sanatorium and Miss Meadows crossed the lawn twice with her eyes on the ground; if she had noticed Albert he would not have seemed out of place in her thoughts, which were of early Greece. Finally Honor appeared on the path below the lawn and at the sight of him turned back towards the school. He came quickly over the damp grass, still swinging the shears.

"Don't go away!"

Honor stopped and looked expressionlessly towards him. She seemed to be poised for flight.

"I never see you now," said Albert. "I wondered - are you all right?"

"All right?"

"Yes – I," - his brows puckered anxiously under the curls - "I wouldn't like for anythink to - to be worryin' you."

Why on earth had he said that? But he didn't like the way she just stood and stared at him - she did look queer!

The colour flooded Honor's startled face. So he thought that, did he! The sort of thing that happened only to servants in novelettes, until it had happened, unaccountably, to one of her own Girl Guides - and her father had promptly married the young man to her and very happy, apparently, they were - but for Albert to suppose - !

Albert, to do him justice, had been thinking no such thing, but, with more perception than she gave him credit for, had been disturbed by her demeanour and her face.

" 'Ere, let me see you smile!" he said.

At such an odd request the colour, departing, left her face expressionless until she twisted it up dutifully like a child.

At this Albert opened his mouth to say: "That's better, now!" but closed it silently, for it was not. He stood, looking disturbed and anxious, staring at his feet in the wet grass. When he raised his head, "That's 'ow it is!" he said.

Honor wanted suddenly to reassure him - he didn't deserve it but she wished she could. No need for any one else to seek that dreadful world in which she had existed lately. She said, "I'm quite all right, it's end of term - I'll be glad to get home."

Albert smiled and held out his hand. "No ill feeling?"

She took the brown fingers and said, perhaps truthfully, "None!" When she let them go she thought: "There he goes - for ever, perhaps," and watched his face.

"It's a bloody queer world," he murmured, thoughtfully, "that it is!"

Realising that he had brought forth the whole of his philosophy to comfort her she said: "Well, never mind!" and contriving to look cheerful turned away.

He stood watching her out of sight and swinging the shears. To take it as hard as that! He wished she wouldn't! "I made a mistake, not 'arf!" he thought, sighing and going up towards the shed.

CHAPTER XXVI

"FLOWERS!" said Miss Meadows, producing a many coloured posy from the school garden and balancing it on top of her purchases. "I wonder where - ? Perhaps this," she said, indicating a jug beside the clock. Shirley removed some matches and three halfpence and dumped the flowers strenuously inside; Miss Meadows noted with approval that the varied collection withstood even this treatment. "That *is* nice, Shirley," she said.

They shook out the antimacassar, laid the table, put the kettle on the gas. "I feel as if I'm trespassing," said Miss Meadows, sitting down when they had finished, "rather odd - and quite pleasant! Sit down, dear." Shirley poised herself on the edge of a chair.

With her lips just reddened, her soft hair shining and the glimpses of her bare toes in her sandals looking, thought Miss Meadows, absurdly young, the child was quite a picture! If only she wouldn't look so – so - but surely no one could forbear to smile at the things those absurd boys said? Her party would be a success.

When they came, their boots stopped clattering in the doorway and they stood and gaped. They had known Miss Meadows would come to entertain them; but not that it would be like this! They took Shirley's hand in turn, a little doubtfully, as though she might not be quite real.

As Miss Meadows' cakes and sandwiches disappeared their tongues loosened. Did Shirley like the pier, the pictures, the country? Had she been on a boat trip? that was fine! The young corporal said tactfully, so as not to seem too pressing, "We'll all take you - you'll like that!" Miss Meadows poured out more tea.

Ginger, whose departure had been postponed owing to some coquetry on the part of the authorities, thought it was the nicest farewell party he could have: glancing at Shirley he wished it might be postponed for ever. He looked round at his companions and wondered who would win. The corporal, perhaps! Miss Meadows, watching their faces, thought, "After so many girls - they're very nice!"

She leaned back in the rickety chair and listened rather vaguely to their talk. I hope they will distract the child a little - I hope it wasn't impertinent of me! she thought. But a girls' school was *not* the place to nurse a broken heart. Too much femininity could be so - ! What dear Unity would say to such heresy, she wondered, I can't imagine. She visualised Miss Bishop sitting in her study, Albert's roses beneath the window, the view of the sea beyond, perpetual footsteps changing classrooms behind the closed door: Unity herself holding the various threads of the school together - or was it someone like Alice who held the threads? All those young heads bobbing, shoulders wriggling, voices chattering! a curious place! I have been away so long, she decided, that I had forgotten, and now tired as I am I shall have to go back - perhaps until next summer - poor Unity might find someone else by then. And what on earth it all amounts to, she thought, her head nodding unconsciously, I hardly know. Very few of them want to learn, even, whereas someone like Ginger

– she came back to the party a little guiltily and asked, "And when do you really go?"

He took his eyes from Shirley and smiled at her. "Two days now, Miss - if they don't monkey me around any more. Them girls," he said, nodding vaguely in the direction of the school, "they gets less interruption - I wanted this next year. Equality of the sexes! I don't know!" Miss Meadows laughed.

Someone passed a cup up, and with the teapot in the air and her eyes on the earnest, freckled face she said: "Yes, it is odd. And some of them, no doubt, would give a lot for the adventure. It ill becomes me, I suppose," she added, vaguely overflowing the cup, "to suggest that academic information stops short of something, for I have so very little else, but I know it does." Ginger rescued the cup and took the teapot from her.

"Yes?" he said.

"But in many ways it *is* a narrow field. Keep your eyes and ears open, my dear boy. Learn the language and - absorb. You won't be wasting time." She looked round anxiously for the teapot and seeing it safely settled on the table said: "School is such a small beginning. Learning - it ought always to be towards something. Never an end in itself - not rounded off. And school is - artificial. The people who say their school days are the happiest of their lives ought to see a doctor I think. Boys and girls - the best of them are straining away from us! And all this knowledge which we accumulate, and try to disseminate, it didn't come out of a vacuum, you know. It came from other people's experience. One ought to connect things up."

"Yes," said Ginger. He looked from her thin, intent face to Shirley's lovely downcast one, at the khaki figures round the table, through the window at the town - there is a connection, I suppose, he thought. She's right, the old girl, no ivory towers for me!

Miss Meadows refilled the teapot, wondered why she was talking so much, let her thoughts slip back to the school. In her imagination an endless stream of short tunicked figures, bareheaded, poured up towards the school. They disappeared into the cloakroom door, but still there were more coming up the drive; like counting sheep. She stirred uneasily in her chair and then some of the ciphers separated from the stream and took on individuality, a casual little figure took a few skips sideways, moved its yellow head. There's one that we won't touch, she thought. Just as well!

Shirley ate her tea and replied politely to the remarks which were made to her. She noted, with little inward comment, the admiring glances she received; she was used to such glances from young men, and sometimes from old ones, and looking at the candid faces around her she tried to make herself agreeable.

When Miss Meadows said that they must go, Ginger and the corporal accompanied them through the town. On the way she thought: "Dear me, perhaps a rather odd assortment? I hope dear Unity - " But they met no one from the school.

The corporal, a little behind with Shirley, said: "You got a steady?"

"No."

They walked on in silence, his palms sticky with relief. Shirley looked away over the road as they passed the Silver Herring.

Miss Meadows, glancing over her shoulder, thought: "Surely I have done right?"

At the gates Ginger said, holding out his hand, "Goodbye, miss. It's been that nice - you'll write to me?"

"I will indeed."

The corporal, with his mouth a little open, watched Shirley branch off towards the back door. "That's settled *you*," said Ginger as they went away.

Shirley went into the kitchen and past Mrs. Prior's chair. She stood at the table with her hat in her hand.

" 'Ave a nice time, dear?"

"Yes."

They looked past each other across the untidy table. Timoshenko went by with his whiskers white.

Shirley said, "That cat's been at the milk."

"I dare say."

In the silence there seemed nothing to be said.

"Want a cupper tea, dear?"

"No, I 'ad me tea."

Timoshenko rubbed round Mrs. Prior and wiped his whiskers on her stockings.

Mrs. Prior said, "You goin' out ternight?"

"Yes." She went upstairs slowly and spent the evening lying on her bed.

Timoshenko peered into Mrs. Prior's face. She said, "God bless you, dear," forgetting that Shirley had gone. He accepted the blessing in silence and uncurled his limbs to wash.

In her room Miss Meadows listened to the familiar noises of the school. On her lap was an anthology of Greek poems, but finding that they harped continually upon young love she let the pages lie unturned.

CHAPTER XXVII

CELIA said, "Why don't you wait until after tea? Then I could come with you. You know I've got this match."

"It's all right," said Honor, "I'm just going for a walk."

Celia went down towards the field. She called out, "Shoulders *back*, Molly! Patricia, will you never smarten up?" with less than her usual certainty, to the girls she passed in the drive. She found herself worrying incessantly about the apathy which had engulfed Honor and was quite at a loss as to its cause. They never laughed over their tea in the evenings now, but drank it in silence, Celia looking anxiously at Honor and Honor through the window at the sea. "I'll speak to that father in the holidays," she thought, bounding past the nets, "she ought not to come back!"

Honor passed the cottage and Albert's son scrambling on the grass. She went through the town to the sea and along the path to the cliffs. Here, although it was hot and still in the town, a little wind pulled at her skirt. She noticed the scent of thyme with half her attention, and the low calls of the gulls.

She walked to the edge of the cliff and stood there so long that a passing tripper glanced back twice to reassure himself before he descended the steep path.

Mr. Walker came over the turf with his eyes on the ground, kicking absently at the tufts and patches of chalk. He had had an appalling morning with the Lower Fourth and as he went he brooded upon his wrongs. Thank God it was almost the end of term! Then he would have peace and leisure to work in and - the company of his mother; he sighed. He groped in his pocket for a cigarette.

When he looked up from lighting it he caught sight of Honor standing at the edge of the cliff; something in the rigidity of her back startled him as he had not been startled for years.

He started running over the turf and calling, "Miss Christow, Miss Christow!" as he ran. Honor turned round slowly to see what was going on.

"Honor!" said Mr. Walker, forgetting himself and pulling up abruptly, "I thought you wouldn't see me - I was surprised – I - I thought I had the cliff to myself." Honor stared politely and suddenly he added, "Come away over here!"

"I was only thinking," she said.

Perhaps she was, but feeling that she ought not to do it so near the edge he drew her away. He put his arm through hers and began walking her energetically up and down. "Someone should take care of her," he thought indignantly, "up here alone!"

"Have you had tea?" he asked her, glancing quickly at her face.

"Tea?"

"Yes," he said with reassuring silliness, "that stuff you have in cups with milk."

"It would be nice."

He steered her off the turf and across the road to a wind-swept bungalow which sported a flag upon a little staff, bearing the legend "Teas." In the rather musty interior they sat in a bay-window waiting for the tea. Honor said nothing and when it came he poured it out and asked, "Sugar?"

"Sugar?"

He put the cup in front of her and said, "Well, just drink it up."

She did so, slowly and thoughtfully, and he said involuntarily, "That's a good girl."

Honor half smiled at him over the cup.

"Better now?"

"Yes."

He leaned back with relief, feeling he needed some tea himself. The bungalow walls were sensibly solid and there she was within reach! He could relax.

When he thought she looked easier he asked, "Would you like anything to eat?"

"No, thank you."

He came round the table towards her and sitting on the edge of it took one of her hands in his. "You seem to need more supervision than you get," he said.

Honor felt her hand, which was cold, growing warmer between both of his. Mr. Walker looked earnestly down at her. "Will you marry me?"

"Will I - ?"

"Yes. I'm afraid this is rather sudden but I think it's a good idea. I haven't much money, in fact I haven't any as money goes, and it goes all the time, but perhaps you wouldn't mind. I don't know whether you'd be happy with me but I think perhaps you might. I - I want you to marry me very much." When she made no reply he added:

"I wish you would."

Honor continued to look at him wonderingly and he leaned over and kissed her cold cheek. "Think it over."

"Yes." She gave a little faint smile and he thought, "It will be all right now!"

They sat on in unembarrassed silence, tinged with mild surprise. Suddenly Honor said, "You know, I - this afternoon - You were very kind." She paused a moment, and then looking round the room as though surprised to see it so altered, forgetful that the alteration was in herself, "I've been unhappy," she said.

"I know."

She searched his face intently, feeling it to be the first one for many days that she had really seen. To come back from wherever she had nearly been to find the world so ordinary and safe; it was - incredible! She moved her hand comfortably in Mr. Walker's. "I'm all right now."

"Yes."

His kind concerned expression recalled her conscience and she said, "Perhaps I ought - ?"

"No," said Mr. Walker.

"No?"

"No"

Of course! she thought, sighing and smiling. It doesn't matter now. It's finished with! And looking up at the increasingly familiar face she knew suddenly that he would blame no one for succumbing to the bright perfection that was Albert Munnings. She said, "Would you kiss me? I would like to marry you. I'm so glad!"

Mr. Walker did so, rather awkwardly, leaning across the

plates.

He paid the bill and took her out on to the road.

Honor looked at the bright turf, the little sunny clouds above her head, the cars shining on the cliff road. She took a deep breath of petrol and sun-sweetened air. "How lovely!" she said.

"By God!" thought Mr. Walker, "I was right." He tightened his hold on her arm. They went down the road and through the town.

They passed Albert's cottage where Mrs. Munnings, holding Geoffrey, stood among the flowers. "Afternoon, sir! Lovely day, miss! " she said.

They greeted her cheerfully and went on up the drive.

CHAPTER XXVIII

WITH a heavy heart Sophie delivered the last kiss upon Geoffrey's cheek. "You'll be seein' a difference in 'im after eight weeks," said Mrs. Munnings.

"I know," said Sophie, holding his hand. "That's just it." She swept his little countenance with loving eyes, determined, if it should change, to memorise every feature.

Mrs. Munnings said, "Wait a minute, dear," and going into the front room she returned with a photograph. "We 'ad that took for my mum."

"Is it - for me?" asked Sophie.

"Yes, my dear."

"How wonderful! I couldn't imagine anything I wanted more. Thank you *very* much." She smiled sadly from Geoffrey to his picture, put it in her pocket, delivered another last kiss and ran round into the drive. She waved to Albert as she passed him and he thought: "That girl's barmy, that's what."

She went round the garden with her treasure, thinking, "Jay will laugh. Well, never mind!"

But Jasmine was in no mood for laughing. She was in the attic by herself.

She sat cross-legged upon the floor, her elbows on her knees, staring at the pile of letters in the dust. Finally she shook back her fair hair and, leaning over, took Jim's cards and put them at the bottom, out of sight. Then she sat back again with her chin in her hands. So that was that.

No one will ever, she thought, remembering his smile, seem quite as wonderful again.

She looked out at the summer sky. When I'm old, she wondered, will I look at the young men of those days and think that they could never be like Jim? For she was sure they never would. She closed her eyes suddenly, visualising death. If the good, the gallant, the beautiful, went out like that, what happened to the rest? Well, at least I'm not good, she thought - I won't die young. And Shirley? - I won't think about that! she decided, quickly opening her eyes.

And do I, she thought, stopping suddenly on the stairs, do I really care? Isn't it just that I'm frightened, because I'm young, and he was young, too? She stood with one foot out over the next step, her hand on the banisters, staring into space. How could I have borne it, she thought, wonderingly, if I had died now before I had lived?

She went down the stairs and stood in the sunlight from the landing window. It was warm on her hands and face. I'm alive - I'll soon be free! she thought, turning slowly round.

"Did you ever see anything like it?" said the Reverend Arthur, holding Jasmine's school bill before May's eyes. "It's not too bad, dear, considering."

"Considering what?"

May, who could think of no immediate answer, took the curtains up to Jasmine's room. When she had hung them she thought: "Well, at least they're better than the old ones," and sat down on the bed. After a moment she smiled, murmuring, "Two more days!" and going down to the garden she picked and shook the smuts out of the flowers.

Nannie said firmly to her employer: "I'll go to the station myself, sir, there's no call for you to break your day. There's Jane can mind the boys." She visualised Margery's bright face under its halo of panama. "Next term I'll keep that Augustus if it kills us both," she thought.

Sylvia added, "toffees, tomato cocktails and flowers for S's room," to her shopping list, but Sir Roger went round to Bond Street and possessed himself of a hat. It was labelled "Jeune fille. Très charmant, très gentil," and he carried it home himself.

Shirley said, "Them's my stockings," looking up from her trunk.

Doris, unabashed, said, "There now, did you ever," and took them out of her case. She packed two dirty dresses, a lump of cake and The Fish. She watched Shirley, her face stony, put the nylon into her trunk. "What yer goin' to do with that?"

"I'll be wearin' it," said Shirley, "what do you think?" Forgetful of the stockings, Doris' kind face crumpled into tears. "I wish you'd act natural," she said.

Shirley wrapped the picture of her family in a vest. "I ain't doin' nothin'."

The tears ran past Doris' chin and splashed on to The Fish. "Someone'd ought to cry for 'im."

Shirley went on with her packing. She looked into the wardrobe and emptied drawers while Doris, surrounded by their peculiar odour, sat on among her scattered possessions, crying for Jim.

Mr. Walker waved to Honor as he went down the drive. She stepped back from the landing window to see Miss Meadows fumbling with her spectacles and peering at her happy face. "Am I - ?" she said.

"Yes," said Honor, "you're quite right - we are - but only just." She gave Miss Meadows a gay, shy little smile and was surprised when the old lady leant over her spectacles and kissed her.

"My dear!" she said, "I wish you all possible happiness. What a delightful end of term - Miss Bishop will be so pleased!" she added, with no reservations, for she knew poor Honor was not outstandingly successful at her work.

Honor said, "Thank you so much!" and went on to her room. She sat down at the window looking at the view. How completely it had changed! It was the same scene which had reflected her misery and now it glowed in response to her release. She felt that she was free from some intolerable burden which would never frighten her again. She saw girls passing below the terraces and their voices rose pleasantly to her ears. When she saw Celia she waved her hand. Suddenly she found herself murmuring: "For our creation, preservation, and all the blessings of this life - " and opening her eyes in surprise at this pronouncement looked from her folded hands to the flowers, the sunny rooftops, the sails upon the distant sea.

Mr. Walker glanced at the spot where he had spoken to Jasmine on a rainy day and remembered how she had looked as she smiled at him, in her white sweater, and wished him a good afternoon. So one can, he thought, going past Albert's cottage and through the gates, one can love two people at once! His heart warmed towards Honor and, in a future fraught with such difficulties as lack of money and his mother, he thought he saw a little happiness for them both. More than a little, though, he decided, turning down towards the sea; and leaning over the promenade railings he brooded: we'll make a success of this! If anything had happened to her, he thought, that day on the cliff - or if anything hadn't happened and she were going home alone! I couldn't have borne it! Well! He lit a cigarette and stared unseeingly at the people on the beach.

When the cigarette went out he relit it and frowned down at the stones. How would Jasmine seem from an aura of domesticity? - but there would be no change in her! For another year he would see her, and her beauty, he could only suppose, would affect him as it had always done. He would endure her misbehaviour in the studio and in the rare moments when she was working he would see, bent over her drawing board, the crown of her yellow head. When he tried to be angry he would meet her golden eyes and smile. And she herself, cheerful and indifferent, would drift through her last three terms at school. He wondered how much thought she would spare him when she heard of his engagement - not much! She would stop and smile, perhaps, and say something to Sophie, and drift on her casual way. Perhaps, poor little creature, they would ask her to put her pocket-money towards a wedding present, which was a way they had in schools. But whatever happens, he thought, pressing his cigarette out on the railings and turning up towards the town, whether she's here or not, there will always be a yellow-headed ghost all over that school for me.

Miss Meadows smiled as she did her packing. Things sometimes worked out very well! A wedding almost in the school as it were: unexpected and - rather nice. And now, she mused, wrapping the Dante in tissue paper, I suppose several misguided young women will apply for that unrewarding post. She took a few books from the shelves and bent her face to the carnations as she passed: Alice was really very kind!

I'm glad, she thought, having done what seemed very little, and sitting down to rest, that I managed to come back. It would be pleasant, when she was once more in her cottage, for however many years remained, to think of the life of the school going on. And for what? The higher education of women - most of whom would rather be left alone, she remembered, hearing footsteps and laughter outside her door. But for some reason, she decided, it is worth it! and she nodded, getting slowly to her feet.

On her way downstairs she passed Shirley carrying a mop and broom. She found it an effort to say, "Did you like my young men, Shirley?"

"Yes, madam. Thank you, madam."

Miss Meadows looked down at the papers she carried, away from Shirley's pale face, but suddenly the girl volunteered: "I been to the pictures with all of 'em - different nights this week."

Miss Meadows said, "And they're - ?"

Shirley smoothed the head of the mop with her rough fingers. "Yes, very nice, thank you, madam. It's just - they're not Jim."

Shirley excused herself and, releasing a smell of soap and polish, pushed open the bathroom door.

Miss Meadows went down to the common-room with her eyes on the ground.

Here confusion reigned. As always, it seemed to Miss Meadows, the entire staff chose the same moment to collect or rearrange their possessions. Cries of indignation, despair, irretrievable loss rose around the room; accusations of carelessness, theft and arson were freely exchanged. Black holes gaped among the bookshelves, a gown lay upon the floor; on the wall a dead headmistress lurched lovingly towards a bishop because Miss Stebbing, helpfully throwing someone a book, had hit the lady's frame; in the empty coal-scuttle Miss Truscott's scarf lay unexpectedly beside a bunch of flowers. "Shocking!" murmured Miss Meadows, moving some papers from a chair and sitting down - "we're far, far worse than the girls." No one answered her, the disorder increased and she was suspected, as she sat quietly brooding, of mislaying the Fourth Form reports. She was thinking how the rigid, unwilling tidiness practised by the girls, somewhat dissipated by a University, came to its final rebellious flowering in the mess at her feet, when Alice opened the door and appeared with a tray of glasses giving forth the musical assurance of ice clattering in lemonade. The staff hailed her joyously, like children, and wet rings and cigarette ash appeared upon all the furniture in the room.

"Eight peaceful weeks - and no girls!" said Miss Crowther, raising her glass. "Ja! Prosit!" replied Miss Stebbing, who was going to Vienna.

Miss Truscott cleared some books from the mantelpiece and in a little Empire mirror thus revealed inspected the progress of her tan. Miss Meadows looked down at the table, thinking of her cottage and a rest.

Matron's sharp eyes looked into the room, noted the general chaos and were followed by the rest of her person, which was subjected, not unnaturally, Miss Meadows thought, to a swift shudder. She announced that the laundry had materialised and that Shirley was distributing it among the rooms. She glanced at the figures around her, mentally clothing them in their washing lists: this was a habit of assessing her colleagues which Matron had long formed. She was just applying the word "combinations" to Miss Cottingham as a mark of grace when the door banged open behind her and Celia burst into the room.

Celia said, looking round, "Have you heard?"

"No?" said Miss Truscott, at the same time mutely thanking Matron for folding up her scarf.

"Honor - Mr. Walker! It's happened - they're engaged!"

Her round face shone with such genuine happiness that Miss Meadows thought involuntarily - poor girl! Other people! - I suppose that will be her role for life.

Matron looked from the amused, surprised, incredulous and sympathetic expressions around her and down at the bright scarf she held. Someone thrust a glass into her hand

and she found that they were drinking, in her absence, to the bride. A wave of colour suffused her countenance and subsided as she drank the lemonade. It was unjust!

Miss Meadows, watching her kindly, thought that at least she must be glad, next term, of a change. She turned her eyes from her stricken face to the window and the sight of Albert carelessly flinging coils of hosepipe around him reminded her again that she was old. As she watched him move among the flowers she reflected, unaccountably, how rarely honesty, thrift, industry or good sense were rewarded with love.

In the dormitory the girls waited patiently while Honor counted the clothes upon their beds. She appeared so pleasantly preoccupied that Jasmine, who had lost her vests, removed three, temporarily, from Sophie's so that they might be rechecked upon her own. Sophie murmured hastily: "And here are your hankies! Thanks!" She gathered up her depleted piles of garments before Honor should notice the change.

As she crossed the recreation-room she was infected, as usual, with the thrill of expectancy in the air: the end, temporarily, of the old routine; freedom for a few weeks! holding the pile of clothes against her heart she leaned over her trunk. When she sat back from it she looked round her at the rest of the room. Eager, inexpert fingers pressed down diaries, tennis-balls, novels, the tins of long eaten and forgotten toffees; as if, thought Sophie, they buried the memories and achievements of a term within the trunks.

She stood up and leaning against a cricket bat which, she supposed, she ought to have put at the bottom, surveyed the room. She saw Margery, packing Augustus' wardrobe with more care than her own, and smiled at her quickly; Matron with her sharp eyes darting over the boxes; Miss Cottingham returning contrabrand - in the form of confiscated books - now neatly and decently swathed in brown paper and addressed, reproachfully, to the owners' parents. Two Sixth Form girls, with reddened eyes, who were leaving that term, crossed her line of vision. She frowned after them and to herself she murmured, "Crazy loons!"

Jasmine's voice beside her said, "Let's go out!"

"Have you finished?"

"More or less." At this she looked at her friend's disordered possessions, passed her two pieces of tissue paper, disguised the cricket bat beneath her own pyjamas and said: "All right - now!"

They slipped out while Matron bent over Margery's trunk. Outside the cloakroom door they found Albert arranging boxes for the van.

"Don't be late for the train!" called Sophie.

"Is it likely?"

They laughed, feeling exhilarated and already almost free. He looked at Jasmine's flushed and expectant face and asked, "You'll be up to some larks now, I shouldn't wonder?"

She laughed delightedly: "I should think we will! The whole of London, let me tell you, Albert, waits for our meteoric appearance!"

"And champagne will be drunk out of slippers and such-like, no doubt?" he inquired sarcastically, for his ideas were out of date.

"I shouldn't wonder!" She started dancing towards the drive and turned to wave as Albert shouldered another box. Sophie looked from one to the other and held her breath. Here was someone who was not outshone by Jasmine - it was odd! But she saw that they grinned cheerfully and derisively at each other before Jasmine called "Come on!" and started running down the drive.

They dropped into the grass at the edge of the wood.

"To-morrow!" murmured Sophie and Jasmine nodded her head.

They lay on their stomachs, thinking disgustedly of the rush of controlled activity in the school, hearing the summer murmur of the wood and feeling the sun upon their backs. Suddenly Jasmine rolled over and put her arms behind her head. She imagined herself sun-bathing in some fashionable spot, perfectly clad - or unclad - for the occasion, and the heads that would be turned as their owners went by . . . some of the heads had faces like Albert's, like Tom's, like Jim's - but those turned immediately to a blank. No use going back! she thought. There was still too much! The sun was shining, the world was waiting, freedom not so very far ahead. She sighed and closed her eyes.

"How can you bear this next year, Jay?" asked Sophie, breaking in upon her thoughts.

"I don't know," she said, "I don't know." Indeed, gazing reflectively at the arc of sky above her, she hardly did.

Sophie said, "You must come over often. You and your aunt – "

"There's Uncle Arthur."

"Couldn't you ditch him for a bit and come to stay?"

"I wish we could!" What fun, she thought, lay ahead for them both! But it would not do to stretch her wings too far in the holidays, they would only have to be folded back into the school uniform next term. She would just taste, as always, the edge of freedom, until next year, it would be hers for good. As she lay in the grass her wide gold eyes reflected the trees and then the illimitable blue at which she gazed. A world - a universe - to be contained within her experience. It was worth waiting for!

Margery, having closed her trunk, also escaped. She cast her eyes downward with a smile, observing, not for the first time, the stiff, rather awkward way that Matron walked. She would imitate that and make Nannie laugh! She too smiled at Albert as she passed him in the drive and then skipped zigzag from side to side all the way down. He scratched his head over this unnecessary expenditure of energy, unaware that she was a ship tacking against the wind. She swung carefully to port below the terraces and sailed quietly along beside the flowers. How much changed, she thought, she had been by one term! The school, she decided, had not beaten her but she it, and now, instead of struggling to control her tears, she was mistress of the situation and of herself. She called suddenly: "Let fly your sheets there!" before she crossed the lawn and cast anchor beside the garden of which she was third owner. Since it was the last day of term and neither of the other partners, she trusted, would miss them, she picked the pansies which were all its flowers and held them up against her face. "They're to be stowed carefully," she ordered the steward as she sailed away, "for they're for a lady, with the Captain's compliments." In the dormitory she tied them with cotton and put them in a tooth-glass to keep fresh for Nannie.

At prayers that evening two Upper Sixth Form girls allowed silent but rather ostentatious tears to fall upon their books. Afterwards, while Jasmine and Sophie practised new hair styles in one of the music-rooms, a song which may have been old when Tom Brown was a boy echoed among the Junior Form rooms; Matron brooded upon injustice in her room, and Miss Bishop's musings, as she sat in her study, were of the universal foolishness of girls.

Margery, curled in a warm, small ball, dreamed that she was already in her bed at home. At the back door Shirley permitted the corporal to take her hand and below the terraces Honor slipped hers into Mr. Walker's and smiled at his shadowed face. The two couples, unaware of each other, passed the gates and went down to the sea. In the school behind them girls lay, wakeful and excited, waiting for sleep to bring the day which would send them home.

When she and Nora had made the last packet of sandwiches for the train Mrs. Prior climbed the stairs slowly and, as if she were God, she looked down from immense distances at her lumbering person as it swayed against the banisters, going up to bed. She did not look towards the holidays, which had no significance, but saw herself, gross and foreshortened, make her slow progress on the stairs: a fat old woman with death in her heart.

Shirley leaned on the rail beside the corporal, looking over the sea. She said, "There now!" and, "Well I never," kindly, not hearing what he said. When he made a suggestion for their entertainment she said, "I don't mind if I do." She found herself sitting opposite him eating an ice. She nodded when he seemed to expect it and sometimes she laughed at his jokes. "Kind he is, and very pleasant. What does it matter?" she thought.

CHAPTER XXIX

ON the last morning girls woke before it was light. Springs creaked, sheets rustled, plaits tied with tape twisted impatiently on pillows. Sophie, observing the shining of Jasmine's open eyes, leaned across the gap between the beds and whispered, "You coming to see Priory before we go?"

"No," said Jasmine, turning her back. Eventually she twisted round and murmured, "Yes. All right." She lay watching the colours form in the cubicle curtains as the day crept up the room.

When the bell rang they sprang for their curtains and dived into their clothes with a zeal they had not manifested all the term. They streamed down the corridor in a turbulent flood, past Miss Meadows' door, behind which she closed her Bible and started looking for hairpins on the floor; past the bathroom in which Celia whistled between her chattering teeth and into the dining-room where Honor, already on duty, paraded vaguely with lists of names in her hands. She smiled softly down the table, as if rising early suited her, and Sophie, as she accepted her tea, gave her a swift and friendly grin. "Love!" she thought, sipping quickly at the scalding fluid, "there's nothing like it. I hope there will be some left for me!" She crammed down her breakfast hastily, in rising excitement, as though if she hurried she might yet escape in time.

Miss Cottingham appeared to read out notices about

trains and then Sophie and Jasmine excused themselves, a custom which was permitted upon the last day, and fled towards the basement stairs.

They presented themselves, rather diffidently, at the kitchen door. Here Mrs. Prior, four-square upon the rug as if it were a quarter-deck, directed operations while Nora scrubbed the table and Maude clattered pans into their final resting place upon the shelves. Timoshenko, looking vaguely discomforted, flinched at the metallic bangs and sniffed disapprovingly as though he knew these preparations presaged a kitchen which would be no fit dwelling-place for him until next term. From the mantelpiece the china spaniels and Jim had disappeared. Jasmine, looking at the bare shelf which, after all, she told herself, she might have expected, since Mrs. Prior had to pack, felt certain for the first time that Jim had gone. She turned her golden gaze swiftly to Doris, drinking tea and propped up against the sink.

"Well, my loves," said Mrs. Prior, lurching towards them on her swollen feet.

"We've come to say good-bye."

"Good-bye, my ducks. 'Ave a good time." She put her hands upon the place which might have been her waist and regarded the two young faces, her head on one side.

" 'Eaven 'elp the young men," she said.

"Ah!" said Jasmine. She put up her face and Mrs. Prior bent her enormous countenance and brushed her cheek.

"Me too," murmured Sophie. She leant forward, carefully judging the distance across the black bosom.

"Be off with you now," said Mrs. Prior. "See you next

term. Enjoy yourselves."

"Yes, Priory, we will." At the door Jasmine added involuntarily, "God bless!"

Mrs. Prior nodded and watched them disappear. She did not reflect that her son would always be young, handsome and a hero to the girls, but it seemed fitting that his expressions should linger on their lips. Long life to 'em! she thought, and, turning round she bawled at Doris to put that cup down and if she wasn't wanted in the sanatorium for God's sake to lend a hand.

Outside the servants' hall they saw Shirley and called to her, "Good-bye, Shirley! . . . Good-bye!" " 'Bye Miss Sophie - Miss Jasmine," her voice floated up the stairs.

She stood looking after them. "How young they are," she thought, listening to their racing feet.

From her study window Miss Bishop surveyed the flying clouds. On the outside of her closed door were scuffles and quick laughter; this morning no prefect enforced silence, for Miss Bishop felt that some relaxation was due. She herself, clad suitably in a dignified garment which the catalogues described as a travelling dress, would soon be relaxing in a first-class Pullman, choosing her lunch. Girls for the early train for the north were already congregating in the drive and an irrepressible child blew a fanfare on the horn of the school bus.

She thought sadly, seeing the term behind her, of how much she had failed. Next term, she decided, she would have stricter discipline, better examination statistics, more tidiness among the staff - she turned her gaze from the horizon and rang the bell for Alice to bring some tea.

Alice was closing windows and fastening cupboard doors. Soon, when the last of the mistresses had departed, she would throw away the flowers in the hall. When the other maids had gone she would linger to see that the school was safe, for these young people were forgetful and she liked to feel that all was well. As the last voice floated over the terraces, the last wheels sounded in the drive, she would continue her faithful tour. She would put newspaper on Miss Bishop's carpet and draw down her blinds against the sun; and then, as the bleak sounds of emptiness grew louder, she would close the door upon them and hurry down to the cottage for Mrs. Munnings' last cup of tea.

The bus for the London train was filling up. Sophie banged a tennis racket on to the seat beside her to preserve it for her friend. Then she crossed her ankles, tipped back her panama hat and watched the others scrambling for seats.

Jasmine called, "I won't be long!" flew past the cloakroom, up the stairs and into the deserted Form room for her book. "I wish I *did* let my head save my legs," she thought, remembering Miss Cottingham's advice.

She banged open the empty lockers, discovered it, and then, forgetting her hurry, strolled between the desks and leaned her elbows on the window-sill. There was the world, bright and inaccessible, lying before her eyes. Her gaze swept the drive, Albert's flowers, the town, the distant sea. She realised with a pang that while she was imprisoned the world was slipping past. So much of it was gone already. She reflected, kicking absently at a desk, upon the men she could have loved - St. Augustine (pre-conversion) - Abelard - Mark Antony - and with agony she envied the Dark Lady of the Sonnets. She leaned farther from the window, her eyes wide. There it was before her, as far as she could see - and beyond the horizon, through other people, other climates, other ways, the shining world swept on.

Jasmine sighed, nodded briefly to the expanse, picked up her book and turned back into the room.

The mistress in charge of the bus was becoming impatient to be gone. Sophie's voice floated up to her, "Jay!"

Jasmine leaned out into the world again.

"Coming!" she called, "I'm coming! Wait for me!"

Greyladies

the new publishing arm of The Old Children's Bookshelf, reprinting vintage women's fiction with links to collectable children's books.

Greyladies will offer you -
- Adult books by favourite children's authors
- School stories from an adult perspective
- A spot of vintage crime

Look for the stylish striped covers

Witty, unexpected, intelligent, quirky
Very niche
Very Greyladies

Greyladies
175 Canongate
Edinburgh
EH8 8BN

0131 558 3411
greyladies.ocb2 @tiscali.co.uk
www. greyladiesbooks.co.uk

Also published by Greyladies

LADY OF LETTERS
by Josephine Elder

Lady of Letters explores many of the themes familiar from Josephine Elder's popular girls' school stories; friendship, love of learning, being true to oneself. It tells the story of Hilary Moore, as scholar, history mistress in a girls' high school, university lecturer and writer.

Thoroughly at home in her academic life, it is in Hilary's friendship with an older science teacher and her romance with a young doctor that tensions arise and her ideals are tested.

The intriguing disclaimer, 'The characters in this book are might-have-beens not portraits' invites speculation on how much of this story is based on Miss Elder's own life.

POPPIES FOR ENGLAND
by Susan Scarlett (Noel Streatfeild)
with an introduction by Joy Wotton

Noel Streatfeild wrote twelve 'romances' under the pseudonym 'Susan Scarlett', now very scarce and sought after. They have many of the characteristics that made her 'own' books so successful, in particular the authenticity of the settings and the believable, often flawed characters that we immediately care about.

In *Poppies for England* she returned to the theatrical background she knew so well. It is 1946 and many are still feeling the aftershock of war. Rationing is still in place and prisoners of war are returning home, only to find their families almost strangers. Two such families, old friends with diverse theatrical talents, join forces to provide the summer concert party in a seaside holiday camp. In this 'gay and cheerful book' hidden talents emerge, romances struggle and blossom, jealousies and artistic temperament are overcome as the families find happiness once more. "Peace was creeping back into the world, and into the heart."

The Old Children's Bookshelf

is packed with beautiful nostalgic old books and prints.

- Girls' and boys' school stories
- Illustrated books
- Scottish children's books
- Pony books
- Folk and fairy stories
- Fantasy and Sci-Fi
- Children's books of both World Wars
- Guide and Scout stories & ephemera
- Annuals, comics, storypapers
- Biographies of children's authors
- Books about children's fiction
- A section of general children's fiction
- New Editions of Old Favourites
- Early 20th century women's fiction

and, of course, *Greyladies* books

The Old Children's Bookshelf
175 Canongate
Edinburgh
EH8 8BN

0131 558 3411   shirley.ocb2@ tiscali.co.uk